A Detective Story… The Hunt for

a Serial Killer

Vanished

Searching for Amanda

David Gatesbury

Copyright © 2016 David Gatesbury

ISBN: 978-1-63491-198-6

All rights reserved. No part of this publication may be reproduced, stored in a retrieval system, or transmitted in any form or by any means, electronic, mechanical, recording or otherwise, without the prior written permission of the author.

Published by BookLocker.com, Inc., Bradenton, Florida, U.S.A.

Printed on acid-free paper.

This is a work of fiction. Names, characters, places, and incidents are the product of the author's imagination or are used fictitiously, and any resemblance to any actual persons, living or dead, events or locales is entirely coincidental. Any true-to-life people mentioned in this book are taken from highly publicized court cases.

BookLocker.com, Inc.
2016

First Edition

To Julie and Eric

Contents

PREFACE 7
Chapter 1 - Raiding a Drug Pusher's House... 11
Chapter 2 - Getting Together with Some of the Guys............................. 17
Chapter 3 - The Study of Criminal Behavior Involving Murder 25
Chapter 4 - Gathering Information on Missing Persons and the Activity
    of a Serial Killer... 36
Chapter 5 - Meeting Amanda's Sister Rhonda at Tokar's Casino............. 46
Chapter 6 - A Visit to the Hospital Raises New Concerns 57
Chapter 7 - Consulting with Supervisory Special Agent Johnson of the
    FBI 65
Chapter 8 - An Interlude with Rhonda and Learning Someone is
    Shadowing Him 72
Chapter 9 - The Bureau Locates the Home of a Serial Killer................... 81
Chapter 10 - Entering the House on Navarro Terrace 88
Chapter 11 - Taking a Ride Out to Lake Laraine 97
Chapter 12 - Poking Around the Lake after Nightfall 107
Chapter 13 - Another Late Night Return to the Lake 116
Chapter 14 - Rendezvous with a Hitman-Contract Killer 123
Chapter 15 - Butting Heads with Georgie 'The Bull' Sypka................... 133
Chapter 16 - A Flirtatious Night at the Races 141
Chapter 17 - An Unexpected Interruption at Dinner 151
Chapter 18 - Facing a Hired Gunman and Shooting it out 161
Chapter 19 - A Witness to Murder 170
Chapter 20 - Meeting with a Nervous Informant 183
Chapter 21 - Learning about the Secret Place 192

Chapter 22 - Entering the Doctor's Lair 200

Chapter 23 - Fitting Together Remaining Puzzle Pieces for Tying Up Loose Ends 209

PREFACE

This is a gripping, suspenseful, and fast-moving detective story that has components of a mystery. While it delves into the darkest side of human behavior, abductions and the heartless, gruesome actions of serial killers are not the main focus. The terrible stories we hear about these killers and the fate of the people who've fallen into their clutches, one is left to ponder about the deterioration of our society.

It would be wise to keep in mind that the character in the role of Buffalo Bill in the motion picture *Silence of the Lambs*, who oversaw the girl kept in the pit, was based upon a real person. To meet the standard FBI definition of a serial murderer requires three or more victims to fall into this classification. How many serial killers have been born who didn't make the grade simply because they were caught and locked up after their first or second murder?

What astonishes a good many people is the little prison time criminals get for kidnappings and abductions in this country. The next time you read or see on television a story about a murderer getting caught, make note of his criminal record and you'll see what I mean. They've already been arrested and convicted of committing serious crimes and it's remarkable how little time they've served. Some of America's most infamous murderers have been incarcerated, only to be released early to prey on the public once again. Having gained their release from jail and determinedly looking for their next target, they now understand the importance of not leaving behind survivors from their crimes. They often start a house of horrors, with their criminal tendencies including kidnapping, torture, and sometimes even cannibalism. As time goes by and their list of victims grows, eventually they gain notable fame for their brutal and horrific escapades. Scars on their victims' lifeless bodies by way of forensics tell of the nightmarish persecution these people have endured.

The world is becoming more and more a dangerous place and for many of us, especially the families of their victims, we cannot grasp why this person was let out on the street. All you have to do is watch the news and it doesn't take long to understand our streets are not safe, and it's even worse after dark. If I see young children playing on the street after nightfall I have to wonder about their parents. . . . Don't they care, and who's to blame when one of them disappears.

I remember President Obama saying, "There are very few African American men who haven't had the experience of walking across the street and hearing the locks click on the doors of cars." Hasn't he ever told his children to be cautious of strangers?

It's highly advisable that if a stranger approaches your car, no matter what race or color they are, you'd better lock that car door and fast! I don't know about you, but I'm uncomfortable when somebody approaches me at a gas station and I'm outside the vehicle filling the tank.

I hope you're not naïve enough to think that every crazed murderer is behind bars, so nowadays how safe can a person feel when walking the streets alone.

John Douglas, a former chief of the FBI's Elite Serial Crime Unit and author of "Mind Hunter," was quoted as saying, "A very conservative estimate is that there are between *35 and 50 active serial killers* in the United States".

Kidnapping laws vary from state to state, and can include just a couple of years in prison for the perpetrator of this crime. If a criminal is caught, tried and convicted for kidnapping, assault, and unlawful restraint in connection with a woman he didn't previously know, do you think after spending just two years in jail that he's cured of the habit? If the woman he'd abducted was lucky enough to escape or law enforcement was able to someway intervene on her behalf before she suffered malicious acts, what would have otherwise been this woman's fate? What is this guy's routine for getting women to submit to his wishes?

After the two years are over and he's let out, what do you think is going to be on his mind after doing without female companionship for a two-year stretch in the clink? There are not only criminal minds to consider, but there are also people with schizoid personality disorders. The mentally unbalanced have legal rights the same as the rest of us. The institutions are full, and the numbers of them on our streets are on the rise. You'd be shocked and amazed at how many people have been pushed off subway walkways in front of moving trains the world over.

So whatever you do, don't take President Obama's advice. Be vigilant and well aware of your surroundings when you step out on the street. If a stranger is standing by your car when you're coming to it, don't go to the car, but seek a parking lot attendant or a policeman for help.

Long after the fulfillment of a serial killer's death sentence, questions still linger, as psychiatrists sift through court records and interviews trying to figure out what was in this person's mind. Was this individual insane or simply an evildoer who exulted over the sadistic torture of women?

One of the most frightening aspects about serial killers is the legacy they leave behind and the culture society has developed in their names, for their deeds are sure to inspire and breed patrons. Some who admire them may come to follow in their footsteps and try to emulate their ways, bringing misery and death on the innocent and unsuspecting that cross their paths. The sad thing is that they're out there now in growing numbers crisscrossing the country in search of their victims.

How are your survival instincts?

Chapter 1
Raiding a Drug Pusher's House

The country was experiencing the worst economic downturn in years, and crime was on the upswing. The city of St. Louis was in the midst of a war on drug-trafficking and distribution, and in an effort to stem the tide of drug smuggling, law enforcement officials planned a citywide crackdown on drug dealers. They intended to raid the locations of four known drug lords simultaneously: two on the north side, one on the west side, and another on the south side of the city. Police squads were aiding narcotics officers, and Chief of Detectives Steven Hastings asked for volunteers from his department to bolster these raiding parties.

Detective Lieutenant Leonard Harris, a tough, no-nonsense, veteran law officer, had nothing pressing on his desk, so he hooked up with a group of officers targeting one of the drug pushers on the list. Subject Booker Jennings lived in a north side three-story brick apartment building on Kossuth Avenue, west of Grand Boulevard. Jennings had a reputation for carrying handguns and a long rap sheet for violent behavior. Authorities had tried convicting him in the past for killing a prostitute, and later, a criminal informant, but were unable to provide strong enough evidence to win over a jury.

Harris attended an early morning meeting on the day of the raid and narcotics officers Derrick Griffin and his partner Julian Ortiz, who'd be leading officers on the Kossuth operation, spoke at the briefing. They told officers participating in the sting that they had been to Jennings's posh third-floor apartment on several occasions to purchase crack cocaine and marijuana to build a case against him. They also announced they had made previous arrangements to purchase twenty pounds of marijuana from Jennings at ten a.m., the time scheduled for the raid. Lastly, Griffin mentioned they had never seen anyone else in the building on their previous dealings with the suspect and they didn't expect any trouble.

Police arrived in force at the designated address at ten minutes before ten that morning and approached the apartment building in orderly fashion. There were two entrances at the building's front, one for first floor apartments, and another leading to second and third floor flats. Griffin and Ortiz wore casual street clothes and entered the building first, moving quickly up a steep flight of stairs while holding their pistols at their sides. Officers wearing black sweat shirts marked with the word POLICE in bold print over bulletproof vests followed them, carrying assault weapons.

Having been involved in this sort of operation many times in the past, veteran Lt. Harris wanted to look out for youthful, inexperienced officers participating in the raid. Tensions ran high, and when the line of policemen stalled, Harris moved forward, taking long strides, charging up the staircase on the balls of his feet to pass some of the officers. Hesitation on the part of the others allowed him to close the gap between him and Ortiz, who followed Griffin, and he fell in line behind Ortiz.

Now third in line at the crest of the stairs, the lead officers took caution at a second floor corridor that took a sharp turn to the left. Harris drew his .45 Smith & Wesson semi-automatic, engaged the slide for chambering a fresh round, and bent his right elbow to keep his weapon pointed upwards. These sorts of raids were always dangerous and there was no way of knowing how they would play out, but as long as they had surprise on their side, the odds were favorable for a successful mission.

The handrail joined with an upright support column before leveling off with the hallway to run horizontally, capping off a row of spindles. They quietly proceeded past an entrance door to a second floor apartment. At the hall's far end was another apartment door set on a forty-five degree angle, and another turn came with the next handrail ascending with another flight of stairs leading up to the third floor.

Griffin and Ortiz started up the stairs to the third floor, but Harris stopped, holding his position as he glimpsed their approach to a closed door at the top of the staircase. Not wanting to be seen when the door opened, he backed up to the angled apartment door in the corner of the corridor, now to his left, his back to the wall. Holding his revolver firmly with both hands and his finger resting against the trigger guard, he leaned to view Griffin knocking on the door before stepping out of view again. Sergeant Harold Kerns, a tall African-American officer, came to stand at the top of the stairs coming up from the ground floor, holding his weapon much the same way as Harris held his. Squad members bolstering the raid remained on the first staircase with their riot guns ready, and there were some taking turns looking over the rim of the second floor to glimpse the corridor.

Harris hoped no one residing in the building would show themselves for the next few minutes, and resisted the urge to look up at Ortiz and Griffin as they knocked on the third floor door again. After Griffin finished knocking, there was quiet stillness, and Harris heard a phone ringing faintly in one of the second floor apartments.

As soon as the phone stopped ringing, Griffin began knocking again, a little harder than the last time, and Harris heard a door in the middle of the second floor hallway begin to open. Officers clustered on the stairs below the handrail spindles, some eyelevel with the second floor corridor's floorboards, ducked to conceal their presence, while Kerns stepped into a corner as a way to avoid being seen.

Harris moved to his right to get a better view of who was opening the door and spotted a large black man holding a sawed-off shotgun. He took aim and shot at the gunman, his bullet hitting the doorjamb at the same time as the shotgun fired. Diving for the stairs leading up to the third floor while pellets hit his left knee, he returned fire through banister spindles. The assailant returned another shotgun blast, missing Harris, and chips of wood from the handrail went flying.

Kerns was unable to see the gun toting individual and remained out of the line of fire, but kept his weapon pointed in the direction of the second-floor door.

The gunman closed the apartment door, but before it latched officers coming up from the first set of stairs took aim between spindles and cut loose with a barrage of gunfire.

Hearing a loud thud of deadweight hitting the floor inside that same apartment suggested they had killed the gunman. Kerns raced across the hallway, leading others to join Harris, a few stopping to force open the door to the second-story apartment to see a dead man lying on the floor, a shotgun lying beside him.

Suddenly, bullets from a chattering machine gun breached the third floor door with shells hitting Griffin and Ortiz, and a pack of officers joining Harris at the bottom of that flight of stairs backed off. The two narcotics officers fell down the stairs onto Harris, and expecting that door to open with a hail of gunfire, Harris stretched to get a clean shot, firing four times at the door with his pistol.

Kerns leaned over the men lying at the bottom of the stairs to fire repeatedly at the third floor door, stopping when two officers carrying pump action shotguns charged up the stairs, firing as they went. The officer in the lead kicked open the door before leaning back and freezing, and then more gunfire was exchanged with whoever occupied the third floor.

The suspect, Jennings, had barricaded himself inside a bedroom, but police quickly overtook the third-floor apartment to occupy it in numbers, taking secure positions for trading lead. The onslaught of police increased quickly, the sound of gunfire deafening; it was only a matter of time before the authorities took him out. Jennings had done time in the past, and wanting to avoid years of jail time, he took his own life with a headshot beneath the chin, which ended it.

Griffin and Ortiz were both wearing bulletproof vests, but had still suffered critical wounds. Griffin had received two wounds in his left leg and Ortiz had a bullet lodged in his right forearm. An ambulance crew hustled onto the scene to take the wounded policemen to the nearest trauma center, while another ambulance transported the two deceased criminals to the morgue to be pronounced D.O.A.

A regular patrolman took Harris to a nearby hospital to have a surgeon dig the shotgun pellets out of his left leg. Given a room where a doctor could examine his leg, Harris immediately removed his trousers for concern they would cut off his pants and then he'd have nothing to wear. He covered his boxer shorts with a hospital gown that closed in the back, provided by a nurse, and then he waited for a doctor to treat the wound.

The doctor entering the room knew Harris from previous injuries for which he had treated him, and he peered down at the holes in his knee and leg.

"Lieutenant Harris, isn't this the same knee I operated on less than a year ago?"

"I guess so. Why?"

The doctor shook his head and proceeded to give him two injections of painkiller in the knee, commenting, "I thought you were going to consider taking a desk job."

"I'm not one who likes to sit around."

After the painkiller took effect, a nurse assisted as the doctor maneuvered a large pair of tweezers to penetrate holes in the tissue to dig out the pellets. He dropped them in a pan one by one.

"This knee is going to swell up and be stiff for at least a week, and until it gets better you may walk with a limp. I'm going to again suggest that you either take a desk job or think about taking a line of work in the private sector that's less hazardous. How many more times are you going to come in here before you receive an injury that's not medically treatable?"

"I'll take it under advisement, but there's not much of a job market out there."

"You'll be lucky if I don't have to operate on that knee again, but before it comes to that you can be retrained for a far less dangerous occupation."

When the doctor finished, the nurse cleaned the wounds before bandaging the knee, and Harris grimaced while adjusting the knee, putting his pants back on.

The doctor said, "I'm prescribing pain medication and I recommend that you do nothing strenuous for the next few days. In the morning, you may find soaking in hot bath water beneficial for loosening that knee up to give you mobility."

By the time Harris left the medical facility his knee was already stiffening up with pain increasing considerably. He knew the doctor was right, as he wasn't getting around like he used to, and there may one day come a time when he wouldn't be as lucky as he was today. Still, there was a question of how he was going to make a living if he got out of law enforcement, as he didn't see many prospects for someone with his training and experience.

David Gatesbury

Hoping to learn of the condition of Griffin and Ortiz soon, he and the officer providing him transportation headed back to the station.

Chapter 2
Getting Together with Some of the Guys

Harris returned to St. Louis Police Headquarters, and another detective named Jorgensen saw him in the hallway.

"Hey Len, I heard you were wounded, so how's the leg?"

"It's nothing serious."

"Hastings wants to see you in his office right away."

Harris went to an office door marked 'Chief of Detectives' and after entering he approached the secretary's desk. "I understand Hastings wants to see me."

"Yes, Lieutenant Harris, he's expecting you. Go right in."

Entering Hastings' office, the two men went back a long way together as old friends, and greeted each other with a smile and a handshake.

Hastings asked, "How's the leg, Len?"

Getting a whiff of the smoldering, citrus-based cologne Hastings wore, he replied, "It's really not bad; just a few pellets caught me."

"You took a shotgun blast to the knee and all you can say is that it's not bad."

Then Harris asked, "How are Griffin and Ortiz?"

"They're in a critical care unit, but are expected to pull through. What do you say to going out and having a bite to eat?"

Harris nodded, "Yeah, sure."

They left the station and went to Reilly's, a restaurant and bar located nearby that was regularly browsed by police detectives as a watering hole. The two friends had drifted apart in recent years as Hastings moved up the ladder in the department, but it seemed like old times as the two sat down at a table together. Hastings ordered a Rueben on a croissant and Harris had a roast beef sandwich on French bread.

Steve Hastings held concern for a drinking problem Harris developed after his wife Valerie was killed in an automobile accident, and listened as his friend ordered a Seven-and-Seven, while he had a beer.

After the waiter walked away, Hastings asked, "You okay with drinking alcohol?"

"One isn't going to be a problem, and I can use a drink after the day I've had."

Hastings nodded, knowing his friend's drinking problem had nearly cost him his badge. "Are you still going to those Alcoholics Anonymous meetings?"

"I went to two meetings, and never once acknowledged I'm an alcoholic, but I've been able to get a grip on managing my problems."

Looking to change the subject, Hastings commented, "I saw you limping. I hope you're not in much pain."

Harris shook his head no.

Hastings then said, "I'm going to arrange it so you can get some time off, maybe as much as a month."

He looked at Hastings, "A month?"

"Look, I know for a fact that you've had several injuries connected with that left knee, and that's the same knee you twisted playing college football. Do you remember the day you learned you were going to lose your scholarship, and we went out and got completely plastered? A few months later, we went in and signed up to join the police academy, a couple of guys who thought they were *hot stuff*."

Harris recalled the memory, "I saw myself as someone of average intelligence, and didn't see much chance in continuing my education. You, at least, had the good sense to get a diploma to make something of yourself, and you've got it made now."

Hastings returned the compliment by saying, "You're a topnotch detective, Len, and if I ever had to go out on a case and needed a partner, you'd still be the guy I'd ask for. I can recall a few times when you and I got caught up in sticky situations and you saved my neck—you're the best friend I've ever had."

The waiter delivered their drinks, and Len replied, "Thanks for saying so, Steve. I know we've kind of gone our separate ways over the years, but I still feel the same about you."

Hastings went on to stir up other memories, "There was a time when I was feeling down because I couldn't get a girl, or a date for that matter, but you always attracted the females. You introduced me to an old flame of yours, Frances, and you came to be the best man at our wedding. We've had three great kids, and life's never been better, but you know that first night we doubled Fran didn't want anything to do with me. She'd gone out with me just to be close to you, hoping to rekindle the relationship she'd had with you, and it was only after she saw the competition she was up against that she settled for this loser."

"You were never a loser. You were a good catch, and I tried setting the two of you up because I believed you'd make a great couple and things worked out wonderfully for you both."

"Maybe I wasn't a loser, but compared to you I was, and it took a lot of work on my part to get Fran to cozy up to me." Hastings then opened his wallet to let Harris see a recent photograph of his wife Frances. "Get a look at her."

Harris was impressed how Hastings' wife appeared, as she had a slender, shapely build. "Steve, I always thought her to be an exceptionally nice-looking girl, and the years have been good to her—she looks better than ever."

"Most people think she looks ten years younger than me and they're surprised to learn she's given birth to three children, all grown now." Hastings then turned the photo to glimpse at it, adding, "When I first met her, I thought her to be pleasantly plump. I like a full-figured woman with a voluptuous figure, and she had an angelic face. After having the kids she started putting on weight, and after trying every diet in existence, she sought help to get her weight down, and now she's skinny as a rail."

Harris grinned, "You know, old buddy, you can afford to lose a couple of pounds. What do you weigh nowadays?"

Hastings replied, "I'll tell you what, I promise not to talk about your drinking problem if you won't talk about my weight."

Nodding in agreement and tapping their glasses together, Harris downed a few swallows of his drink.

Harris then took notice of a senior detective named Ron Warren walking by their table, an honest, diligent cop he respected.

Warren acknowledged the two men's presence, "Hi, Steve. Say, Len, you were the last guy I was expecting to see here this evening.

After hearing about how that raid went, I thought you'd be in the hospital. So how's the leg?"

"I'm going out ballroom dancing later."

Warren grinned, nodding his head, "Oh yeah, like it's an everyday thing for you to get wounded by a shotgun blast."

"No, but seriously, it's not that bad. I'm going to walk with a limp for a while."

"You were lucky—both those scumbags were hardcore criminals with rap sheets a mile long. Jennings ran that neighborhood with a climate of fear from that apartment building with his mother living on the first floor, and she was the only person shedding tears over her son's death. Everybody else within a six block radius was celebrating when they got the news Jennings died in a gun battle, ending his life with a bullet to the head."

Harris said, "Why don't you sit down with us, Ron, and have a drink?"

"Okay, but I've got Jack Gallagher with me."

Hastings nodded, "Tell him to come over and join us."

After the other two detectives joined them at their table, Hastings remarked, "Len and I were going down memory lane, talking about the old days. You wouldn't believe how the girls used to flock after this guy." Hastings reached over to gently pinch Harris on the cheek, "His features haven't changed all that much, maybe a little more rugged, but he still has that baby face the females like."

Warren and Gallagher chuckled, and then Warren said, "I don't know if you've heard, but Jack is opening up his own detective agency here in town."

Harris said, "Good for you, I hope things work out. But what made you open up your own office?"

Gallagher, dark-haired and the youngest of the four sitting at the table, gripped his glass, "I took up corporate work for a couple of attorneys investigating the theft of industrial secrets at a chemical plant. The work became quite lucrative and with the money I made I was able to make an investment toward starting my own agency."

Warren commented, "In my day, detective work took a whole lot of thought and footwork, but these young guys have the smarts and the advantage of today's technology to acquire information. They have miniature camera lenses and listening devices to help them, and look how most of the kids today are operating computers at almost the same time they can walk." He gently elbowed Harris, "We were born at the wrong time Len."

Hastings commented, "Yeah, but while they're becoming a computer whiz they're lacking in social skills. Some of these kids can't even make change." He then turned to Harris, "You ought to start your own agency. I can get you all kinds of keyhole work—men checking on their wives and vice versa."

"I haven't the business sense to manage a company. For now, I'm soaking up time cushioning my pension, but today's raid may be the last one I'm volunteering for."

Hastings stated, "You must've been out of your mind taking a spot on that sting operation. What are you trying to prove?"

"These younger guys have much more to lose than I have, and I thought I could give them assistance."

Ron Warren kept rubbing his nose, finally commenting with a disturbed expression, "My nose itches, am I getting a cold or what?" He then squinted, looking at Hastings, "It's that damn cologne you're wearing. I know that's what it is because my nose acts up every time I step into your office. Where'd you get that goofy stuff, and don't say Macy's or Dillard's."

"I got it at a high-class clothing shop in the Plaza Frontenac shopping center some time ago while picking up a blouse for Fran." Hastings looked at Harris, "I told you how Fran has trimmed down and is still losing weight. She'd purchased this blouse for a wingding the city was having in the mayor's honor, but they didn't have her size so it had to be special ordered. When picking up the blouse, it occurred to me that I'd been thinking about purchasing cologne for those celebrity VIP bashes the city holds, and I asked the salesman what male colognes his shop carried."

"The guy sets three fancy bottles on the counter and one at a time he puts a couple drops on his wrist and forearm to let me get a whiff. I don't know anything about colognes, and my smeller isn't the best, so I asked if there's one out of the three he recommends. He draws my attention to the third bottle and says, "This is the one I wear. It has a very distinctive, risqué scent.

"Now I notice this guy's looking deep in my eyes, and all of a sudden it hits me that he's gay and flirting with me. I nearly climbed over the counter to punch his lights out, but this calm voice comes to me from the back of my mind, *Hastings, you're not above the law. You belt this guy and you're sure to find yourself arrested for assault and battery and he'll probably sue you.* What else was there for me to do, but say, "Okay, put it on my wife's charge account?"

Everybody busted out laughing, and Jack Gallagher asked, "What's the name of it?"

Hastings replied, "Vintage something. The salesman described the fragrance as a blend of unique but masculine primal scents in wood and musk with citrus and floral notes."

Harris gazed at Hastings, wondering about what he'd just said. "You can recall all that, but you can't remember the name of the cologne."

A few other detectives gathered to listen in on the conversation, and Warren commented, "I think I'm allergic to that stuff. It's powerful enough to set off the damn sprinkler system in this place, and as long as you go on wearing it, you ought to be carrying a fire extinguisher to guard against spontaneous combustion."

More laughter broke out, and Warren caught sight of a popular blonde waitress named Angie walking by who had a reputation for holding a straight face while making off-the-cuff remarks. He stopped her, "Hey, Angie, get a whiff of the cologne Hastings is wearing and give us the lowdown on what you think. It's a blend of unique but masculine primal scents."

The woman stopped to lean over Hastings to catch the spicy, heavy scent, and then she gave him a look. "Tequila—yeah, that's what I smell, tequila. I hope you have to be over twenty-one to purchase it because it's sure to give people a mind-numbing high. I highly recommend that you don't get behind the wheel of a car when wearing it—the arresting officer won't need a Breathalyzer to put cuffs on you."

Everybody was laughing and some were on the verge of falling on the floor when Warren said, "You know something, you're right. I think I smell tequila too—it must be those citrus notes that are in it."

While on a roll, Angie remarked, "Citrus notes, like hell, that's tequila—the fumes from that stuff can melt the chrome off the bumper of a '57 Chevy."

Angie grinned, pointing her finger at Warren, "Ron, you're laughing so hard you're in tears."

Still laughing, Warren shook his head no, "I'm in tears because I'm allergic to that damn cologne of his."

Angie now broke into a giggle, turning to look at Hastings, who was no longer amused by jokes about his cologne. "Instead of wearing it on your body you should dump some in your car's tank to increase your gas mileage. It would make a good substitute for fuel injection cleaner."

The place was now in an uproar, and Warren said, "Angie, here comes Gary Heitzel, a detective we all suspect is gay. I'll ask him what he thinks."

Warren signaled for Heitzel to join the party, "Heitzel, we're trying to describe the scent of the cologne Hastings is wearing. Would you like to give us a take on what scent you pick up?"

Thinking his description would differ entirely from everyone else's, Heitzel appeared glad to give his opinion. "Sure, I'll give you my best shot."

Warren gave Angie a wink without Heitzel noticing and began thumbing at the detective as he leaned over Hastings to take a slow, gentle whiff.

Heitzel then voiced, "Citrus based with a confluence of grapefruit and lime, hints of pepper and lavender, and bottom notes of oak and sandalwood. I also believe it contains patchouli, which is a warmly scented oil derived from an Indo-Malayan shrub."

In the deliberate motion of shaking his head yes, Warren said, "That's the best description I've heard yet."

Angie nodded, "You can tell this is a guy who knows his colognes." She leaned back as she gave Warren a look with her eyes bugging out, "Be careful though. They say it's known to bring out the primal, animal instinct in you."

Angie next looked at Hastings, "I'll tell you one thing though, you need to leave the window open when you uncork the bottle to apply that potent stuff to your skin. The fumes could blow up the whole house, and it may take months for the bomb squad to determine the accelerant was that crazy cologne."

Their laughter went on at Hastings's expense, as almost everyone went on running down the cologne he wore.

Chapter 3
The Study of Criminal Behavior Involving Murder

Later, Warren, Gallagher and the others moved on to mingle with other law enforcement patrons at the bar, and Harris and Hastings resumed talk about the old days at their table.

Hastings finished his drink and, after ordering another round, lit up a cigar.

Harris saw an opportunity to give Hastings a hard time about his smoking, remarking, "I thought you'd given up smoking those nasty things. I recall you once telling me that doctor's orders were for you to stop."

Hastings took a deep drag, and then expelled smoke as he spoke, "I don't know if it was doctor's orders as much as it was Fran's orders, but I'm down to smoking three a day." He then had another thought. "Say, do you remember when you were still wearing blue and you hooked up with a young kid named Mark Kramer? You sort of took him under your wing, becoming his partner for a short time until he was killed."

Harris recalled Kramer, "Yes, he and I had received a radio call about a burglary in progress and when we went to the address we made a search of the grounds. He was shot in the alley by a kid not yet seventeen years of age."

"That's him. His sister disappeared."

"Which one? He had two sisters."

Hastings commented, "Yeah, I forgot you dated the older sister, the foxy blonde with the sweet smile—she's the one missing."

Harris nodded. "Amanda was the one I dated, and Rhonda was the younger one. They're a nice family, good people. So, what is this about Amanda disappearing?"

"It seems whenever the economy takes a nosedive it brings out the worst in criminal behavior. As you well know, over the past few months the gruesome remains of prostitutes have begun turning up in the metro area. Thus far, three victims found are black, but, of course, Amanda Kramer was no prostitute. Her father called me up voicing concern about wanting to find his daughter alive and asked if I could connect him with a reliable detective. My answer was that we're doing everything possible to find her, and hiring a detective would not only be expensive, but there's little chance he'd be able to find her before the police could."

Hastings paused to take a drink. "I thought that since I'm giving you some time off you might want to look into the case. I've assigned Ron Warren to lead the investigation into the deaths of the prostitutes, but the FBI has intervened, so I don't know if he'll be able to give you the latest up-to-the-minute progress we're making. However, if you're interested, I'll give you Mr. Kramer's phone number."

Harris said, "Sure, I'll take it, but what was his response when you told him hiring a detective could get expensive?"

"He said, he's lost his son and now one of his daughters is missing, and he's willing to spend his entire life savings to find her. When speaking of his wife passing away about a year ago, he got emotional, sounding terrible over the phone, out of breath and wheezing like he's having serious health problems."

"I remember Amanda's father once telling me how his father escaped Tito's socialist Yugoslavia with his family in a small boat during a thunder storm, crossing the Adriatic Sea to reach the Italian shore. He had undergone torture for denouncing communism, and succeeded at bringing his family to the United States. Wanting to Americanize his family name, which was Kurasovic or something like that, he had it changed to Kramer."

Hastings handed over his business card with Mr. Kramer's phone number written on the back. "I told him someone would contact him, and that was a few days ago, so try to get in touch with him as soon as you can." He then had another thought, "I recall Amanda Kramer well. She was a knockout, and I thought for a time you and she were going to marry. Why did you and Amanda stop seeing each other?"

"Naturally, Mark Kramer's death devastated that family, and the day they laid him to rest Amanda told me she wasn't going to see me anymore."

He clasped his hands around his glass, "When she and I first met, she was a freshman in high school and I was a senior. I was embarrassed dating someone that young, but she was the most beautiful girl I'd ever seen. Ordinarily, you'd get a hard time from classmates dating a girl that young, but that was overlooked in part because she was nice-looking and had a charming personality. I don't think I ever met a person who didn't like her. At first, I tried avoiding her, but every time I turned around she was standing there, and what she liked most was that I could make her laugh—we had a lot of fun together. After graduating in 1999, I picked her up in front of school on a couple of occasions, and it was a little weird, but she was happy to see me pulling up in my car.

"Anyway, I was a young officer on the force when Mark joined the department, and when he was killed it was over for the two of us. She wasn't going to get involved with a cop and have her heart broken again when he was killed in the line of duty. I never asked because I didn't want to make matters worse, but I believe the family thought I'd let them down by failing to look after Mark, blaming me to some degree for his death. I made it my business to see her once more, telling her I loved her and asking her to marry me, but she said no. I suppose to merely look at me reminded her of what happened to her brother. She had looks and amiable traits, but she was never the same after her brother was killed, acting very cold toward me the last few times we spoke. I took it that was her way of breaking ties with me and giving me a sendoff."

Harris put the card in the inside pocket of his sport jacket and swished around the ice in his glass while thinking about ordering another drink. "Are you gonna have another?"

"I hope I'm not going to be at fault for you falling off the wagon."

"No, I just thought I'd have another to help kill the pain in my knee." Smiling, he added, "You know, for medicinal purposes."

The two men soon departed and Harris went to his home on the southwest side of the city. He popped two pain pills and poured himself a tall glass of Kentucky Straight Bourbon Whisky to wash them down with. There was no hiding from the truth that he used liquor as a crutch to help him live in what he saw as an empty, lonely existence. Always a heavy drinker, his drinking significantly increased after his wife Valerie's death, but seeing his liquor consumption running out of control, he managed to cut back on the habit. He had little choice, as to go on the way he was would make it impossible to function in this world as a homicide investigator.

Sitting down in the living room and carefully propping his left leg up on the coffee table, he reached for his wife's picture which he kept on the end table. Staring at it, he thought how much he missed her, as they were a happy couple. If there was anything their marriage lacked it was children, and although doctors hadn't given them much chance for having a child, they hadn't given up hope. They'd spoken a few times about adoption and giving it consideration. They saw years ahead of them for making such a move, and suddenly, she was gone. In that moment, swept away was a future full of expectations, and for a time it was as though he didn't have much to live for.

For months, depressed and grief-stricken, becoming a miserable drunk, one night when feeling downheartedly bereaved and melancholy, he nearly shot himself in the head. What kept him from pulling the trigger was looking at Valerie's picture, as he knew this was something she wouldn't want him to do. From that moment on he began pulling himself back together. Realizing without some sort of routine he was sure to fall back on the bottle again, he concentrated on his work, and for a time this was the only thing that kept him going.

Something that helped Harris climb out of his fit of alcoholism was the study of serial killers, a sobering phase of his education in law enforcement. Reading correctional institution records and coroner's reports, he'd analyzed statistical information with regards to the history of these enigmatic psychopaths. Vicious, soulless, and evil to the core, these prolific murderers are committed to taking the lives of innocent people to feed and gratify a thrill while getting perverse pleasure from these unspeakable acts. It made him wonder what awakens the ravenous appetite of this type of killer to emerge and take hold, whereby for a time they willfully take control over another person's fate. Being in control can bring on an exalting feeling of power, feeding a savage but primitive rationale as the killer gives into perverted thoughts, an overwhelming defilement of the soul that energizes the capacity to kill. Some find fulfillment in the rapture of this magnificent grand illusion, and once they've crossed this line they become something inhuman, for it's only a matter of time before they do it again.

Harris had previously taken college courses covering Criminal Justice to scrutinize the characteristics of murderers, while focusing on the basic fundamental motives for such acts. He found the main motives for murder to be: love or the absence of it, money and greed, pride and jealousy, revenge, mental illness/obsession, crimes of passion/sex and lust. Other factors inducing the urge to kill are gang initiation and violence often related to drug trafficking, mob contract/murder for hire, thrill killing, hate crime (religious, racial, deteriorating marriage), and robbery.

His studies of human behavior entailed examining the roles of certain emotional risk factors such as personality disorders. Men who kill their wives are almost invariably personality disordered, and he'd learned that physical abuse, domestic violence, and rage often come before the act of murder. Deaths of a spouse or an intimate partner usually come after an escalation of violence, beatings and bludgeoning. Estrangement, separation and abandonment are motivational factors in many cases for creating rage. One clear pattern is that a high degree of domestic homicides occur after a verbal or physical confrontation during a failed reconciliation, or when a wife first announces her intention to leave.

Police report male jealousy as the most frequent motive. After a prolonged period of internal conflict, chronic, and aversive tension, the act is carried out on impulse in a violent episode. "Overcontrolled" murders are common, where paranoia and depression is linked to passive aggressive and dependent personality disorders. Homicide-suicide incidents often involve amorous jealousy on the part of the perpetrator, whether real or delusional, for their partner's infidelity.

Marital or intimate killings often result in greater violence, or "overkill", involving lengthy and excessive violence, inflicting harm far beyond what is necessary to ensure a kill. It is not unusual for these fatal assaults to continue long after the person is dead, as victims in most of these prolonged attacks have multiple stab wounds and dozens of bodily injuries. There may be two or more separate actions of stabbing, cutting, or shooting, but most resulted in stabbing and/or throat slashing. This act of overkill in most cases doesn't apply with mariticide (husband killing).

Knowledge Harris acquired in case studies helped aid him in his career for solving numerous homicide cases. Murder is seldom simple, and predominantly an unplanned event. Psychoanalysts have diagnosed killers' prevalent pathologies and emotional problems in an effort to pinpoint the root cause for murder. The mindset of some killers ranges from ruminative to obsessional, and often taking on the "Othello Syndrome." Such relationships are more often than not chronically chaotic, fraught with jealous suspicions, and verbal and physical abuse. "Homicidal husbands" commonly escalate to a dangerous level of anger and anxiety prior to the act. In many cases, they threaten to do what they end up doing for responding to the intolerable stimulus in the face of a wife's departure. The worst scenarios lead to "Family homicides," which are often precipitated by separation from the partner.

What he'd learned in the past as a detective helped prepare him for taking up a psychiatric study for delving into the mind of the serial killer. The actions of these people definitely place them in a separate classification. Their 'Modus Operandi,' approximately translated "method of operation," sets them apart from the others, and can sometimes by description make a person's skin crawl. It's a term often used in criminal profiling, and examining the actions and methods employed by these perpetrators offers clues to the offender's psychology. Work in this field can assist in the identification and apprehension of such criminals while determining links between crimes.

Getting into the minds of these psychologically unbalanced killers is difficult, as their ungrounded thinking usually has no logic to it, and it may be that their behavior is linked to a degenerative gene. The environment of their upbringings linked to child abuse can impact their mental development, but it may just as well be that they suffered oxygen deprivation for a lengthy period of time at the moment of birth. Studies have proven that these considerations can lead to a flawed mind-altering mutation, resulting in their having warped ideas about people and in particular, the opposite sex. It's a well-known fact that many serial killers show a propensity for torturing and killing animals in their youth, which accelerates into a diseased, unstable mind that has crazed, violent impulses. A predisposed fault in a person's personality can cause this killer instinct to take root and prevail while surfacing to give a person an unrestricted drive to kill and mutilate the bodies of their victims.

Few see themselves for what they are and what they've become, but for some an internal struggle begins. They're conscious of their criminal behavior and how it caused them to take a life. They know they've done wrong in the eyes of God and man and want to repent as a way to come to grips with their actions. Overtime they are tormented by feeling the need and strong desire to do it again and again. Judgmental reconciliation leads to excuses and forgiveness, and an innermost urge to kill again pushes aside clear thinking, overriding civilized reasoning. The period of intercession has fallen to the wayside, as the insertion of another victim put through living hell is the only thing that can quell this unremitting and incessant drive to kill. This hostile, aggressive tendency that needs quenching is immured for but a short time before the murderer is compelled to conspire, solicit, and incur upon the unlucky, the unsuspecting, and the sadly unfortunate. What happened once is imminently and ultimately certain to occur again and again until the killer is exposed and put away. Some might say they are sick and can't help themselves, but they get fulfillment, and even enjoyment, out of torturing innocent people to death.

Serial killing took the public's fascination in the late 1880's when a murderer calling himself "Jack the Ripper" began slaughtering prostitutes in London's Whitechapel District. However, many of modern day's serial killers, by comparison, make this individual look like a boy scout.

Harris's study of courtroom records covering American serial killers chronicled in depth some of the most infamous murderers in modern history, starting with the Zodiac Killer. These were killers whose atrocities rocked the nation, as they cruelly etched a place for their names on the list of the worst criminals in the annals of history.

His thoughts for the moment were for the relationship he'd had with Amanda Kramer. It seemed that having this missing person's case may serve to keep him occupied so he wouldn't drink during the time he had off with this injury. However, this also gave him reason to recall the death of Mark Kramer, and he carried a guilt complex for not being able to do anything to save this young man's life. Having collared the teenager who'd fatally shot Mark, he remembered standing over his dying partner and watching life drain from his body. This was an image that had surfaced in his mind more often than he wanted to recall, and he'd sometimes relive it in his dreams for feeling so helpless to save him. What gave Harris additional cause to rehash this terrible incident was that he'd played a role in Mark wanting to become a cop, as he'd looked up to Harris. He'd seen Harris as the kind of law officer he wanted to be and strived to emulate him.

He remembered Amanda well, a woman he wanted to marry, but it wasn't to be, for she had no desire to be married to an officer of the law. He fell asleep in the chair thinking about both Amanda and Mark after drinking almost half of the bottle of bourbon. Awaking in the middle of the night, feeling the urge to use the restroom, as he stood up, the stiffness in his knee caused him to misstep and fall flat on his face. He got up from the floor and after stumbling into the bathroom to relieve himself, he soon made it to bed.

Waking up the next morning, he was looking at foreclosure on his house before finally getting a grip on life to turn around his grim financial situation. Nowadays doing a much better job managing his life and keeping up with invoices, he sat down to write checks to cover the house payment and utility bills. Later, looking in the bathroom mirror, he thought himself a mess, but then he showered, shaved, and prepared to start his day. He stopped and gazed at Valerie's photograph once more as though making a gesture of apology for his drinking, and without a spoken word promised to try harder to stop.

He phoned Mr. Kramer and when he didn't get an answer, he neglected to leave a message, stopping instead at a greasy spoon to have a light breakfast.

Afterwards, he phoned Mr. Kramer again and this time he got an answer, hearing a drowsy voice sounding deep and withdrawn. "Hello."

"Good morning, Mr. Kramer, my name is Harris, and I received your phone number from Chief of Detectives Steven Hastings."

"Yes, I'm sorry I can't speak too clearly. I came to the emergency room of St. Mary's Hospital a few days ago complaining of chest pains, and the next thing I knew they were performing bypass surgery on me."

Thinking this man must've just came home after being hospitalized, Harris said, "Well, perhaps I should call you back in a day or two to give you some recovery time."

"No," the voice said urgently, "I want you to come to my house today so you can start looking for my daughter immediately."

Having a bad time understanding Mr. Kramer, Harris replied, "You want me to see you now?"

"Yes, please, as soon as possible."

"It may take me a half hour or so, but I'll be right there."

Harris drove to the Kramer residence in his tan Chevrolet Impala, and memories of coming to this brick home on the south side returned to him as he walked up to the door. He hadn't seen Amanda's father in years and saw little chance of this man remembering him. Mr. Kramer must've been watching for him to arrive, as he opened the door wearing a robe and slippers, "Are you the detective I spoke to on the phone?"

"Yes, I am."

The frail and seemingly feeble man gently caught hold of Harris's sleeve to pull him inside.

Not knowing what response he would get with his next comment, Harris said, "My name is Leonard Harris. I knew your son Mark well, and for a time I dated Amanda. Do you remember me?"

The aging man's eyes flashed at Harris, as if giving his features a look over, "Yes, yes I do, and it's good you know Amanda. You may know the circle of people she ran with and something about the routine she followed."

"I haven't seen Amanda in a good many years, Mr. Kramer, but I'm willing to investigate her disappearance, if that's what you want me to do."

Mr. Kramer made a strong effort to communicate verbally, "I had this wretched heart attack out of concern for her safety, and I want you to find her."

"I understand."

His hand shook as he reached for a piece of paper on the fireplace mantle where there were graduation pictures of Amanda, Mark, and his youngest daughter Rhonda, photos Harris remembered seeing before. He handed the paper to Harris, "This is my youngest daughter's phone number. Her name is Rhonda and she can write you a check from my savings account to get you started looking for Amanda."

On the piece of paper was chicken scratched handwriting, but he could make out the name Rhonda and the phone number Kramer had written down.

"I wish I could be more help to you, but in my condition I'm quite helpless. I went in the hospital the next day after last talking to Hastings and he told me he'd be sending someone."

Harris gave a reassuring nod, "You can rest assured that I'll do all I can to find Amanda for you and I'll get in touch with Rhonda today to start my investigation." Harris handed him his card, "Here's my card, in case you need to reach me, and I'll also see to it that Rhonda has my phone number."

As if out of breath, Kramer strained to add, "Rhonda is sometimes difficult to contact. She's employed as assistant manager at Tokar's Casino, but you can catch her there tonight after six in the evening."

"Where is Amanda employed?"

"She works for Anthony Tokar, owner of the casino, managing his affairs as his personal secretary."

The old gentleman settled down when telling Harris goodbye, and over the course of the next several hours, Harris had trouble reaching Rhonda by phone. He tried her number at different times throughout the day, leaving no message. Confident he'd soon catch up to her, he went to police headquarters to fill out paperwork to arrange time off for his knee injury. While there, he intended talking to Ron Warren to see what he knew about Amanda's disappearance since it was currently under investigation by the department. He was also curious to find out if there were any new developments regarding the gruesome murders of those prostitutes.

Chapter 4
Gathering Information on Missing Persons and the Activity of a Serial Killer

After completing the necessary paperwork at police headquarters to arrange time off, Harris went to Steve Hastings' office. In the short time he spoke to his secretary, he learned Hastings wasn't available and he may not be back at the station for hours. He caught the scent of cigar smoke and that peculiar cologne worn by the chief of detectives. His knee beginning to ache, he took a pain pill, and stopping by a water fountain to wash it down, he saw Ron Warren standing behind a counter reading paperwork. Hasting's had indicated that Warren was the one to speak to, as he was handling both the missing person's cases and directing the investigation involving black prostitutes.

Harris approached him, "Ron, I understand you're conducting the investigation into those murdered prostitutes. I've taken on a case involving the disappearance of a woman named Amanda Kramer, looking into it as a favor to her family, and I was wondering if you can give me anything helpful."

"You're asking for privileged, confidential information Len, but I don't mind letting you in on a few things because I know you'll keep a tight lip. This is a hot item to say the least—it's beginning to get nationwide attention, and if the media finds out you have anything to do with this case they'll be breathing down your neck. I'm giving you my cooperation strictly because I think you're an OK guy, but unfortunately, I can't say the same for your old buddy Hastings."

Warren appeared a bit steamed and resentful, "He burned me a few times to make himself look good for becoming Chief of Detectives, and getting that promotion has blown-up his ego. I haven't got too long before retirement, so I don't mind if you tell him I said he's a jerk. It's my hard work that's made this department operate efficiently, and just this morning he dumped his problems on me, but I've come to the point where I don't care anymore."

"Whatever you and I talk about stays with me, Ron."

"Moving up in the ranks gave him a big head. I saw a change in him the minute he took that position, and now he acts like he's some kind of a ladies man."

"Ron, he's a family man."

"Oh, yeah, don't fool yourself, a guy that wears cologne that potent is on the prowl for female companionship, and if you don't know that, you're not the detective I thought you to be."

Warren took a manila folder from a nearby file cabinet and handed it to Harris, "These are photos of the first three victims. We found the remains of a fourth victim this morning, the body mangled and badly decomposed, and like the first three victims she's a black prostitute. We got a break making the identification with her being a local living on the streets for only a couple of months. She kept tabs with family and friends on the north side where she turned tricks to make a dollar, and they reported her missing ten days ago. A plaster cast was made of undisturbed tire tread impressions found at the location of where they discovered the body."

Harris examined photos of the first three victims while listening to Warren and a photo marked #1 in the upper right hand corner indicated the first body found. Her remains were nothing more than a skeletal structure assembled on a table, hair still connected to the skull.

"The killer focused on women living on the fringes of society, leaving no family members reporting the first three victims missing. We received our first lead a month ago by mail here at the station, a typewritten letter with a map, and a red X on the map pinpointing exactly where to find the remains of that first victim. We found what was left of her lying on a stack of debris in an abandoned lot on the north side of town, and as you can see, she wasn't much more than scattered bones. This is the method by which we've found all four victims: correspondence arriving here at the station in the nature of a short letter and a map indicating where to find a body.

"We discovered the second victim in much the same condition as the first. However, with the exception of the first murder victim, the others were located across the river in the metro east. Plastic straps bound the hands and legs of the decomposed bodies, which may have been used to make it easier to transport them, and there are obvious indications they underwent torture. Each one had limbs and ribs broken, injuries perhaps delivered by a brutal kick. The killer placed the bodies in high weeds or thick woods at secluded outdoor areas, and not one of them had a stitch of clothing or articles of identification, their identities confirmed by various means.

"Whoever this sadist is, it wasn't enough to murder these women and expecting to get away with it, he wanted credit and attention for his handiwork. He's entertained himself by sending us letters and maps, correspondence that has drawn a lot of media attention. He's been careful thus far not to leave fingerprints, but we've detected DNA from saliva applied when he carelessly licked one of the envelopes to seal it. No match came up in CODIS and the National DNA Index System of known criminal offenders, but we are still checking with other database systems nationwide, and the FBI has taken over control of the investigation.

"One detail you'll have to keep to yourself is the typewritten letters and maps come off a computer printer say very little, but the FBI agent leading a specialized team thinks the maps carry significance. Getting his kicks marking the location of victim's bodies on a map, he's certain to get a thrill when it's announced on the news that a fourth victim has turned up. I understand they found scarring on the wrists and ankles of this last female, indicating he'd secured chains or cuffs to hold her in bondage."

Harris remarked, "Amanda Kramer is not a prostitute, nor is she black, so even though she was reported missing, she may not have been abducted by the same individual who killed these other women."

Warren acknowledged this with a nod. "That's true, and she was reported missing just four days ago, but you never know about people's lifestyles. I've done murder investigations to learn a woman can lead the life of a high-priced call girl with practically no one knowing about it until she's found murdered. Another young Caucasian woman reported missing is a dancer at a topless lounge in East St. Louis, and she's held several other occupations while residing here in Missouri. Her name is Deborah Kutraba, an immigrant from Albania who may be of Bosnian or Serbian descent. She's married with three children, and to put it the way her husband told it, she is a hardworking girl trying to support a family. The husband had a heavy accent that was difficult to understand, also mentioning he was having a bad time finding work. You know how it is, a girl can make a lot of money working as a dancer and the cost for a babysitter can get expensive. So, the way I see it, they're making it the best way they know how, and he's a stay at home dad."

Warren presented to Harris an envelope that held still photos from security cameras where Amanda Kramer worked. The photos were taken at the casino's underground garage and showed the Toyota Camry she had driven as it left her place of work for the last time.

"These surveillance photos are the last taken of the Kramer girl, and the last accounting for her whereabouts. It's difficult to make out with any certainty that it's her behind the wheel from glare reflecting off the glass, and the picture's a little fuzzy anyway. Technicians have tried to computer enhance the imagery to give them clarity, but as you can see, it's done little good."

He also presented additional photos of the two missing Caucasian women, "These are fairly recent photos of Amanda Kramer and Deborah Kutraba."

Harris mainly gave attention to the photo of Amanda Kramer, who still looked very attractive, "What else can you tell me?"

"I can give you this Kutraba girl's address," and Warren wrote information down for him on a piece of notepaper.

Warren added, "I'd like to give you more, but I'm restricted on what I can say about this case. Should information leak out jeopardizing the investigation or subsequent arrest and prosecution of a suspected serial killer, I'd lose my badge. If I had any evidence linking Amanda Kramer's disappearance to these other killings I'd tell you, but except for the fact that she's missing I have nothing clearly indicating that someone abducted her. Two days after receiving the missing person's report on Kramer, a patrolman found her car downtown, not far from the riverfront on Wharf Street, six blocks south of the Arch grounds. That's not an area I'd recommend for somebody to go casually walking after dark. There were no prints or indications of a struggle, but the driver's seat may have been moved back to accommodate a person taller or larger than her. So, while suspecting foul play, we can't say with any certainty that somebody took her from that location or if someone simply parked her car there and took the keys.

"My gut feeling is that Amanda Kramer was probably abducted elsewhere and whoever took her left her car at that location, but we haven't enough facts or evidence to draw any conclusions. After all, like I said, the Kramer woman was only reported missing four days ago, this Deborah Kutraba was reported missing forty-eight hours ago, and we've yet to find her car."

Harris returned the photos to Warren, "Thanks Ron."

Someone in office personnel dropped a typewritten note on the counter, and while Warren read it, he commented, "There's no end to the hours I've spent on unsolved deaths and disappearances." He then looked at Harris, "I'd say the FBI agent handling the deaths of these prostitutes is a decent enough guy that he might be willing to give up more information. I'll put in a good word for you and should I get anything more I can release to you I'll let you know. He's not at the station now, and I couldn't give a definite time for when to catch him here."

"I'll try to stop by again soon to speak with him. What's his name?"

"Howard Johnson."

Harris continued looking at Warren, who nodded yes, "Really, that's the guy's name."

Warren added, "I don't know if you're aware of it, but the mayor announced this morning that there's to be a meeting at city hall to discuss the murders of the prostitutes at noon today. If you're going to it, you haven't got much time."

Harris thought it best to make that meeting, and when arriving at city hall he had a difficult time finding a place to park. There were television news crews and newspaper people gathered in the building's spacious lobby where he came to listen to the mayor speak on an elevated platform. After telling the crowd that immediate family members have been notified, he detailed the names of four victims before introducing a female criminologist named Juliet Palmer, heading the Behavioral Science Unit for the FBI.

The woman came forward. "I know you have questions, but at this time I can only tell you that we have leads we are pursuing. The FBI was asked to assist local law enforcement in this case, and has taken an interest in it mainly because it involves multiple murders of females that transcend state lines. While the body of one victim was found in the St. Louis area here in Missouri, the other three victims were discovered in Illinois, but they're all Missouri residents. Our primary role at this time is to ensure the continuity in evidence collected.

"Serial murders comprise less than one present of all murders in a given year, but it is estimated that serial killers may have done away with as many as ten times their known victims. We have a serial killer in the St. Louis area walking about in our midst, so beware and avoid contact with strangers. Many serial killers rely on charm to seduce their victims, and yet are rage personified, getting excitement and arousal out of terrorizing their victims. These rages satisfy an animal instinct pleasure, controlling pain and suffering as they wield the power of life and death. Strangulation for most of these killers is a component of sexual gratification—the grandeur of having importance by dominating others and controlling their fate.

"Often those targeted are runaways caught in the drug trade or a prostitution circuit, casualties by their way of life. Women living a transient, rocky, wasted lifestyle are weak-minded, unsuspecting and easy prey. Having been molested and abandoned at a young age, enduring harsh treatment and suffering violent episodes at the hands of possibly their parents or guardians, they're often robbed of their childhood.

"The science of anthropology has made great strides in the past 125 years. Quite often in such cases it's by the study of bones that we determine the deceased's age, sex, and race for identification purposes. The first two prostitutes found were badly decomposed, little more than a collection of bones, but an odontologist identified the victims by dental records, and their remains speak to us through forensics.

"Whoever did away with these prostitutes is merciless in how he deals with women, for before he's finished with them, they are probably praying for their deaths to come. The medical examiner said she believes the first two deceased women died from suffocation as a result of manual strangulation. She gave special attention to the laryngeal skeleton when performing the autopsy for determining their hyoid bone was broken. Exerting pressure on the neck to suffocate a person often breaks the small U-shaped bone at the base of the tongue.

"As for the third victim, he crushed her entire larynx and thyroid cartilage to collapse her airway, which he may have accomplished by a punch, a Karate chop, or perhaps a kick. For investigators, this says he's taken self-defense courses or may have had training in the armed forces. He may have just as well had experience in law enforcement, and simply delivered the blow to end the victim's misery or to silence her screams. The killer may have been emboldened to make this death blow as an exhibition of power to instill fear in others he may have abducted and have little choice but to watch.

"The killer hogtied and strapped up the fourth victim, probably doing it as a form of torture or punishment. Hanging someone that way for an undetermined period delivers hideously cruel pain, and the lungs are expanded so they cannot fully function to exhale, leading to asphyxiation or heart failure. The fact that her shoulders were dislocated gives evidence of this, and ligature marks were found on the victim, indicating he may have used various forms of restraints such as rope, zip-ties, or handcuffs. The killer's inordinate capacity for homicidal violence is rooted in a dysfunctional family history, as he may have endured beatings from his parents. Psychiatrists say society breeds serial killers who have a twisted hatred for women, compelling the individual to abduct and torture them as payback for the mistreatment they suffered as a child.

"During the act of performing torture on their victim, these people are living a fantasy. In most cases, the perpetrator was a victim of torture and in a certain sense they may be reliving the experience of their own victimization. By delivering torture to their prey they imagine themselves as regaining something they'd lost when experiencing a violent episode directed at them. Often a person of low esteem, the satisfaction of exerting power over their prisoner, for whatever reason, may give them a feeling of exaltation and by this act they've returned some of the dignity stolen from them. It's evident that he may periodically get some uncontrollable, compulsive urge to attack women as payback for mistreatment he experienced, and he may enjoy these power trips of making the female species suffer.

"While most serial killers are white, the hair follicle of an African-American male was lifted from one of the bodies. Believing this single hair was not transferred by some form of contamination, we have good reason to think our suspect is black. When profiling this individual, we again have concluded that he may have been in the military, and only perhaps recently was discharged. Since getting out of the armed forces he may have had a hard time finding employment or feels he is not suited for the job he now has. He may have undergone a recent divorce, which has increased demeaning feelings of his inability to function in this world on his own. This is an individual who may feel uncomfortable or even inferior when in the company of certain women. In his personal life at home, he may easily fly into a rage, which may have played into the failure of his marriage.

"Once he's overpowered a female and she's subject to his will, torturing her in a controlled environment gives him a sense of superiority. His mind may host multiple personalities, as he may usually act like an ordinary person in order to hold a job, but when exercising his authority over his captives, he demonstrates egregiously monstrous behavior. In a strange way, these episodes may feed his ego, giving him weird, gluttonous compensation for other things he's lacking in.

"Many in my department feel that most of these predators are beyond rehabilitation. Take the pervert who likes to abduct and fondle children. If this individual has a sexual preference for little kids, how are you going to alter his way of thinking? It's like you're a heterosexual, and a psychoanalyst is convinced that with treatment he can change you into a gay or lesbian. Taking into consideration he exhibits violent behavior, he may have avoided serious criminal charges up till now. This means he has no criminal record, making it more difficult to identify who he is. If he's committed violent crimes in the past besides these murders and eluded authorities to go on preying on the public, he may live under the delusion he can do as he pleases without consequences. What makes this individual dangerous is that he's obviously convinced himself that he's not going to allow witnesses to survive his wrath."

Harris left city hall thinking about the predatory killer who'd murdered these four women, his mind immersed in things serial killers do to their fellow human beings. While Harris's investigative experience told him there was a good chance that Amanda Kramer's abduction had no connection with the deaths of those four black prostitutes, he could not discount that possibility. Surmising that after having secured her in a confined, out-of-the-way space, her abductor could be holding her anywhere in this town. He may have driven her car to the riverfront and from there caught a cab or used a bus route to return home. Seeing those gruesome photographs of dead women Warren provided left him uncomfortable, for this person might have a number of women caged in such a way that they're helpless.

Still having no luck reaching Rhonda Kramer by phone, he intended seeing her that evening where she worked at Tokar's Casino in nearby St. Charles, Missouri. St. Charles is a city in the county seat of St. Charles County, with a population of fewer than 70,000, making it the ninth-largest city in Missouri. A municipality located northwest of St. Louis and a thirty minute drive from the St. Louis city limits, the casino was located on the Missouri River. A fairly large facility, it also offered a private gentleman's club for high rollers who have an itch for amorously attractive young females who like to tease.

Harris wasn't exactly pleased with Amanda and Rhonda Kramer's employment at a gambling casino, and this casino in particular, for their involvement with its owner, Anthony Tokar, complicated the investigation. Tokar had a dark, nefarious reputation with likely connections to organized crime, and if he had anything to do with Amanda's disappearance it would be difficult to prove. The fact that Amanda managed Tokar's affairs as his personal secretary meant she had insight into his private business dealings, giving her access to crucial information that perhaps made a man like Tokar uncomfortable. The casino owner was known to employ unsavory and unscrupulous people recently released from prison who were anxious to acquire large sums of money fast to make up for lost time. Some were rough characters with long criminal records, in which Harris thought to be capable of making an individual vanish without a trace. They weren't the types of people you'd want to turn your back on or think about crossing if you wanted to sleep peacefully at night.

Chapter 5
Meeting Amanda's Sister Rhonda at Tokar's Casino

Harris arrived at Tokar's Casino at six-thirty that same evening, a huge building with that name in bright lights to draw the eyes of people from afar. Entering the lobby, he passed by hotel accommodations offered by the casino's inn that was part of the complex. He walked through a wide corridor lined with fancy shops carrying high-priced clothing, souvenirs, and two restaurants, one offering Greek cuisine and the other offering Italian dishes.

Two warmly decorated drinking establishments caught his eye. One presented a brightly lit sign showing galloping race horses with the name *The Kentucky Derby,* which played prerecorded horse races on a big screen for people to bet on. A computer controlled the races, having multiple outcomes for it to choose from, with the ability to change the colors of horses and their numbers. The other place was *The Viking Lounge,* and what made it remarkable was the long replica of a Viking fighting ship that made up the bar, a majestic dragon's head protruded from the bow.

Moving along, clusters of exotic plants and palm trees surrounded the casino's broad entrance, which was a spacious sky lighted atrium. He went to a counter to register for receiving a card issued by the casino that gave him access to the gambling establishment and all the trappings it offered. Harris made the card visible to a watchful female guard in a dark blue jacket standing at the casino's entrance who observed him pass through. His eyes were soon drawn to a lovely young female dressed in a sleek black uniform, wearing the same black top and slacks all the female casino employees wore. The cool brunette with big brown eyes gave a bright smile as though recognizing Harris, and coming to greet him, he thought she may be Rhonda Kramer.

"Len Harris," she said, before welcoming him with a hug.

At first having trouble seeing her as the grownup younger sister of the girl he once dated, he expected her hair to have changed to light brown like Amanda's.

He grinned, "What's it been, about a-hundred years?"

She had that same choked up laugh she'd had as a teenager, "It seems about that long."

He lowered his voice when saying, "I tried phoning you numerous times today. I don't know if you're aware of it, but at the request of your father, I've taken up investigating the whereabouts of your sister."

"I know Dad was trying to get through to Steve Hastings to ask him about hiring a private detective to look for Amanda, and I'm glad you're the one who took the job."

"Hastings hooked me up with the case by asking me to speak with your father, and I agreed to do what I can to find her. I've got some time off as a result of an injury, and I don't intend charging your family anything unless some unexpected expenses crop up."

Rhonda had an anxious expression, "I thought I noticed you limping. Are you okay?"

"My knee is a little stiff is all, but it's nothing."

The pair began walking casually about the casino, "The reason Dad wanted to hire a detective is because with each passing day the chances of finding Amanda gets slimmer and I agree. We're very concerned about her, and it's a situation that's fast growing unbearable. It's bad enough when your sister's missing, but there's also those dead prostitutes they're finding around St. Louis and over in Illinois."

Moving about in no definite direction, they meandered away from the ringing slot machines and sound of clanging and shifting levers as she continued, "I'm sorry you couldn't reach me by phone. I may have impulsively switched the ringer to low, a habit I got into doing during the daytime when I know I'm working the night shift. I've tried to avoid hitting that switch on the phone for concern Amanda might call, although I never turn off my phone in case she leaves me a message."

She turned her head to face Harris, her fluffy long hair enveloping her face and plump cheeks. "I can give you my home phone number, but it's best to catch me by my cell phone, and I check my messages on a regular basis."

"I didn't leave a message because I thought it better to talk to you in person, but I do want to get your home number just in case." He nodded in the direction of the slot machines, "I wonder if the noise of those things can lead to hearing loss."

She gave a warm smile, "The noise gives a vibration in my ears during the allergy season when my sinuses are acting up, and I use ear plugs." Her expression changed more serious as she remarked, "Dad and I are going crazy, and we don't know what to do, but you're someone I have confidence in. Years ago when that kid shot and killed my brother, he may have just as well shot my mother and father too because it practically destroyed them. I can attest that it took years off my mother's life. Not a day's gone by that I haven't replayed in my mind the time I heard the news of his death."

Harris momentarily looked down, picturing Mark in his mind while remembering the night he died in that alleyway, recalling apprehending the kid that shot him, "Yeah, it still haunts me too. Mark was in every way like the kid brother I never had, and there have been few people I've met with whom I've been as fond of."

He stopped walking to look into this beautiful young girl's clear eyes. "I fully understand you and your father's concern for Amanda, and I promise to do everything I can to find her. Something that may prove helpful is that the FBI is looking into the deaths of those prostitutes, and in doing so they're also taking an interest in Amanda's case. While it's highly unlikely your sister's disappearance is linked to their deaths, they may still come up with some valuable information for helping to find her, so keep your chin up."

They'd moved far enough away from the noisy slot machines to speak in a normal tone of voice, and poker, blackjack and craps tables surrounded them. Harris then asked, "One thing I'd like to know is, what made Amanda take up working here at the casino for Anthony Tokar, and for that matter, the same question goes for you? On the outside looking in, these places are alluring and exciting, but in my opinion, they draw the lurid, criminal type that I detest. Part of what draws the people is the money and the carnival atmosphere, many of them are addicted to the gambling scene, but you and Amanda don't fit in this. You're worthy of a better calling in this life."

"Like I said before, when my brother died, it was like the end of the world for us, and it changed Amanda in a way that I never could've predicted or imagined. She loved you and had aspirations of getting married and having a family, but that all changed the night Mark died. For a short time, I thought you could take the place of my brother toward helping my family heal because my parents thought you'd make the ideal husband for her. My brother's death changed her though, she turned cold, and my folks and I couldn't believe it when she broke off from seeing you. It was as though the way she perceived life changed overnight, and while I can't say she became a selfish person, she no longer wanted things that tie a person down. Most of my mother's emotional distress came from Mark's death; she cried for days, but she also took it to heart when Amanda ended her relationship with you, and there was no reasoning with Amanda.

"Anyway, when she took up with Anthony Tokar years later, he wined and dined her. He eventually asked her to marry him, but she wouldn't say yes for probably the same reason she wouldn't marry you. You could say she'd taken up with the good life, and even though she saw marriage was out for Tokar, the two had a lasting and meaningful relationship. Unfortunately, it was taking up with Tokar that led to her to falling into drug dependence for a spell, but she was strong-willed enough to overcome that. However, she didn't break off seeing Tokar afterwards, which is something I couldn't relate to or understand.

"I guess, over time, I was lured by, as you say, the bright lights and excitement of the casino and the prospect of making good money here as an assistant manager. Amanda got me the job and looked after me as best as a sister can to make certain I didn't start carousing with the shady characters that hang around here. In some ways, I've done better than Amanda by establishing a career here, and at the same time, I've tried looking out for her. While she's stuck to Tokar, I've been groomed as a professional for managing this business, and I'm afraid seeing what goes on behind the scenes at this place might have played a part in her disappearance."

Harris scratched his chin, "Yeah, and how's that?"

She pointed to a wide black door that had neon lights over it that read **Tokar's Private Gentlemen's Club**. In lights was a female posed like a French floozy as though resembling a playboy bunny with her rump in the air.

"On the far end of the interior of the men's club is Tokar's office where Amanda spent almost all of her time. That place is off limits to me, but a few times after Amanda disappeared I pushed my way in, asking questions to those who knew my sister to find out what happened to her."

She motioned for Harris to look at a large, blown up photo hanging on the wall from the last New Year's party held at the casino. Girls employed at the casino had grouped together laughing in the photo, and she pointed out a girl closely resembling her who stood next to her in the picture.

"A lot of people thought this girl to be my sister because we look so much alike. Her name is Nadia Popovich, but we all call her Natalie here, as we rarely use our real names at the casino. Incidentally, I'm known as Bianca."

Another female, dressed the same way in a black outfit came to interrupt Rhonda to ask a question, cutting short their conversation.

"Len, will you excuse me for a minute, there's something that needs my attention. It's important that you and I talk, and we're slow tonight so I'm going to arrange to be free in less than an hour. My car's in the body shop and I need to make arrangements to pick up a rental my insurance company is paying for."

"I'd be glad to chauffer you around town."

She pointed at Harris as she walked away, "I want to stop by the hospital later to see someone, and I'd appreciate you coming with me."

"Sure, that's not a problem." He then used his thumb to draw her eyes to the gentlemen's club. "I'm going to see your boss for a few minutes before we leave."

Rhonda gave a bright smile, "Good luck with that," and she continued on her way to take care of a small problem a dealer was having with a customer.

He went to the entrance of the gentlemen's club where a doorman wearing a dark suit stood watch, and he looked at Harris while holding out his hand, "Your card, please."

Harris presented his badge, "I'm not here to be entertained. I've come to see Mr. Tokar on an important matter if he's available."

The doorman had a miniature walkie-talkie with an earpiece he listened through, and before speaking into it, he asked, "I'll need your name, and the purpose for you wanting to see Mr. Tokar?"

He put away his badge, "I am Lieutenant Leonard Harris, and I'm here on police business investigating the whereabouts of a missing person."

The doorman spoke into the mouthpiece of the communication device, "I have a Detective named Harris here who wants to see Mr. Tokar regarding the investigation of a missing person."

He listened briefly before saying, "Yes, I've seen his detective's badge."

The door opened for him to enter the establishment, which didn't look much different than the casino, but there were no slot machines. Dolled up girls working the floor wore little more than a sparkly, snug fitting red swimsuit, and they hung on the arms of male patrons playing games at the tables.

A hostess dressed much the same way greeted him with a warm smile. "Mr. Harris, please come this way."

The young lady escorted him across the gentlemen's club to Tokar's office and while walking they passed two men of Latin American descent who were leaving. They were well dressed, but Harris highly suspected they were drug smugglers. One had the build of a stout football player, his hair worn in a short, stubbly, skinhead haircut, and he had cold, dead eyes and had a nasty scar across his left cheek. The other had a darker complexion, black wavy hair and a black moustache, appearing more businesslike.

Harris came to a door marked OFFICE and the female leading the way opened the door for him, holding it open until he entered a room with a vacant desk. He thought this would've been the station Amanda Kramer ordinarily occupied. After closing the door behind her, the girl opened the next door which took him to Tokar's office. Harris saw

Tokar as a man with an off-colored complexion, as though he was Hispanic, Caucasian, and possibly oriental, wearing an expensive silk blend suit and strong cologne, his hair wet with mousse.

Tokar got up from his desk and in a gentlemanly manner came to greet Harris with a smile and a handshake, "Hello, Detective Harris, won't you please have a seat? I understand you're here investigating a missing person, and am I right to assume its Amanda Kramer you're trying to find?"

The casino owner's smooth-talking manner did little to impress Harris. He thought everything about this guy was phony and fake from the word go. Wanting to seem friendly to the successful businessman, he simply replied, "Yes, as a matter of fact it is, and I'm also a friend of the Kramer family."

Tokar returned to his seat behind the desk, nodding. "Oh, yes, I remember Amanda once mentioning she had an old and dear friend who was a police officer. Well, I'm pleased to meet you, and I hope you're here to report the police department is having some success locating her?"

"I wish I could say that is true. We're following up on a number of leads, but so far everything keeps taking us back to this casino. The last persons to see her before she disappeared are her fellow employees, and the main reason for my coming here is to find out if there may be something we missed."

"I turned over to the department what our security and surveillance cameras filmed that day and they show her leaving in her car, but we have no idea what happened to her after that. Other detectives have interviewed my staff and me, and I don't know what I can add that I haven't already told them."

Harris calmly replied, "Yeah, we keep going over those videos and reports expecting to turn up something. I came out this way on the mere chance that you might've remembered something that slipped your mind since that first interview. You know, it's common for people to recall something later that they forgot to mention before, and those are often the kinds of things that give us an important lead."

"If I had remembered anything of importance I assure you I would've phoned to tell investigators about it. Amanda is one of my most valued employees, and I'm sure you know Amanda's sister Rhonda works here as well. Both girls are intelligent, hard-working, reliable people and what they contribute does a lot toward keeping this place going."

At that moment, there came a knock on the door, and in entered a man with thinning hair, wearing black rimmed eyeglasses and carrying an assortment of paperwork. Seeing Tokar was busy, he turned around to leave.

Tokar said, "Allen, come on in." He then made introductions, saying, "Lieutenant Harris, this is Allen Schaeffer, the casino's business manager. Allen, this is Lieutenant Harris, who is one of the investigators looking for Amanda."

Schaeffer, who looked brainy, mild-mannered and somewhat shallow in character, shook Harris's hand, and said in a soft-spoken voice, "Pleased to meet you." He then turned to Tokar. "Tony, I need your signature on a few things and then I can return to my office for processing these invoices."

As Tokar gave attention to the paperwork, Harris said, "I've taken up enough of your time Mr. Tokar, and I appreciate you seeing me."

After signing the first document, he looked up at Harris, "I apologize for the interruption Harris, but we're constantly under a logjam of paperwork here. If there's anything I can do, you're welcome to stop by my office anytime to discuss the case. Like I've said, I need Amanda here and it means everything to me to find out what's happened to her."

"It's helpful to know that, and one thing you can count on is that we'll keep on searching for her."

Harris shook hands with Tokar, and then left the room to wait in the adjoining office space for Allen Schaeffer. When Tokar's business manager exited the room occupied by Tokar, he approached Schaeffer as he closed the door.

"Excuse me, Mr. Schaeffer. I was wondering if you could shed any light on the disappearance of Amanda Kramer. You see, all our leads keep taking us back here to the casino and I would imagine there's little that occurs here that you don't know about."

Schaeffer appeared uncomfortable, holding firmly the paperwork Tokar had just signed, and avoiding eye contact with Harris. "My position here is strictly connected with the business aspect of running the casino. I have little to do with how the casino operates out here on the floor."

"Yes, but you know Amanda Kramer by having seen her on a daily basis. It's only logical you must be somewhat familiar with her routine and duties here at the casino. We're counting on someone with the kind of insight you possess to provide information to help us find her. Investigators think it rather odd that her parking space was out of view of surveillance cameras when there are so many set up to cover parking areas around the casino. That's either a strange coincidence or quite convenient, depending on how you want to look at it."

Schaeffer commented, "I have nothing to do with security, but I think you may have better luck talking to the casino's floor manager."

"Well, like I say, there are few people who would've seen Amanda Kramer as often as you have or know her routine here at the casino as well. What's more is that I spoke to one floor manager and she told me the gentlemen's club was off limits to her, so she couldn't tell me anything. What's important to understand is that we think she is still alive, but her whereabouts is time sensitive in that she may not have long to live. Depending upon how circumstances play out, the law could contend that someone withholding information about Amanda's disappearance could be partly responsible in the event of her death. Their failure to speak out to prevent Amanda's murder could result in prosecution for criminal negligence and leave them facing years of imprisonment. At the very least, they could be prosecuted for manslaughter for having done nothing to assist law enforcement at this critical time, and you'd be wise to think about that."

Schaeffer looked nervous, shaking his head, "I don't know what I can tell you that I haven't already told the other investigators."

Harris stood in Schaeffer's way, giving him a look of disgust to let him know he didn't believe him. To get further under his skin, he stated, "I thank you for your time then, but it may become necessary at a later date to bring you in to the station for questioning. If nothing else, I want to get you on record making a statement on what you know about Tokar's shady business dealings."

Schaeffer wore a worried expression as the two men exited the office space to enter the gentlemen's club and Harris moved on to reenter the casino. Thinking he shook up Schaeffer and that the key to Amanda's disappearance lay here with Tokar and his cronies, he found a restroom and thoroughly washed his hands before going to look for Rhonda.

She came to him, "I was beginning to wonder if you stood me up and left without saying goodbye."

Harris replied, "Maybe you can tell me something that may be of importance. Amanda was and perhaps still is romantically involved with Tokar, but can you tell me whether their relationship was more on or off near the time of her disappearance?"

"Amanda is Tokar's favorite, but he has many favorites he caters to and treats like they're his one and only. They were on the off going side of romance, but he didn't see it that way, and treating people as property he owns, he generally sees life the way it suits him best. Amanda gave me the strong impression she'd had it with him and was ready to move on with her life by finding work elsewhere. A couple of months ago, she met Jim Abernathy and they dated only a few times before two men took him by surprise and beat him up in the lobby of her apartment building.

"I didn't see Jim after the fight, but from what I understand they gave him a rough going over, clobbering him and kicking him until he was nearly out cold. Bruised ribs and a jarred back, he could barely walk for a week. He told Amanda that the one that gave it to him the worst had fists like sledgehammers."

"Did he say what these two men looked like?"

"Amanda said Abernathy described the men as tough-talking thugs wearing trench coats, telling him that if they found him at that address again they would finish the job. Jim was good for Amanda in that he had a lot of patience with her, showing he cared deeply for her. I think the way their relationship was going he was on the verge of asking her to marry him. Jim's work is forming and finishing concrete and he looks like he can take care of himself, but the two that assaulted him must've made their point because he feared for losing his life. I know he didn't want to break off from seeing Amanda, but for a time he was out of commission, losing almost two weeks of work because of his injuries."

Harris looked down as though dwelling on the incident, "It sounds like they really did a number on him. It's tough taking on two, especially when they have the element of surprise on their side."

Rhonda broke his concentration. "It doesn't take a lot to imagine these two men were enlisted by Tokar. I think he wanted to get rid of Jim to either win back Amanda or to make it easier to abduct her. She knew almost as much about his business dealings as he did, and she hinted more than once that Tokar was into big money in connection with drug smuggling and distribution."

Rhonda then asked, "Do you still have time to make a couple of errands?"

"Sure, you want to pick up a rental car and then you wanted to drop by and visit a friend at the hospital."

She smiled, "It's the girl I pointed out to you in the photo named Nadia who, as I said before, is known at the casino as Natalie. You might find this visit interesting because in an odd way what happened to her may pertain to Amanda's disappearance."

Chapter 6
A Visit to the Hospital Raises New Concerns

Harris and Rhonda picked up the rental car and from there he followed her to Barnes Hospital in midtown St. Louis to visit a friend of hers getting medical care. After parking the cars in the parking garage, they began their walk to the room occupied by this girl.

While strolling through corridors, Rhonda spoke, "I think I'd better let you in on a few things before we see Nadia. I intended to tell you this earlier at the casino before I got pulled away to take care of a problem, but Nadia had borrowed my car when her car was in the garage for repairs. She'd gotten off from work and the plan was that she would return later to pick me up at the casino when I got off, and at that time I'd run her home."

Rhonda stopped walking to face Harris as she continued, "After she left the casino, a man driving a four-wheel-drive vehicle or SUV sideswiped her and ran her off the road. He accosted her and dragged her out of the car before brutally attacking her, beating her half to death on the side of the interstate highway. Len, he beat her so badly that he broke her jaw and fractured bones in her face, and I believe it happened because she was driving my car."

Becoming emotionally choked up, she clamped her hands over her nose and mouth, her complexion turning red as she became teary-eyed, and she said something he couldn't understand. He pulled her out of foot traffic in the hospital corridor, and drew her close before carefully pulling her hands away from her mouth.

"Okay now, tell me again what you just said."

Sniffling, she went on to say, "It happened after I'd gone into the gentlemen's club pressing people to tell me what they knew about Amanda's disappearance, and now Nadia is in terrible shape. Whoever this man was, I'm convinced he must've thought Nadia was me, and he beat up the wrong girl."

Crumpling into his arms as tears flowed, Harris took a deep breath. "I've only just begun working this case today and there's much about it I don't know. But what happened isn't your fault and there's nothing we can do about it now except to try and find out who brutalized her."

In near hysterics, Rhonda then blurted out, "I'm wondering if this man was one of the men who attacked Jim Abernathy at Amanda's apartment building. Am I going to be the next one who's assaulted or maybe disappears?"

After Rhonda calmed down, they resumed walking to Nadia's room, and she stopped to freshen up in the Ladies public restroom. When she came out, she said, "Nadia comes from a large family, and although Nadia holds no grudge against me, some family members believe I'm at fault for what happened to her."

"I guess I can't blame them for being upset, but you did nothing to hurt this girl and it's not your fault she was attacked."

When finally entering Nadia's room, they saw close family members gathered there for her, and Rhonda and Harris drew what they perceived to be unwelcome looks. There was tension in the room as Rhonda approached Nadia who lay before them with her head wrapped like a mummy, her eyes looking back at them.

"Nadia, this is another detective investigating the assault. His name is Leonard Harris."

Harris spoke in a quiet manner, "Hi Nadia. Did you get a good look at the man who attacked you?"

Nadia nodded yes, and Rhonda pulled from her purse a notepad and pen to hand to her, "Can you write down his description?"

Nadia wrote, and Rhonda read out loud what she was writing, "A man, like a mountain, wearing a suit, with dark hair worn short and choppy, maybe using mousse because it looked wet. He didn't speak a word, but used his fists, knocking me down with one punch, and then hovered over me. I tried blocking the blows and I remember his head and neck appeared abnormally fat or wide, as if he had a form of…"

Rhonda had difficulty making out the last word she'd written, and Nadia's father came forward to peer over her shoulder, speaking very distinctly, "Gigantism." He then added, "She described him as abnormally large in his proportions, perhaps not so much extremely tall, but big and brawny in an odd sort of way."

Nadia nodded yes, raising her arms and hands as if motioning to show he was a large man.

Rhonda then spoke to Nadia's father, "Mr. Popovich, I'm so sorry about what's happened."

Mr. Popovich gave a kindly nod. "I know, and some members of my family flew off the handle when first learning of circumstances surrounding Nadia's injuries, but that's all over now and we apologize."

With that, Mrs. Popovich, a woman with sad eyes and big hips, rose from a chair and walked over to give Rhonda an affectionate hug, patting her on the back. She then spoke sincerely, "We know you are a good friend to our daughter, and we understand this wasn't your fault." She then held her hands out, "I didn't mean to act so angrily when speaking before, but this is one of my babies."

"I understand, Momma Popovich." Then Nadia's mother returned to her chair.

Her father then said, "I told Momma that there are lunatics driving on our highways and it is dangerous out there, but our Nadia is alive, and I have faith she's going to be fine. However, judging by what I've heard, there does seem to be a chance this man was targeting you when this incident occurred."

Harris then asked Nadia, "Did this man who attacked you have any distinguishing features, any marks or scars on his face?"

She paused and then resumed writing, and Rhonda again read what she wrote, "He had a light complexion, and dark eyebrows. He had a flat nose as though it had once been broken and a large mole the size of a dime on the left side of his face."

Harris took an interest in the mole she described, "Can you indicate exactly where this mole was on his face?"

Nadia wiggled her index finger to draw him closer and touched his cheekbone on the left side of his face, just over an inch away from the outside corner of his eye.

Harris then asked, "What can you tell me about the car he drove, I understand it was a four-wheel-drive vehicle?"

Nadia grabbed her father's arm, as though wanting him to speak, and the man moved in closer. "Well, yes, we gave all of that information to the police, but Nadia said it was much like a Chevrolet *Carry All* I once owned some years ago. Mine was one of the last made because by then they'd begun using the name Suburban, and GMC had a version of it with a very similar body style. They were bulky vehicles, ideal for pulling a boat, and we would pile into it and jam it full of everything you can think of for going on a camping trip. Nadia described this model as dark brown, but the side trimming was light beige, and what makes it unique is that she insists it was an older vehicle like mine, rarely seen on the road anymore. She also thought it similar to the one I'd driven because it was a rust bucket, and the driver had no trouble nudging the car she was driving off the road."

Harris smiled when looking at Nadia, "A man of size with the description you've given will have difficulty hiding from the authorities. We train our police to identify people and makes of automobiles, and you've given important information that may be helpful for bringing this person to justice. Hang in there now, get well, and Rhonda and I will come back to see you again."

He then motioned toward the door and waited while Rhonda took Nadia's hand. "I leaned on the casino to pay you while you're off work. In case someone asks, and I don't think they will, I told them you were running a work-related errand picking up office supplies when this man ran you off the road. My insurance agent told me your injuries are covered, so make copies of the hospital bills and give me the originals so I can send them to him." She then added reassuringly, "You're going to be okay, and I promise to do all I can to help you get through this."

Nadia gripped her wrist tightly, shaking her head yes, and then Harris and Rhonda left the room. They exited the hospital to soon arrive at Rhonda's home, which was located in an upper middleclass neighborhood in the western suburbs.

Harris pulled in behind the rental car Rhonda drove before stopping in the driveway, and when he shut off his Impala's lights and the engine, he noticed the front yard was dark. He stood outside his car leaning on the open door as Rhonda got out of the rental and came to hand him a piece of note paper that had her home phone number and address. He then gave her a business card with his cell phone number.

He stuffed the paper inside his shirt pocket, "Speaking for myself, I don't like coming home to a dark house. You already have a light above your garage door, and it wouldn't take much to change it out for a motion detector light that will come on when you pull into the driveway."

"I know and I generally park in the garage anyway, but driving this rental, I didn't have my garage door opener. My father suggested the same thing, telling me he'd install a light for me, and as soon as he gets back on his feet again, I'll ask him to. Once he's feeling better, I intend keeping him occupied doing a few light chores to keep him active until this blows over and we have Amanda back. . . You do think she'll be found safely, don't you?"

"I think the chances are fair to good for a favorable outcome, but it's important that she be found soon."

There was quiet before Rhonda said, "I remember when you used to date Amanda and I'd make a nuisance of myself pestering you. I don't know how many times you tried getting rid of me so the two of you could have time alone together. Once you even offered me a dollar to get lost, and I wouldn't go, but I'm sure you had plenty of opportunities to trap her in the backseat of an automobile."

Harris rubbed his chin, "That's going a long time back, a lot of water under the bridge, so they say."

"I enjoyed giving you a bad time, and don't tell me there wasn't any paybacks, like those times you teased me about my breaking out with acne, and my braces. The worst time of my life was when I wore braces, and I can remember feeling terribly embarrassed to smile when wearing them. I never gave a hint of it, but I had a crush on you, and I was even a little jealous of my older sister."

She just then had a thought, "I heard about you losing your wife Len, and I just want to say I'm sorry. Actually, Amanda told me, and she didn't learn about it until a few weeks after it occurred or both of us would've surely shown up at the funeral parlor to give you support."

"Thanks for saying so. It's been a difficult adjustment living alone in that house—everything there reminds me of her." He then looked her in the eye, "Well, it was nice seeing you again and if anything should come up, no matter what the hour, I want you to phone me."

"I'll keep in touch," and she gave him a kiss on the cheek.

Watching Rhonda at the front door, she gave a wave before stepping inside, and seeing her awakened many memories from those days when he dated Amanda.

He'd only driven five minutes from her home when he received a cell phone call from Rhonda, and she sounded upset, "Len, I think someone's prowling around in my backyard."

Harris made a sharp U-turn to return to her house, "Where are you at?"

"I'm in my bedroom wearing my robe. I was getting ready to shower when I heard a noise outside the window."

"Stay where you are, I'll be there in less than two minutes."

Quickly driving back to her house, he switched off his car lights when turning onto her street, swerving to the curb to park a few doors from her address. He quickly got out of the car, crouching while letting the door close quietly until the dome light went out and he heard it catch. Removing his .45 from the shoulder holster inside his sport jacket, he pulled the slide back to chamber a round and ran swiftly in the dark across neighbor's lawns to come to Rhonda's fenced in backyard. He opened the gate without making a sound and now held the semi-automatic clenched with both hands in a forward manner outstretched before him.

Moving surefooted, he peered about to get a closer look at where bushes and shrubbery clustered next to the back of the house. Light from a partially open window showered an area near the middle of the house, enabling him to target the face of a prowler peeking in the window. He came forward stealthily holding his weapon firm and steady, his finger resting against the trigger and ready to squeeze it.

Hearing the shower running inside the house, he came in close to press the muzzle of the weapon against the side of this person's head.

"Freeze! Move and I'll splatter your brains all over the place."

Now seeing this individual's youthful appearance, he placed his finger against the trigger guard, and holding the grip of the pistol with one hand, he collared the teenager with the other. He then called out,

"Rhonda, I don't know if you can you hear my voice, but I've caught a peeper."

Her voice carried from inside the house to where he stood, "I'm coming to the patio door to go out on the porch."

Rhonda came to open the patio door in her robe, and turning on the porch light, her jaw dropped. "Robert Jensen, what are you doing outside my house in the dark of night? This man is a detective and he could've shot and killed you."

The young man, who wasn't much more than a boy, looked embarrassed, and was speechless.

Harris continued holding him by the collar as he moved forward, "Do you want to call the police?"

"No," replied Rhonda in a disappointed way for finding out her peeper is a neighbor she never would've suspected. "He lives in the house directly behind mine, and I know his parents. I'm phoning his mother."

Rhonda still looked surprised when dialing her cell phone, "Bobby, I can't believe you were sneaking around my house looking in windows."

She spoke on the phone to a neighbor explaining the situation and how this young man had nearly gotten killed."

His father rushed over with his hair mussed, wearing a T-shirt and shorts.

Seeing Harris holstering his .45, the neighbor slapped the boy alongside his head, speaking angrily, "What's the matter with you sneaking around people's houses after dark? This man could very well have shot you and he'd be in the right. He doesn't know whether you're an armed intruder looking to burglarize the house or what.

"Get home now," and looking to Rhonda and Harris, he used a soft spoken voice, "I apologize for this disturbance. Nowadays, you need to watch your kids every minute and that's impossible when you're working class people like us. It's that damn Internet—the kids have access to everything under the sun available at their fingertips, and I wouldn't be surprised if an entire generation grows up to be perverts. The temptation to browse is enormous, all they have to do is type in the word *girls* and you know what kinds of sexually exploitive pictures are sure to pop up."

After the neighbor left, Harris shook his head, "That kid has no idea what's happening in your life, nor does he have any idea how close he came to meeting his maker tonight."

It now dawned on Rhonda that over a period of time this boy may have been looking in her window on other occasions. "When I shower, I like the water hot and steamy, and I often open up the bathroom window first so the mirrors don't fog up. I'll have to leave the door open to my bedroom from now on instead."

Rhonda's left eyebrow raised, "I'm sure he got an eyeful tonight." She then gave Harris a curious look, "He wasn't exposing himself in some way when you caught him, was he?"

Harris had a peculiar grin, "At the moment I snuck up on him he was merely peering in."

They took chairs at her kitchen table and talked for a while. Rhonda told him that if he was ever in the vicinity and dropped by to find her not at home, he should use a key she kept under the flowerpot on the front porch to let himself in. She also mentioned that with her father needing assistance with his recovery, the casino was allowing her flexibility in her work schedule and she expected to have her evenings free.

Harris left that evening with thoughts about Rhonda, as he'd always been fond of her, and he was looking forward to seeing her again soon.

Chapter 7
Consulting with Supervisory Special Agent Johnson of the FBI

Harris arrived at police headquarters at eight o'clock on Wednesday morning to further discuss facts involving Amanda Kramer's disappearance with Ron Warren. He discovered FBI personnel there, knowing they were FBI agents because they looked dressier and more polished than the regular personnel roaming about the station.

When catching up to Warren, he was given a slight nod indicating Warren wanted Harris to follow him, and he spoke as they walked together, "Supervisory Special Agent Howard Johnson is here. I told him you are a hardnosed detective investigating the disappearance of Amanda Kramer and afterwards he expressed an interest in wanting to talk to you. Hastings told me you once dated the girl, and I mentioned this to Agent Johnson, as if to say you had a special interest in finding her. I also told him I thought you'd be an asset to the investigation, so just don't say anything to piss the guy off."

Following Warren to an office occupied by Johnson, Warren said, "Agent Johnson, this is Lieutenant Leonard Harris who's working the case involving Amanda Kramer."

After Warren walked away, Johnson said, "Won't you please be seated and tell me what you've learned that may be important for helping to solve this case?"

"From what I've gathered, I don't believe the disappearances of Amanda Kramer and Deborah Kutraba are in any way connected to these prostitutes turning up dead across the metro area. I'd say it's more likely that Amanda's disappearance is linked to her work as the personal secretary of Anthony Tokar, the owner of a casino located in St. Charles. Tokar is said to have connections to organized crime, and holding a trusted position in his employment for some time, she may have had a front seat witnessing his illegal business dealings, which has now led to her disappearance."

Johnson gave a short nod, as if acknowledging his awareness of Tokar's links to organized crime. He then rolled his chair back from the desk and folded his arms, "Tokar is suspected in her abduction, and we are presently monitoring calls from his home, cell phone, and his office phone. We also believe he has his hand in narcotics and money laundering with regards to drug trafficking. He's yet to say anything to implicate himself in the Kramer girl's disappearance, but I'll keep you posted if anything changes. Tokar lives a secretive lifestyle and is always on the move, making him a difficult suspect to keep track of, and if we're going to put him away, we need more on him."

Harris stated, "If Tokar had anything to do with Amanda Kramer vanishing, it was done with these other murders in mind as a way to keep heat off him. With law enforcement officials focused on the deaths of these prostitutes, most are looking for a nutcase to pin it on. Should we zero in on a suspect considered responsible for the murders of those prostitutes and Amanda Kramer isn't found, this serial killer may be held accountable for her death as a way of closing out the case. However, I think Tokar's reason for getting rid of her was because she knew too much about his shady business practices. He may have done away with her to silence someone he'd begun to see as a potential liability, as from what I've heard from her sister, she was thinking about walking out on him."

Johnson commented, "We had agents approach Amanda Kramer once for learning a few things about Tokar, but she refused to talk. If she told Tokar about our speaking to her, the idea of their breaking up may have made him worry that she'd give us crucial information at a later date. Should we not be able to locate her, regardless of how the investigation with the prostitutes comes out, I'm in agreement with you that her case could eventually end up in an unsolved cold case file."

"There's a girl named Nadia Popovich who was run off the highway by another vehicle when she was driving Rhonda Kramer's car, the sister of Amanda Kramer. Both of these women work for the casino, and Nadia bears a strong resemblance to Rhonda Kramer, wearing the same style of uniform when working. It was after Rhonda made inquiries into her sister's disappearance at the gentlemen's club located inside the casino that a Chevrolet Suburban rammed the car driven by Nadia and forced her off the highway. She was then savagely beaten on the roadside by the driver of the SUV, and it's highly likely she was mistaken for Rhonda Kramer after she'd questioned people about Amanda's whereabouts at the casino."

Johnson said, "I've seen the report on that altercation and, while we're uncertain about whom the assailant was, we've considered that Anthony Tokar had it done. At the same time, the bureau isn't as yet convinced that Tokar murdered Amanda Kramer, and we don't see how he could be holding her captive without the help of other people. The bottom line is that we deal with tangible evidence that can be substantiated in a court of law. Up to now we've yet to confirm whether he knows of Amanda Kramer's whereabouts, giving us little chance of dragging him before a grand jury. For one thing, if there are others who've conspired with Tokar to get rid of Amanda Kramer for her knowing information regarding his dealings why haven't we picked up on it through his phone conversations?"

Harris replied, "It may be that Tokar is clever enough to know he's under investigation and smart enough not to talk about Amanda Kramer's disappearance over the phone. I'm sure he's not in the habit of discussing his illegal business dealings over the phone for concern of the authorities listening in, and her abduction and disappearance falls into that same category. But I'll tell you this much about Tokar, he owns a great deal of real estate in both St. Louis and nearby St. Charles—homes, apartment buildings and warehouses where he could be holding Amanda Kramer. While the deaths of these prostitutes are sponging up the authorities' time and resources, it's the perfect opportunity to make her disappear. My investigative experience tells me he's fully aware that he's suspected in the Kramer girl's disappearance and he may have arranged to have another girl kidnapped named Deborah Kutraba to divert suspicion away from him. It's an old tactic used by criminal minds, persons under suspicion of murder have killed complete strangers for absolutely no reason at all but to throw off investigators and draw their attention elsewhere."

Johnson replied, "The Kutraba woman is part of this investigation, and I can't as yet confirm if what you're saying is true, but if it is, Tokar has a more diabolical mind than I'd have given him credit for."

Harris then remarked, "Some killers have been rated with the intelligence of a genius, and while I'm by no means claiming Tokar is intelligent, I'm simply saying murderers use outrageous techniques to throw off investigators. You know as well as I do that Tokar has spent his entire life skirting the law, and while working for him Amanda must've had insight into many of his affairs. You don't know Amanda Kramer, but I do and she's a smart girl. It may very well be that the only time she lacked good sense was when she got mixed up with Tokar.

"The city has long suspected Tokar of trafficking in drugs. I went to his office yesterday and bumped into a pair of Latinos that should've been carrying signs that read 'drug smugglers for hire.' One of them had a husky build and a bad scar across his left cheek, the other came across as more businesslike in appearance and had a moustache."

Pulling open a cabinet file drawer, Johnson removed a document and placed it on his desk top, opening it to present mug shots of two Latinos. There were also recent surveillance photos of the pair getting out of a new, white four-wheel drive Cadillac Escalade they use for transportation.

Johnson explained, "I imagine these are the two you're speaking of, Salvador Garcia and Rafael 'Choco' Cordero, two Puerto Ricans. Garcia, the one with the moustache, is either number three or the number four man in the Camacho Cartel working out of Puerto Rico, and his scar-faced sidekick Cordero is merely his bodyguard and chauffer. We've had this drug ring under investigation for over a year now, and in the next two to four weeks we expect to activate a sting operation for clamping down on their operations. Cocaine and marijuana coming in from Mexico and Central and South America are entering the country through Miami, New York, and New Orleans.

"We know people who've fronted money for opening the casino are charging Tokar outlandish interest rates while pressing him for a piece of the action, making the casino business not as lucrative as he'd prefer it to be. However, at this time we are unable to provide concrete proof that Tokar has a hand in drug distribution, and if he does have any involvement, he's as of late begun backing off from this activity. Tokar may or may not be aware that the Camacho Cartel is under investigation by various government agencies, but he might be shying away from drug trafficking for going legitimate.

He has purchased abandoned property on the north side of St. Louis in a depressed industrial-commercial area, picking up much of it for back taxes. He's amassed a considerable amount of acreage under various names and corporations to hide the fact that he's accumulating this property. Buildings scheduled for demolition are on much of the land and there are rumors that Tokar is considering opening up a horserace track with political backing from the mayor. I think our best chance of finding out more lie with continuing phone line surveillance, and another break could come when we learn of Deborah Kutraba's whereabouts or when we at least find her car."

Johnson then pulled out maps and typewritten letters sent by the serial killer for indicating the locations of dead prostitutes found thus far, "Now getting to the flipside of this investigation. The killer of those prostitutes sent us these letters and maps, and even though he's trimmed down the maps to deceive us about their origin, our cybercrimes unit has determined he acquired them off an internet website."

He displayed the maps to allow Harris to look at them, "These maps came off a standard computer printer, but they have distinctive characteristics that help identify the provider's database. We've recently concluded that there are two links that could've made them, one is *Safari Sitescan International*, and the other is *Search and Discover Online Mapping*. In just the last hour, we've narrowed it down to *Safari Sitescan International*, and we've subpoenaed the internet service to supply us with customer's IP addresses that are of a unique link for pulling these particular maps. It's not likely the user pulled these from multiple internet addresses with public access, so our hope is that hits linked to the same address from this surrounding area will take us to the serial killer's residence.

"Tracking on fixed format files can be done, although there's a lot of red tape, as all information connected to the Internet is well guarded, but it shouldn't be long before we receive information needed to identify the killer. When that happens, things are going to start moving around here. And because you cooperated by sharing information with me, I'm going to give Ron Warren authorization to contact you the moment we have that address so you can be in on this guy's capture. If we don't get that news today, we're certain to have it tomorrow, but in return, I'm counting on you to continue your investigative work and keep me informed of anything that might impact this case."

Special agent Johnson then shook his hand, "Harris, you seem like a detective who has his head fixed straight on his shoulders. The possibility exists that this arrest could lead to the rescue of other women held in captivity, and if it should lead us to discover the whereabouts of Amanda Kramer, I hope she's found safe."

"Thank you Johnson and I'll keep in contact with you through Ron Warren."

Leaving Johnson's office, Harris knew that neither Garcia nor Cordero was who had assaulted Nadia Popovich on the side of the highway, as they did not fit her description of the perpetrator. It came to him that the pair could be the two tough talking thugs that roughed up Amanda's boyfriend Jim Abernathy, although these men weren't described as Latinos. Harris believed one of the men that worked over Abernathy was likely the person that had brutally beaten Nadia on the side of the highway. The girl had gotten a look at her attacker, describing him as exceptionally large with a light complexion. Abernathy had mentioned that the one that gave it to him the worst had fists like sledgehammers, leading him to believe he may have been the guy that broke Nadia's jaw.

Harris stopped at Ron Warren's desk to thank him and Warren handed over to him copies of files connected with the case. Some of the information relating to the other missing Caucasian girl named Deborah Kutraba and the vehicle she drove. He then drove out to this female's address and after showing his badge to the husband, he was given entrance to the house. The place was very much in disarray with rs running wild from one room to the next. He tried ing with the husband, but accomplished little, for his strong foreign accent made it difficult for them to understand one another for trading information.

Afterwards, he went to Rhonda Kramer's home to pay her a visit, and knowing she wouldn't be arriving home until later, he used the key left under the flowerpot to get in the house. Rubbing his knee, which had begun throbbing, after taking a pain pill, he stretched out on the couch to relax and as soon as the effects of the pill kicked in, he dosed off.

Rhonda arrived home to find him asleep on the couch and she gave him a gentle nudge, "What do you say to going out and getting a bite to eat."

Harris sat up, and after rubbing his eyes, he noticed the angle of the sun had changed through a window since first lying down on the couch.

"This dinner is on me Harris."

He nodded, "Fair enough."

Rhonda showered and put on an eye-catching, knockout black evening dress that had a deep V-cut in the front. Escorting her to his car for providing transportation to a popular steak house in West County, Harris complimented her on how gorgeous she looked in the dress.

Chapter 8
An Interlude with Rhonda and Learning Someone is Shadowing Him

After arriving at the restaurant, the waiter took their orders and soon returned to their table with glasses of water and goblets of red wine. Rhonda initiated conversation. "I took my father to see his physician this afternoon, and because his recovery is slow he recommended I consider taking him to stay at my home. I think he's right, but I'm finding difficulty making time to move him and his personal things to my home."

Rhonda expressed another thought, saying, "Sitting in that doctor's office gave me time to think, and something came to mind about Amanda's disappearance that I've already told the police. There's a doctor who's an acquaintance of Tokar and who became a regular at the gentlemen's club that paid Amanda a lot of attention. His name is Vincent Dvorak, a very influential and prestigious surgeon, and she spoke of him on several occasions. Have you ever heard of him?"

Harris interjected, "Rhonda, I don't want you sticking out your pretty neck by going around the casino or that gentlemen's club asking a lot of questions. These people put Nadia Popovich in the hospital, and for certain knowing they've injured the wrong girl, they may make another attempt at silencing you. I'm serious about this Rhonda—I don't want you to end up like your friend Nadia. We know practically nothing about the people we're dealing with, and asking a lot of questions could lead to you disappearing next. I spend far too much of my time with the coroner investigating the deaths of young women who've gotten involved with the wrong people, believing they could trust a man like Tokar. That's the root cause for why Amanda is missing now. It makes my stomach churn to see a young person with a bright future lying on a slab at the morgue."

Rhonda's eyebrows raised, "Okay, I promise not to keep on asking questions, but I'll keep my eyes and ears open just the same. Getting back to this Doctor Vincent Dvorak I was telling you about, he's a renowned cosmetic surgeon whose been on several television talk shows. Amanda said he kept after her, constantly crowding her and asking her out, steadfast about convincing her to go on a trip with him, but she found him annoying and bothersome. He'd come to the gentleman's club trying to entice her with an invitation to *Lake Laraine*, a private lake development where he has a home on the opposite side of the lake from Tokar's weekend home. There was something odd about him that turned her off, and she went on for some time avoiding him and his flattering come-ons.

"Thinking him strange or perhaps touched in the head, she kept rebuffing his proposals to get her to say yes to a romantic rendezvous. He'd flaunt himself at her by telling her things about himself, divulging tidbits about his surgical ability as though to project a worldly image. He probably is a man of distinction in certain circles, as he's done work on movie stars and the rich and famous. Whenever she'd encounter him, he'd act awkwardly eager to keep her in his company, but she did everything she could to sever ties with him without going so far as to outright insult him. One time when she was talking to him and tried excusing herself, he detained her with a firm clasp of her wrist as if exerting power over her. From that moment on, she felt uncomfortable about being alone in his company. Like many men who find Amanda attractive, he desired her and wanted to see more of her."

Harris placed his hands together, interlocking his fingers with his elbows on the table, looking as though dwelling on the past. "Amanda was a beautiful woman, and what I remember best were those plump cheeks and dimples that formed whenever she'd laugh. I was taken by her looks and sweet disposition from the first moment we met, and you've got that same radiant smile."

Rhonda froze, looking down at the tablecloth, "I wish you wouldn't talk about her in the past tense."

"I suppose I phrased my wording that way because I haven't seen her in such a long time. After she dropped me, I had a bad time getting it through my thick skull that our relationship was really over and done with. I didn't think I'd ever get over losing her, and it wasn't until I met Valerie that I was able to turn the page and put that chapter of my life behind me. Valerie and I were quite compatible, and she was well-liked by others, leading me to think if the two of you had met you would've hit it off as friends."

The waiter delivered their food to the table and this brought a pause in conversation before Rhonda went on to add, "Like I was saying, this Doctor Dvorak has close ties to Tokar. I once met him at Tokar's weekend home located at that *Lake Laraine* I just mentioned, a subdivision on a lake of roughly one hundred acres. The lake is scenic with mature trees and landscaped yards, some terraced as the land runs down to meet the water's edge. I don't remember seeing any big boats on the lake, as I remember it to be a quiet place, except for the clamor and ruckus made by Tokar's partygoers."

Rhonda cut a bite size slice of steak, and after she'd finished chewing and swallowed, she had a sip of red wine before continuing. "There was quite a turnout at Tokar's lake house the day I met the distinguished doctor, and after showing up, he did as Amanda said he'd always done in the past. He followed her around and annoyed her, and I thought it comical the way he kept after her. I noticed Dvorak was chummy with Tokar too, as the two apparently spend much of their time together on the weekends when they were both at the lake."

Harris looked at her, "Lake Laraine?"

"Yes, that's the name of the lake, and something else Amanda told me about that day at the lake was that Dvorak made a few distasteful remarks that infuriated her. I didn't hear what he said, and as far as I know this was the only time he used rude and inappropriate language in her company. It must have been something degrading for a female to hear to have angered her so, and it took her awhile to regain her composure after hearing it. I guess the doctor reached a point where he'd lost patience with winning her over using his charm and because he felt rejected, he resorted to insulting her. The incident happened when there was strain on Amanda's relationship with Tokar, and if the doctor knew about it, he may have thought he could say almost anything to her and get away with it."

Thinking about everything Rhonda had just told him, Harris held a stoic expression. "Beauty can unfortunately attract lunatics of all types. I may have to look up this Vincent Dvorak to ask him a few questions."

Rhonda then added, "Come to think of it, I know where Amanda keeps a card in her apartment that gives her accessibility to this Lake Laraine. It may be that she has a key to Tokar's lake home as well. It's a private, gated community, and if you'd like to take a drive out there sometime to see Tokar's lake home we can."

Harris remarked, "Dvorak and this Lake Laraine are beginning to interest me, and yes, I want to stop by Amanda's apartment tonight and pick up that card. I may spend some time snooping around at that lake over the weekend." He gazed at Rhonda. "This private lake community might present some unique opportunities to study Tokar and his followers to see what they're all up to."

On their way back to Rhonda's house they stopped by Amanda's apartment and Rhonda went in by herself to get the card they'd need to give them access to Lake Laraine. When returning to the car, she said, "I found the card, but I didn't see any keys, so she may have the key to Tokar's house in her purse."

"That's OK. I mainly wanted to acquire the card to gain entrance to the lake development."

Upon their return to Rhonda's house, she said, "I neglected to give you a tour of the house last night, but I'd be glad to show you around if you've got the time."

Harris nodded and after following her into the house they walked through the living room, dining room, and kitchen. They then went down a connecting corridor where he saw a hall bath, giving a quick look into each of the bedrooms.

She stopped at the door to the master bedroom. "I'll have to keep the curtains drawn from now on since I now know I've got a peeper for a neighbor. I'm even considering putting up blinds with those curtains to ensure I have privacy."

Harris came to stand beside her in the doorway, and they stood close facing each other with their backs against the doorjamb. "You've got a fine home here, much larger than mine in the southwest part of the city. But as far as the blinds go, yes, I think that would be a good idea. That kid may not be foolhardy enough to come into your yard and risk getting caught peeking into your bedroom window any time soon, but I wouldn't put it past him to have a set of binoculars."

Gazing up and down Rhonda's slim fitting black evening dress, he added, "I'll say this much though, if I was a neighbor his age, I'd be definitely tempted to have a looksee."

Her head tilted to one side with her long dark hair swinging over, and Harris commented, "I don't know if whether I mentioned it before, but you do look lovely and quite ravishing in that dress."

She nodded, "You paid me a nice compliment earlier, and I appreciate that." Then her eyes fell upon the nicely made up queen-size bed that had a collection of pillows strategically placed on it. Her big brown eyes then turning to him with a look of innocence, "Do you approve of the way I have the bed made-up?"

Harris now began acting cynical, "Rhonda, I've seen that look of cunning in a female's eyes before, and let's not forget that your parents raised you as a girl of high moral principles."

Standing in the confines of the doorway, Rhonda wanted to make it clear she was open to the idea of intimacy and playful fooling around. Switching her position for squaring up to face him, her breasts rubbed against his chest, and she looked deep into his eyes. "What exactly are you trying to say?"

"Let's quit fooling ourselves. You know exactly what I'm getting at."

"You know, even good girls like a little affection every now and then."

"I imagine so, but it's a little innocent affection that gets things sparking and the next thing you know you're stoking the coals of passion."

She ran the fingers of her right hand down the lapel of his sport coat. "What object would you usually use to stoke a fire with?"

"All right, I'm getting in a tight position to maneuver, so I'm outta here," and as Harris turned to walk away, she in a teasingly, feisty way hung onto his arm.

"You know, I'm not my big sister's kid sister anymore—I'm a woman."

"Yeah, and how many other poor, defenseless victims have you lured to the threshold of your bedroom?"

She lifted her head up to look him in the eye. "It just so happens you're the first to make it this far and that's because I'm more than just a little choosy about the men I ask to my home." Now deciding to be the cynical one, she remarked, "Harris, I hope you're a better detective than you are a romanticist. I don't mind a little foreplay, but the way you're going about it, it's disappointingly killing the mood."

He nodded as though giving recognition to what she'd said, "For what it's worth, it's having the direct opposite effect on me and I may have to take a cold shower the minute I get home. It may help to say that I try to avoid distractions when working a case and it just so happens that I'm on a rather important one right now that requires my undivided attention."

Rhonda looked disappointed and leaned her shoulder against the hall wall, folding her arms, crossing her legs, and nodding to the bedroom. "You could take your cold shower here. I've already taken one, but I wouldn't mind scrubbing your back."

"All fun aside, I haven't even so much as kissed a female in over a year, leaving me working from a defensive position. I want to thank you for the most wonderful evening I've had in a long time. You look beautiful, and you've just given me about the most flattering invitation I've ever received from a woman."

Rhonda replied, "If you're out of practice, a couple of laps around the bases may be what you need to get back in shape."

Harris came to her, took her in his arms while placing his hand around the back of her neck, and kissed her ever so sensuously on the lips.

While holding her in his arms, he gave her a caring look. "I hope you're not home too late tomorrow so we can go out to the lake and have a look around before it gets dark. I want you to point out Tokar's weekend home and maybe we'll swing over to the other side of the lake to have a look at the doctor's place as well. It may be a good idea, if you've got them, to wear a wide brimmed sunhat and sunglasses, and we don't want anyone out there recognizing us so we need a laidback look."

He then gave her one last kiss before letting her go to stand on her own. "You may not believe this, but I found tonight quite exhilarating, as you've awakened in me some spontaneous feelings I'd pretty much forgotten."

Rhonda shifted her body inside her dress for pulling out wrinkles. "You sure took your time about giving a girl a little cooperation. And if you were stalling because you're out of practice, I want you to know you made a few points with that kiss. I guess I'll have to concede to the bell and give you this first round, but this wrestling match isn't over yet."

Harris smiled, "I enjoyed every minute sparring with you and letting you chase me around the ring. There were a few times you had me on the ropes, and I'm afraid if we'd gone on much further you would've landed a knockout punch."

Rhonda kept a straight face. "If I had gotten you on your back, I'd never have let you get up off the canvas, but go home now and take your cold shower."

As Harris put his hand on the door to leave, Rhonda said, "Seeing you again has been a welcome distraction, but I'm terribly worried about Amanda. I've never known such a profoundly unsettling feeling worrying about her, and while I have a gut feeling she's in bad trouble, I can't give up believing she'll be found okay. I hope your people get a break finding her soon because I'm climbing the walls thinking about what may have happened to her, and it's beginning to wear on me in a big way. Is she dead or held prisoner at the mercy of some fiendish degenerate who enjoys exerting his will over a helpless victim? I'm also concerned Dad could have another heart attack worrying about her."

"I shouldn't be telling you this, but over the next twenty-four to forty-eight hours there may be a break coming in the investigation. I'm not saying Amanda will be found, and if she is there's no telling what the outcome will be, but I'm expecting important news soon."

Rhonda moved closer. "What is it? Tell me what's going on."

"I can't say anything more, and there's always a chance that something could go wrong, so don't get too hopeful. Just hang on tight to your britches for a little bit longer and stay optimistic, and if you've been saying prayers for Amanda, this is the time they're needed most."

She embraced him with tears in her eyes, "I hope she's found soon."

"You know, a detective has a difficult time keeping his mind on what he's investigating when the case involves an attractive woman."

She cracked a smile and they kissed one last time before he stepped out the door.

On his drive home, Harris noticed a distinctive set of headlight beams on a car in his rearview mirror that in his mind seemed to be following him for some time. This car's headlights were somewhat unique by way of the placement of the flasher part of the lens. He knew the headlamp assembly lenses of a good many automobiles and recognized this to be a sporty, low riding, Nissan Altima because he had considered purchasing one at one time. He'd rented an Altima on a vacation trip once and thought the car a cheap version of a Porsche, quick handling with fast acceleration, prompting him to give thought to buying one for his wife.

It wasn't unusual for a Nissan Altima to be following him because they were quite common on the road. The optics of the Altima's headlights had a lengthy, elongated eggshell design and he was sure he picked up on the notable location of the turn signals. However, getting used to seeing those headlight beams behind him was beginning to make him feel uncomfortable. For one thing, he thought he'd seen Altima headlight beams keeping pace with him the night before when getting off the highway while on his way home.

Getting off the exit ramp and turning onto a busy boulevard, he saw the Nissan kept following him. Without signaling, he cut a sharp right-hand turn and sped down Eichelberger Street with the Altima giving chase, and then made a sharp turn onto Tamm Avenue. Noticing the other driver doing the same, he turned down an alley and hit the brakes hard, then watched as a gray Altima passed by and sped away.

Harris backed up his Impala and punched the accelerator for pursuing the Altima down Tamm Avenue, but it was already out of sight, leaving him no chance of getting a plate number off the car. The driver was obviously following him, making him wonder why and for what purpose, and his first thought was that Tokar had made arrangements to have him followed. Now certain of this, he intended to watch for those distinctive headlights in his rearview mirror from now on, and figuring it wasn't Tokar himself trailing him, he wanted to know who it was.

Chapter 9
The Bureau Locates the Home of a Serial Killer

Thursday morning, Harris received a call on his cell phone and 'Police Headquarters' showed up on his track indicator for identifying the caller. Expecting Ron Warren, he answered it by saying, "Hey Ron, what's up?"

"You must've scored a few points with Agent Johnson. He asked me to tell you he has the IP address he subpoenaed from the Internet Provider in connection with a home here in the St. Louis area. The first two maps sent to the station pinpointing the locations of prostitute's bodies came from the same residence, and the next two came from Powell University. It just so happens that an individual listed as living at the home address in question has a position of employment at Powell University as a maintenance man. Now I can't say another word about this except that we're having an important closed meeting here at the station at eleven o'clock this morning and Johnson gave authorization for you to attend. Don't be late and don't speak a word about this to anybody."

"This means a great deal to me Ron. Thanks."

At ten minutes before eleven, Harris arrived at the station to see an unusual amount of activity, looking as though the investigation looked ready to move into high gear. He went to the detective's bureau to meet up with Ron Warren and Supervisory Special Agent Johnson, and minutes later, Johnson spoke to a group of high-level law officials in attendance. No people connected with the media were allowed in the meeting.

"The address of the suspect is in a municipality called Overland in St. Louis County, and their chief of police is Martin Ulrich, who's standing beside me now. He'll be coming along to lend what cooperation and assistance he can in the arrest of this individual."

Ulrich and other high-ranking law enforcement officers stood silent as Johnson went on speaking. "The man we're targeting works at Powell University doing maintenance work and since early this morning I've had him under surveillance. I won't be giving out his name or his home address to the media until he is apprehended and we have the crime scene secured. We have warrants in hand, and we're going to make the arrest at his home with no more than six agents taking him into custody. The names of those six agents acting in that unit are Blattner, Weatherly, Parks, Cavanaugh, McCord, and Williams. I'm going to now ask that those few agents I've mentioned step forward and come with me to another locale that's in the vicinity of the suspect's home. It's there that we'll set up a command post for concentrating our efforts and coordinating our next move.

"At one time or another we've had over 150 law enforcement officers involved in this investigation and many of you have been instrumental in identifying this individual. I can imagine you're disappointed for not getting the opportunity to participate in this climactic endeavor to bring this man to justice. However, we can't take any chances; this is a dangerous individual who has time in the armed forces. He may be armed, and I feel our success depends on the utmost secrecy.

"I know you all understand the importance of keeping the lid on this and for those of you who aren't coming along, you have my thanks and gratitude. As soon as we have this animal in cuffs, we'll send word to you and hopefully, after all the work and sweat we've put into this case, we'll have something worth celebrating."

With that, Supervisory Special Agent Johnson and the FBI personnel whom he delegated to be involved in the apprehension left the building. Ron Warren caught sight of Harris and signaled that he should follow him outside, and the two got into an unmarked police car to take a place in line with other cars leaving the station. The Overland chief of police rode with Agent Johnson in the lead unmarked federal car. They traveled to a shopping center located at the corner of a busy intersection in Overland and arrived at a coffee shop called *the Java House,* located at the northern end of the mall.

Law officers gathered at a section in the back to isolate themselves from the few customers occupying seats in the place. A plainclothes detective told the manager in strictest confidence that they'd come with regards to a police matter they needed to discuss and they didn't want any interruptions. Convening around a circular table, Johnson presented an enlarged satellite photo covering a four-block radius to convey his plan of how they would go about closing in on the suspect's residence.

"As mentioned earlier, the subject is employed by Powell University as a custodian. We're using extra precaution because this individual held the rank of Corporal in the armed forces, which means he may be carrying a weapon, and he also has martial arts training. Perhaps most importantly, I want everyone to know this individual was an explosives technician, which means the house may be wired."

An inconspicuous man with thinning hair, wearing a blue suit and a red, white, and blue diagonally striped tie was sitting in a corner of the shop. Keeping a low profile to avoid being recognized while sipping coffee, he had a limited view of goings on and leaned to turn an ear for listening to what was being conferred.

One of the agents, McCord, said something to turn Johnson's attention to Overland police cruisers converging on the coffee shop, and he raised his head to look outside, remarking, "What the hell?"

Johnson looked to the chief of police, "What is this, a police convention or are we gearing up for a riot? This is exactly what I hoped wouldn't happen—I don't want this blowing up in our faces."

"I'll take care of it," said Chief Ulrich, stepping aside and talking into a handheld police radio to voice his displeasure, instructing cruisers to avoid a ten block radius of the shopping center.

The man with thinning hair, and blue suit came forward, and knowing Ron Warren, he addressed him, "Ron, what's going on?"

Warren shook his head, "Why don't we just bring in the television news crews and a goddamn chopper to give everybody a bird's eye view?"

Johnson asked, "Who is he?"

"James Whiting, a reporter for the St. Louis Post Dispatch newspaper."

Whiting's eyes enlarged as he pointed at Warren, "It's that psycho serial killer, and you're getting set up to take him down."

Johnson angrily blew up, looking to the Overland police chief, "Look, if you've still got a car out there, I want this man locked up for twenty-four hours."

Whiting excitedly held up his hands in a pleading gesture, "No, no. I represent the press and I was just sitting over there when I caught on that something was happening. I merely want to be a bystander acting as an eyewitness for getting the exclusive story. I have First Amendment rights—I promise not to phone anybody or get in the way."

Disgusted about the newspaperman's presence, Johnson's eyes turned to Warren, "Can he be trusted?"

Warren nodded, "I think he'll be okay."

"I didn't mind allowing some of you people to be in on this because you are somehow directly involved in this investigation. I suppose if I'd given the guy's name and address there'd be squad cars and news crews jamming his street, but should one more thing happen to jeopardize this operation, I'm kicking everybody out. After that, it'll strictly be FBI personnel handling the operation—I don't need you people."

Johnson looked at Whiting, "You can accompany Warren to the site after the arrest is made. From then on, I don't care if you call for a photographer, but until then, I'd better not hear so much as a peep out of you."

Making use of the enlargement showing homes behind the shopping center, Johnson's index finger encircled an area of residential yards backing up to fencing as he resumed speaking. "Our subject lives in a quiet community on an elevated street running behind this shopping center called Navarro Terrace. One of these houses that have its backside to this retaining wall behind this mall is the suspect's home. These are older homes with large fenced-in yards, no alleyway access, and our agents have previously studied this photo for determining positions they'll be taking. The retaining wall behind the coffee shop is twelve feet above a parking area specified for employees, and while I suppose we could scale it, I don't think that's necessary."

Johnson then raised his voice a few decimeters, "Our suspect gets off work at three o'clock, and agents that have him under surveillance will keep us posted as he makes his journey home. We've given local law enforcement officials the route we expect he usually takes when traveling to and from home, and we've asked that they not intervene by pulling him over for a simple traffic violation. We'll have our people take their stations at the house at precisely two-thirty, so we'll be set-up and waiting for him when he arrives home. I want him taken down quickly and briefly questioned before we enter the house."

He noticed the newspaperman, Whiting, jotting down information on a notepad, and looked at his watch, "We'll be leaving in another half-hour. We have to be careful, while we think the suspect is operating alone in this, we don't know for certain whether he has a partnering associate inside the premises. We've phoned the house a number of times and no one has answered our calls, and phone records indicate the home phone is only in use when he is off work. Those six agents whom I've designated for making the arrest will travel to the house inside an FBI box truck that is set up to look like a FedEx delivery truck. This vehicle is outside on the lot now and it will be driven by Judy Pressler, who is dressed in a uniform to look the part."

Johnson looked around for Judy Pressler, an African-American, and upon seeing her motioned for her to come and stand beside him. "This is Judy, she'll have a package to deliver to the residence, and when she gets to the door she'll knock and ring the doorbell. After she makes a diligent effort to draw someone to the door and is convinced no one is available to answer it, she'll place the package next to the door. That will be the signal for those six agents to approach the house to take their positions. Judy will then return to the FedEx truck and leave while those six hold their stations and wait for the suspect to arrive.

"The subject drives a dark green minivan, and our surveillance team will have already given us word on whether he's traveling alone on his ride home. If he is, and we expect he will be, we'll wait until he begins walking from his vehicle to the entrance of the house to move in with our weapons drawn. I want to emphasize that we want to take him alive, but don't forget he's experienced in martial arts, so I expect him to be combative. Be careful about how you take him down. I couldn't care less if we fill him full of holes, but psychoanalysts are going to want to study him for years for determining the root cause of his bizarre behavior."

He glimpsed his watch once more. "The bureau has located the suspect's ex-wife and taken her in for questioning, which will eventually be done at the station. Various spousal abuse convictions against the husband resulted in a divorce and the couple has not lived together for over two years. During the time the two were married, he had a stint in the army, whereby afterwards he had trouble adjusting to civilian life, exhibiting anger and violent behavior. The wife acquired restraining orders, but they did little to keep him from kicking in her door and beating her on a regular basis. However, this changed about a year ago when he took up residence in his mother's home after she took to living in a rest home for the elderly. Violent behavior toward his wife became subdued from the moment he took this change of address, and that's about the time he began abducting women, so his maniacal ways were then directed at his captive prisoners."

Johnson adjusted the enlargement while pointing out a house that sat back from the street more than most of the homes that had small front yards. This particular house had a large front yard, and a short backyard that fell short of fencing running along the retaining wall.

"Without my having to give up the address, let me just say that we're targeting this bungalow that sits back from the street. Judy is familiar with the house, as she earlier cased homes along Navarro Terrace on foot while wearing a different set of clothes and stuffing pamphlets with advertisements in the mailboxes."

Harris looked fidgety, crossing his arms and looking elsewhere before once again turning his eyes back to examine the enlargement.

"Do you have somewhere else you'd rather be Harris, or is this beginning to bore you? Maybe you'd feel more comfortable taking over and running this operation."

Harris's eyebrows rose, "I was thinking about his captives and how his last victim was discovered hogtied with her arms pulled out of the shoulder sockets. Depending upon whether there are women inside that house and what their condition is right now, a few minutes may seem like an eternity."

Johnson straightened up, drawing breath, "We moved on this as quickly as possible after learning the address, but that's a good point, the current situation inside that house may be hellish."

He then heard the voice of the agent who had the suspect under surveillance coming through a Nextel device, "Johnson."

Johnson replied, "Go ahead."

"He just left the university to go to his vehicle."

Johnson's brows raised and his forehead wrinkled, "I thought he didn't get off until three?"

"He may have received permission to get off early without the university giving us notification or he's anxious to get home and simply snuck out without anyone paying attention."

"Okay, we're heading for his house now to get set up," and then Johnson stuffed the Nextel inside his coat. "He's starting home, so let's get the ball rolling."

Johnson looked at Harris, "I want you to stick with me. I'd forgotten you have a personal interest in this case and there may be someone in that house that you know."

Chapter 10
Entering the House on Navarro Terrace

Johnson, Harris, and other field agents comprising the arresting team went outside and got into the FedEx truck to start their brief ride to the house on Navarro Terrace.

When addressing the Assistant Special Agent-in-charge, Johnson handed him a photo of the suspect obtained from the license bureau, "Blattner, its imperative that we stay in constant communication. The suspect's name is Terrance D'Angelo, and believing there's little chance he has an accomplice, Harris and I are going to get out of the truck with Judy to approach the house. She'll go straight to the door while we circle around back to inspect the rear of the residence. As already discussed, after Judy has made a thorough attempt to draw someone to the door to answer her knock or the doorbell, she'll set the package down and start back to the truck. You'll let me know the moment that happens and while you're all taking positions out front, Harris and I will see about gaining entrance to the house from the rear."

The moment the truck stopped, Johnson put on his sunglasses, and he and Harris exited the truck's passenger side to follow Judy Pressler as she marched toward the house. The other agents in the truck kept watch while Judy went straight down the walk carrying a package to begin knocking on the door and ringing the doorbell. They viewed Johnson and Harris making their way to the rear of the house, the land having a gradual declining grade to the backyard.

Johnson and Harris had begun scouring the backside of the house with Johnson taking steps leading up to a small porch where there was a backdoor entrance. Hearing a muffled sound coming from inside the house, he removed his sunglasses and placed them in his shirt pocket, but he still could not see any activity inside. Gripping his semi-automatic pistol and bringing it out, he tried the door handle, but found it locked, and then he came back down the steps to notice there was no basement entrance to the house.

All the while listening to Judy's persistent pounding at the front entrance, Johnson and Harris met at a basement window approximately three feet square that appeared spray-painted black on the inside. When hearing a pause, they glimpsed one another and Johnson said, "We need to get inside this house, and if you don't want to perform the break-in, I guess I'll do it."

Grateful to have been asked to provide assistance, Harris nonchalantly replied, "I'll do it. You said this guy was an explosives technician—if this house is blown to hell, it's been nice knowing you."

Johnson gave a final warning, "Be on the lookout for trip wires, and if you see any we'll have to stop to bring in the bomb squad to disarm the place before moving in."

They heard Judy resume knocking at the front door and this time when she stopped they heard Blattner's voice come through over the radio.

"Judy left the package and is returning to the truck."

Johnson responded, "OK, let's move to take your positions."

Pressed for expecting the suspect to arrive home soon, Harris drew his .45 caliber pistol, and squinted when kicking the window frames where they met vertically in the middle. They swung inward with the glass panes shattering from the impact, and they immediately heard a loud playing television operating somewhere in the house.

Harris saw a basin sink inside below the window, and he stooped to carefully plant his right foot in the sink, his eyes scanning the dark interior that awaited him. Moving to squat with both legs in the basin, he felt the crunch of glass beneath his feet and peered about with the barrel of his automatic following his line of sight. Finding himself in the basement laundry room, clumps of clothing scattered everywhere, he gripped the sink's rim with his left hand to hold his balance as he stepped down on a bare concrete floor. Seeing only one door to enter and exit the room, the loud noise made by the television made him think the set was playing in the next connecting room.

Johnson followed, climbing through the window with his weapon in hand, and the two came to stand before the room's only door. Both men feeling urgency to comb the basement for prisoners, they moved forward to enter a room much darker, the only light coming from a big screen television that was playing loudly.

Catching the dim outline of a staircase coming down from the main floor on his right, Harris moved to take aim for the door at the top of the stairs.

Johnson saw a light switch on the wall next to Harris, and whispered, "There's a light switch behind you."

With the flip of the switch, recessed fluorescent lights in the ceiling came on to brighten the area and they saw a clean and tidy room where a red velvet couch faced the television. Turning their attention to a door across the room, they looked at each other as if both wondering what lay beyond that door, never forgetting the suspect could've wired the house with explosives.

Outside the house, agents took places of concealment behind a bush, a tree, two taking positions at the corners of neighboring homes, and two more squatted behind trashcans that provided cover.

The voice of the agent trailing D'Angelo came through urgently over the radio, startling Johnson. "He's off the highway now and only a couple blocks from his house driving at a reckless high speed."

"We're ready for him," Johnson replied, and with that, he gripped the door handle and opened the next door to see a torture chamber containing two black women. One woman of thin build was lying on her stomach on a mattress, and her eyes opened wide to look back at them as though uncertain of her fate. Her wrists bound by a zip-tie fastener, one of her legs were shackled by a chain anchored to a metal, upright support beam, restraints that gave her limited mobility. Their attention quickly turned to the bizarre sight of a completely nude female strung up by her arms and legs, appearing lifeless with her body and back arched in a U shape. Elevated by rope attached to an overhead gas pipeline running across the ceiling, her head, breasts and hair hanging down, the two moved forth to support her.

Harris brought out a pocketknife to cut ropes rigged for holding her up, and they let her down gently to rest on the mattress alongside the other girl. The touch of the body's skin and its stiffness gave no doubt to her being stone-cold dead, and Harris removed a waded cloth that had been jammed into her mouth.

Johnson went to get a sheet from the laundry room to cover the body with, and on his way back carrying two bed sheets he turned down the television's volume so he could hear himself think.

The woman shackled to the post finally found her voice and was soft-spoken, "She's gone—she died last night around midnight from how he left her hanging. Like some kind of a monster possessed by the devil, he took joy in torturing her and watching her die a slow death. The pain she suffered was excruciating, and hardly able to draw air, the more she squirmed, the more the rope tightened. Even with how he had her gagged, I ain't never heard anybody scream the way she did, and after what all he'd done to her, I believe she was ready to embrace death."

She leaned to one side to allow Harris to cut the zip-tie binding her wrists together, giving out a faint grunt as he carefully cut through the durable plastic to give her hands freedom. Still having one foot shackled by a chain linked to the metal support beam, she latched onto his arm as she began crying, realizing help had finally come to rescue her. Feeling redemption after having given up hope, she wept over what she'd endured, and for having had to live with the fear that she could've shared the same fate as the other girl.

Johnson had draped the survivor with one sheet, and proceeded with covering up the deceased girl with the other. It was then both lawmen noticed a streak of blood spatter covering a large portion of a wall that must have come from one of the previous victims.

The female spoke with tears streaming down her face, "He'd test me by acting as though he'd gone, and if he heard me screaming for help he'd come down and beat me with a rubber hose. I called out for hours today but nobody can hear me with that television drowning out the sound of my voice, and when I heard glass breaking a minute ago, I was afraid he'd returned. As much as I wished for it to be police, I believed my turn was coming and after this next time I'd be in the waiting arms of God's angels. I'm speaking this way because my father is a minister, and thinking about him and expecting I may die soon, I've tried to make peace with the Lord.

"I may not deserve to see the gates of Heaven, but I don't believe I deserve the hell where that evil man is sure to go. His thing is having power and control over people, getting enjoyment out of watching them struggle and suffer. He'd twice strangled me with his bare hands, and both times, when I was at the point of suffocating, he shouted in my face to look in his eyes. It was as though the last thing he wanted me to see on this Earth was his eyes, and I watched him do the same to the others as a sadistic way of torturing and tormenting us."

Choked up with tears flowing, she looked to the body that lay beside her. "I only know her as Naomi, and she was a fighter, much like another that died the same way she had."

Harris asked her, "What's your name?"

"Claudia Jones."

Blattner's soft-spoken voice came through Johnson's hand held radio, "Green minivan."

"He's here!" Her eyes enlarged with fright as she yanked at the chain to try and get free, but Harris calmed her, and Johnson put his index finger to his lips to indicate he wanted quiet.

He then told her, "We've got him covered with a half dozen agents outside awaiting his arrival, and they'll take him down before he reaches the house."

Out front, the minivan came to a halt, and the unsuspecting Terrance D'Angelo, a broad-shouldered, stocky built, dark-skinned man, got out of the vehicle to start walking toward the entrance of his home. Agents closed in from their positions to confront the suspect, who looked like he may be a handful for the team of six to take down.

When nearing the front porch, D'Angelo saw what he was up against, and he took a threatening stance as though he wasn't going to let them apprehend him without a fight. Blattner, knowing the subject had martial arts experience, held his Taser gun pointed at him in preparation for using it, while the others converged with their pistols aimed at him.

Stopping within ten feet of confronting him, D'Angelo saw himself surrounded with no chance for escape, and he made a sudden move as if lunging for one of the agents. Blattner leveled his Taser and fired the weapon, which caused D'Angelo to fall to the ground, convulsing.

In the basement, Harris and Johnson remained still while listening and heard what sounded like a scuffle over the radio. For when agents stood huddled over the suspect, one stooped to handcuff D'Angelo and he sprung to reach and grab the agent's throat.

Hearing a single gunshot, after the commotion settled down, Blattner addressed Johnson over the radio. "I'd taken him down with my Taser, but he still had enough fight in him to catch Ted Cavanaugh by the throat. When we couldn't get him to release his grip, Cavanaugh shot him in the stomach, but I don't think the wound is life-threatening."

The woman chained to the support beam broke down, releasing more tears, and Johnson replied, "Keep him cuffed at all times, but get him to a hospital. We also have a surviving victim here in the basement named Claudia Jones, and you can release her name to the media after contacting her family, and we'll need you to bring bolt cutters to free her. There's one victim who didn't make it who we'll have to send to the medical examiner's office, and her only known name at this time is Naomi. Let's get crime scene investigators in here right away to go over the residence, and then see what needs to be done in order to secure the premises."

An ambulance whisked D'Angelo away to a trauma center, and minutes later, a second ambulance pulled up to give Claudia Jones transportation to the nearest hospital. A third emergency vehicle would transport the deceased woman to the medical examiner's office.

News crews began arriving on the scene, and a newsman was granted time to ask the lone survivor one question. "I understand your name is Claudia Jones, can you tell me how you felt when you realized the FBI had come to your rescue?"

The woman looked overcome by all of the attention and at the same time relieved for having escaped a nightmarish fate. "Euphoria—it was as if I'd been reborn."

Johnson and Harris stopped to listen as the newsman pressed the emergency crew to allow him one more question. "What do you have to say about the man who held you prisoner in that house?"

She shook her head, "I ain't ever met any human being so evil, deranged, and sick, taking pleasure out of torturing us and seeing life drained from a person."

The doors closed on the ambulance, the newsman then looked around to interview others, and a uniformed policeman pointed to the unit of six that made the arrest. "Those are the agents who took him down."

An unmarked federal car picked up Agent Johnson, and after it sped away Ron Warren drove up to provide Harris transportation back to the station. On the way back, Warren asked questions about how things were inside the residence, and Harris gave sordid details about D'Angelo's house of horror and the dungeon room in which they found the surviving victim.

At the station, FBI, detectives and uniformed police filed into a room adjacent to another room used for interrogations, separated by a one-way mirror, and they viewed Mrs. D'Angelo making a statement. A heavyset Caucasian woman sat facing FBI agent Juliet Palmer, who asked her, "Why do you think your husband may have killed other women at another location?"

The woman began, "When my husband was stationed at Fort Bragg in Cumberland County we mostly lived on base, but for a time we lived on the outskirts of Fayetteville, North Carolina. During the time we lived there a woman claimed my husband attacked and choked her, and Terry denied it. He insisted this woman was mistaking him for someone else, but the situation didn't look good for him. He was my husband, we'd been married less than a year, and I thought I knew him well enough to believe what he was telling me was the truth. He claimed the only way to avoid imprisonment was for me to give him an alibi whereby I'd have to tell I knew of his whereabouts every minute on the night of this woman's assault. In the upcoming days as the trial neared, he became nervous and skittish to the point that he couldn't hardly sleep or even sit still. I gave him support at the hearing by giving testimony that our baby was sick throughout that night with colic, and we were up taking care of her all night long."

Palmer remarked, "So you lied under oath to protect him?"

"Well, our baby was sick and irritable with acid reflux at the time, but she also had colic and I hardly got any sleep that night nursing her. Exhausted from caring for her, I may have fallen asleep for an hour or so, and in all honesty, I cannot account for his whereabouts every minute of that particular night. The trial ended in a hung jury, and the victim was reluctant to go through another trial, leaving me convinced he was innocent from the beginning. I believe Terry's mother gave this woman an unspecified sum of money in the hopes that it would end her ambition to put her son through another trial."

Palmer reiterated, "All right, so you stretched the truth, and now, with this most recent turn of events, you're convinced your husband may have choked this woman with the intention of killing her?"

She nodded, "After we left North Carolina and returned home to St. Louis, I saw changes in my husband's behavior. He'd grown demanding and suspicious of me in a distrusting way, becoming quick-tempered and easily thrown into a rage. He'd beaten me several times and for that, I leveled charges against him for spousal abuse, and then I looked to get help from a social worker for acquiring restraining orders. Every time we met, he'd throw a fit, and I couldn't get away from him—he demanded to see his daughter, which the courts allowed him because of his parental rights.

"I thought about moving out of state to another town, but as obsessed as he acted, I believed he'd surely come following me and it might make things even worse. There came one night when he came by to see the baby on an unscheduled visit, and choosing not to make a fuss, I let him in the house. All evening long, he had a strange look in his eyes and as it got late, I asked him in a nice way to go, sensing at the same time that his mood and temperament was changing. He'd always blamed me for all of his problems and standing there staring at me with the oddest expression, I told him, 'Terry, you ought to see a psychologist,' and this threw him into a tantrum."

The woman was on the verge of tears, "He began strangling me, and I tried doing everything possible to pull his hands free from my throat, but I couldn't. I was slipping out of consciousness while looking at him, and then he began shouting in my face, 'Look at me! Look in my eyes!'"

She paused long enough to get composed for finishing her statement, "I was on the verge of passing out when he finally let go of my throat. It was then that I knew he'd choked that other woman, and there were two other unsolved murders near where we stayed at the base that were female strangulations."

The woman became emotional and Harris left the room to phone Rhonda to tell her about how he assisted the FBI in the capture of a serial killer. In doing so, he also explained there was no indication that Amanda had ever been inside the house, and confirmed their date to drive out to Lake Laraine later that same evening.

Chapter 11
Taking a Ride Out to Lake Laraine

Early Thursday evening, Harris drove to Rhonda's home and waited for her to shower and get into a change of clothing before going out to see Tokar's and Doctor Vincent Dvorak's weekend homes at Lake Laraine. Rhonda came forward wearing a wide brimmed hat, sporting sunglasses that had extra-large lenses. She had on an almond halter top with cutaway shoulders, a black wraparound waste band, white short shorts, and white tennis shoes.

"I'm ready if you are," and they walked out the door.

Harris grinned, "Laid back look—inconspicuous, the hat and the glasses are fine, but you look like you're dressed for going to a fashion show at the yacht club. The idea is not to draw attention, and if seen outside the car you're certain to draw attention—guys, in particular, are going to be scoping out those legs."

"I thought the idea was not to be recognized and I went for a summer look since we'll be at the lake." She raised a brow, twitching her right shoulder as they began strolling together down the walk to the driveway.

Rhonda, now wondering if they were going in Harris's car, asked, "Which car do you think we ought to take?"

"We're taking your rental. In case a snoopy somebody takes down the plate number, it'll throw them off."

Rhonda handed him the keys and after they got in the car, Harris started its engine. She turned to him. "Dealing with abject fear that something's happened to my sister, the capture of that nutcase today did nothing but fuel fiendish ideas about what she may be going through."

Harris tried preparing her for the possibility that bad news may come, "I know you hate to hear it, but the clock is running against Amanda. As much as I don't want to paint a bleak picture, the time that coincides with this weekend is vital to her survival. It's in all likelihood going to take something radical on my part to learn where she is. It may be that her whereabouts has nothing to do with people linked to this lake, but right now it's my best lead. Depending on what I see while we're out there, it may become necessary for me to go out to that lake after dark to observe goings on."

Soon taking an entrance ramp to get on the highway, he checked his rearview mirror and accelerated to pick up speed for easing into traffic. "I've avoided mentioning it because I thought it would make you nervous, but for the last two nights a gray Nissan Altima has followed me home. Why, I don't know, but if it's in any way connected to Amanda's disappearance, and I think it is, it means someone regards my involvement as a serious threat."

He gently but reassuringly patted her on the leg and noticed how smooth her skin felt, "Don't give up hoping that we'll find her."

Rhonda noticed Harris's sport coat was unbuttoned to expose what was a compact leather pouch connected to his belt, and asked, "What's that pouch for?"

"I'll tell you about it later."

He went on to comment, "I remember reading something written by a columnist about this *Lake Laraine* some time ago in the newspapers. It was originally a summer retreat for well-to-do people who had classy homes of unique architecture built there, but nowadays most of the homeowners live there year-round. The lake development began forming in the late forties, and they'd built many of the homes in the 1950s when the economy was gaining steam after the Second World War. I remember the writer speculating that the lake's developer had named the lake after a bright-eyed actress who was popular at the time named Laraine Day."

Harris then said, "You said you once came out to this lake to attend a party at Tokar's place. Was that the only time you've been here?"

"No, I came out here once before the party on a Sunday when Amanda asked me if I'd like to take a drive and tour the lake, and I remember it was a sunny day. Amanda was engaged to Tokar at the time, and I believe she was using this opportunity to spy on him. She saw him kissing and fondling a female on his pontoon boat, and I told her, 'Tokar owns a casino and has girls around him constantly, so you shouldn't be surprised.' While out that way, she showed me Tokar's house and pointed out Dvorak's home on the opposite side of the lake.

The two later had a big fight and she very nearly quit him while considering moving to California to start fresh, but they made up, although after that little tiff she gave him back his ring. From then on their relationship began to whither, he tried winning back her trust, but she gave me the distinct impression she had no intention of ever marrying the guy."

When arriving at the lake, Rhonda handed over to Harris the access card for giving them entrance through the gate. After he inserted the card in the slotted box, it chucked out the card and he took possession of it, and an electronic arm blocking the way immediately lifted to give them entry. They traveled further in, proceeding down a hill, when Harris got his first view of the lake, and the body of water was quite scenic. In front of them, a cross street ran before the water's edge, and a sign indicated that to the left was North Lake Drive and to the right was South Lake Drive.

Harris's eyes continued scanning the lake as they coasted slowly down the hill while approaching the cross street.

Rhonda explained, "This view gives the impression that the lake is U-shaped, but the shoreline meanders in all different directions and there are many coves."

Harris asked, "Do we turn left or right?"

"To get to Tokar's place you turn left, and Dvorak's is to the right."

Turning left, they rode for as much as a half-hour on a snaking road that followed the lake's shoreline to reach Tokar's home near the end of the drive. Rhonda pointed out the house and Harris made a mental note of the number 119 on the mailbox, and slowly passing the residence, they both gave attention to cars parked nearby. They moved on for a short distance to where there was a circle, and they saw the dam holding back the lake's water covered with gravel, having enough space for a vehicle to drive across it. Turning around to go back the way they'd come, Harris closely scrutinized cars lined up in Tokar's driveway that descended from the road to run alongside the house to the backyard. He'd hoped to see a gray Nissan Altima, although not one of the cars was a Nissan, but around to the back he saw an automobile covered by a tarp. Behind the home, Tokar's guests were seen wearing summer clothes, most in shorts or wearing swimsuits and sunglasses. Some were tending to a barbecue pit on decking at the water's edge, with a few relaxing in lawn chairs soaking up sun on this warm day.

Rhonda commented, "It looks like Tokar is entertaining friends today."

Suddenly, appearing from the opposite direction was a black Buick Lacrosse, and Harris put on his sunglasses and leaned toward the driver's door glass. He placed his hand to his face as though shading it from sunlight for a quick disguise, and stopped to give the driver time to park. Two large men got out of the car; the driver was a pale, stone-faced individual who had silvery white hair with bushy black eyebrows and a cold set of eyes. The passenger was a curious looking individual of stocky build, looking kind of freakish in how his features and bone structure appeared oversized by comparison to the average persons.

"Look," Rhonda excitedly said, pointing at the larger man getting out of the car's passenger side wearing sunglasses.

Harris caught her wrist to pull it down, "Don't point."

As Harris drove off, she nearly choked, "Harris, that guy fits the description Nadia gave of the man who ran her off the road and assaulted her. He even has a mole on the side of his face like she described, and what was that one word she used that I had trouble pronouncing."

Harris nodded, "Gigantism, and yes, I know, but it wouldn't be smart to give it away that we spotted him. Didn't your mother ever tell you that it's impolite to point?"

"Yeah, but what are you going to do about it?"

"I'm not going to do anything just yet, except report it to the station, but I'm coming back here again tonight to check out the festivities at Tokar's and maybe play photographer."

"Can I come along?"

"Absolutely not, this isn't going to be a night for amateurs—the last thing I want is for somebody to recognize you snooping around here. It's important you keep a low profile and simply maintain your working schedule to make these people think we're still in the dark, having never seen these friends of Tokar's. We don't want them to know that we even came to this lake—you and I were never here and you didn't see those two men. Do you understand?"

Rhonda nodded her head yes, and anxiously said, "Those two men may also be the ones who beat up Amanda's boyfriend Jim Abernathy."

Harris gently patted her on the inside of her leg, "That may very well be, but let's not get overexcited about it until we can provide proof that they did it."

Rhonda quickly remarked, "Yeah, but that's not going to be something easily proven."

Harris understood she was excited for having seen the man who hurt her friend Nadia, wanting to see him arrested and prosecuted, and even probably more worked up for thinking he may be behind Amanda's disappearance. "I agree that it won't be simple, but let's keep our shirts on, and keep in mind that seeing those two is a good sign we're on the right track. If I'm lucky enough to photograph them, perhaps your friend Nadia and Jim Abernathy can make an identification to start the wheels of justice turning."

They continued riding around the lake, and drove on past the entrance avenue for viewing the lake's south side, taking in the view while admiring homes built on the lake. In some locations on this side of the lake the shoreline of lots raised to greater elevation, and they spotted sportsmen in two fishing boats in a cove. When nearing the end of South Lake Drive, Rhonda pointed out a mailbox in front of a brick home that had *Dvorak* with the number 114 printed on it, and she spouted off, "There, that's his home."

Harris drove on to the end of the road to a circle situated much like the one on the other side of the lake where they viewed Tokar's home near the dam. He pulled into an open space on a vacant wooded lot on the right that wasn't a lakefront lot, and after parking, turned the car's engine off.

He removed the pouch connected to his belt and opened it to display a variety of small tools and metal instruments it contained. "I'm going to take a short stroll back to Dvorak's house to have a look around, and if nobody's home, I'm using my little locksmith kit to get inside and have a quick look around."

Rhonda's eyebrows rose above her sunglasses. "What if you find him at home—I saw a detached garage and he may have his car parked inside it."

He took a second to admire Rhonda's legs. "I know you feel as though you're at the end of your rope worrying about your sister, but try to chill out." He leaned over to place his left hand gently to her cheek for giving her a long kiss. "I won't be gone long."

Harris walked back up the road to Dvorak's house, intending to have a look around to end any suspicions he had about the doctor so he wouldn't have to spend much time investigating him. The brick home looked well-constructed, and the roofline of the detached garage ran over to connect to the house, providing a shaded, open breezeway between the garage and the home. After making a pass around the house, he then gave the garage a quick look-over, but was unable to tell if there was an automobile in the garage because curtains covered the windows. He then went to the home's entrance to ring the bell and knocked on the door several times, but no one answered.

Feeling confident no one was home, he opened the leather pouch he carried and withdrew a slender six-inch metal probing device with which to pick the lock, and in no time had the door open. Placing the tool back inside the pouch, he then entered the house, locking the door behind him by simply twisting the turn piece on the knob. Making a quick walkthrough, he thought it odd when locating an oversized 42-inch wide door to the basement, and it seemed even stranger to make the distinction that this was a metal door.

Starting downstairs to have a look around, Harris immediately noticed a light switch, and flipped it to power a light over the stairs and recessed florescent ceiling lights in the basement. Leaving the door at the top of the stairs open, another light switch at the bottom of the stairs turned on additional light fixtures on each side of a fireplace in a large paneled room. The broad faced fireplace was on the garage side of the house, playing a key role in how this room's furnishings were arranged, and there was shelving displaying books and knickknacks on each side of it. After scanning the area, he concluded there were no basement windows, and he thought this peculiar.

It struck Harris that Dvorak was a man who knew how to live, as the room had a crescent shaped camel colored couch positioned to face the fireplace and a coffee table situated before it. Embossed vinyl tile closely resembling light oak parquet gave the room a warm appearance, and the open space seemed ideal for entertaining a group of people. He went on to a louvered door that opened into a utility room where the furnace was located. Another door gave access to a pristine clean, nearly empty closet space, and a third door opened to an impressively large bathroom with a Jacuzzi. Yes, Dvorak was a man who appreciated the good life.

Deciding to vacate the premises, Harris turned off the fireplace lights and started up the stairs to leave. Nearing the top of the stairs and the metal door he'd left open, he became alarmed by what sounded like someone entering through the front door. For a second wondering if it was Rhonda; he knew this couldn't be, for he remembered locking the door behind him after making his entrance into the house. Uncertain about what to do, while remaining on the stairs he flipped the light switch, turning out the basement lights and dropping back a step while quietly closing the metal basement door.

Standing in pitch black, he brought out from his coat pocket a miniature, three-inch-long LED flashlight that produced a bright beam. Concerned there may soon be a confrontation, he used his flashlight to descend the stairs and return to the basement level. He went straight to the louvered door to find sanctuary inside the utility room, switched off the flashlight and stood still in the dark. Wanting to avoid being recognized, as he'd surely lose his detectives' license for not first securing a search warrant, he withdrew a handkerchief to cover his nose and mouth, tying it behind his head. Having no intention of using his .45, he still brought it out and pulled back the slide for engaging a cartridge, and then held the weapon crossways against his chest.

Stiffening up when hearing the faint sound of the metal door opening, his intent, if necessary, was to clonk on the head whoever it was with the butt of his weapon the moment they opened the louvered door. The person switched on the lights, and the footsteps he heard indicated they were coming downstairs to leave him boxed in, and with the faint flick of a switch, lights flanking the fireplace came on.

Harris stood frozen, staying calm as he viewed the floor tile in the fireplace room through the louvers, the slant of the louvers limiting his sight into the main room. Awaiting the opening of the door, he heard sounds and raised the weapon above his head, but he was unable to determine their origin before everything surprisingly fell silent. He waited another minute before stepping out of the utility room to have a look around. It was as though whoever it was that had come down the stairs had disappeared into thin air, but had left the lights on.

He removed the handkerchief to stuff it inside his coat pocket, and as baffling as this situation was, he felt relieved for having avoided a conflict that may have resulted in the use of his firearm. Inserting his pistol into his shoulder holster, he examined the fireplace and a few ornamental pieces on the shelves because that's where he'd last sensed this individual's presence. Wherever they'd gone made for an unexplained mystery that perplexed Harris, leaving him bewildered. Something else mysterious is that he now smelled the faint aroma of an exotic food dish reminding him of fish and rice, and even though he wasn't hungry, it aroused his appetite.

Going upstairs, while still uncertain about what happened to this person, he knew it was to his benefit not to have confronted whoever it was because he had no business being in this house. He knew a face-to-face confrontation would've most assuredly meant someone acquiring a serious injury, and if identified later as the intruder, such an incident could cost him his career in law enforcement. He saw the turnpiece on the doorknob in the locked position, and twisted it to enable him to open the door before stepping outside and once again turning it when closing and securing the door.

In Dvorak's driveway sat a sleek, black Lexus, which Harris supposed was the doctor's automobile. He noticed an elderly white-haired gentlemen raking up dead leaves and branches in the yard across the road from Dvorak's residence. The home was merely a bungalow, quite small by comparison to most of the lakefront houses, and the man concentrating on yard work had little interest in Harris, seemingly not even noticing him.

Relieved to be out of that house, he drew a deep breath, and then returned to his car. He sat in the driver's seat beside Rhonda and gave her a look, "I just had the strangest experience I've ever had in my life. It may be that the doctor is not only a physician, but he may be a magician as well."

Rhonda replied, "I saw Dvorak pull up in his driveway, and I thought about tapping the horn a few times, but unsure whether you'd want me to, I thought I'd better not. It only took him a few seconds to reach the door anyway so it may not have helped to hit the horn. So how did it go, did you stumble into each other?"

"I used my locksmith tools to get inside and after casing the place, I was on my way back up the stairs from the basement when I heard him enter the house. To avoid a confrontation, I went back down in the basement and hid in a utility room that had a louvered door and waited as he turned on the lights and came down the stairs. No more than a minute later, he vanished into thin air. Something odd about that house is that there aren't any basement windows, but I suppose some are built that way, and even stranger yet is that I have this weird craving for Chinese food."

Rhonda grinned, "Chinese food . . . well, let's go get a bite to eat someplace."

The two stopped at a Chinese restaurant and Harris kept sniffing at the food until Rhonda finally complained, "Stop that. Why do you keep smelling the food, what's the matter with it?"

"Nothing, but I could swear my nose caught a whiff of a Chinese dish when I was inside Dvorak's house, the aroma was fish and rice. It aroused my sniffer to the point that I can't get it out my head, along with the doctor disappearing."

"Would you have preferred bumping into him instead?"

"No, I'm glad I got out of there without him seeing me, but it's just strange."

The experience at Dvorak's lake house stayed with Harris for some time, but he eventually put it aside and concentrated on returning to the lake that same night. His focus was on the two men he'd seen at Tokar's house who'd shown up in the Buick Lacrosse, for one fit the description of the person who assaulted Rhonda's friend Nadia. In addition, these two men could possibly be the thugs who had beaten up Amanda's boyfriend Jim Abernathy. Harris thought things were starting to look up and beginning to gel, but he knew poking around Tokar's lake house after dark could make for unexpected trouble.

Chapter 12
Poking Around the Lake after Nightfall

On Thursday at dusk, Harris returned to Lake Laraine and took South Lake Drive to the circle near Dvorak's home, pulling into the same vacant wooded lot where he'd parked earlier in the day. When driving by Dvorak's home it looked deserted, and still wondering about Dvorak's vanishing act, he was having trouble comprehending exactly what happened for the doctor to have disappeared. Wearing dark clothing, with the cloak of nightfall falling across the land, he turned his attention to surveying Tokar's party pad on the opposite side of the lake. Stealthily moving about, he saw no one outside Tokar's home, but using binoculars enabled him to view people carousing inside the residence. When all seemed quiet, he crossed the dam carrying a leather bag and stopped near a mature crape myrtle bush that gave him sufficient cover.

Assured in his mind that his movements had gone undetected thus far, he began fidgeting with his photography equipment, a .35 millimeter camera with a telephoto lens. He'd paid a lot for this equipment, but it was getting outdated, although it still achieved the results he wanted, and he had a clear visual shot through a window for studying people inside Tokar's lake house. On the basement level men were seen playing billiards, some standing around smoking, talking and drinking, and he was curious about the topic they were discussing.

Harris saw the two men who he'd seen arrive earlier in the Buick Lacrosse and had success taking a number of pictures of them, which he hoped would later identify the pair. He kept glimpsing a man with dark hair that always had his backside turned to the window, and the identity of this person stirred his curiosity as well. Throughout the night this individual never took a turn playing pool, so the opportunity never came to take his picture. It may have been near eleven o'clock when Harris carried his equipment back to his car and loaded it into the trunk. Returning back across the dam again to examine cars parked around Tokar's home, he took down the license plate numbers of a few of them, one of them being a burgundy Mercury Marquis. What surprised him was sighting a gray Nissan Altima, and although there were probably hundreds of these models owned by people in the St. Louis area, he took down the plate number just the same.

Intending to return Friday night to perform more surveillance of Tokar's home, Harris thought he might get an opportunity to recognize the dark-haired man who had his back turned to him all evening long. Curious about what kind of car Tokar had covered with a tarp behind his home, the automobile sat parked next to a stack of fireplace logs laid out in a neat row. Unable to guess what make of car was underneath the canvas, for all he knew, Tokar could be a classic car collector and it may be a vintage Duesenberg road car from the thirties.

Not wanting to push his luck, when crossing back over the dam to return to his car he heard rustling in a nearby wooded area, and he ducked while pulling out his .45. Pointing it in the direction of the sound he'd heard, he caught a glimpse of a rambling doe darting across high grass, scared off by his presence.

He spoke to himself in not much more than a whisper, "Okay, Harris, you're getting jumpy. It's time to head on home."

Giving Tokar's lake house one last look, he saw the silhouette figure of a man walking outside to take a smoke, gazing at the lake's rippling water while doing so. Harris didn't think it likely that whoever it was could see him in the darkness, and he went on to quietly cross the dam without a problem. He later phoned Rhonda to let her know he'd photographed the two men they'd seen in the Buick Lacrosse, mentioning he was going to develop the film in the basement dark room of his home. He would get the photos to Ron Warren first thing in the morning in an attempt to identify who they are.

Harris got up early Friday morning to make a trip to police headquarters and showed the photos to Warren.

"Ron, can you help me with identifying these two men? They are associates of Tokar's and may be somehow involved in the disappearance of Amanda Kramer."

Warren looked at the photos. "You must've taken these with your telephoto lens, they're not bad, and the one with the frosty white hair looks familiar. Yeah, his name is Lou Emanuel Solano, and he's been in organized crime almost from the time he could walk. The name Solano could be of Spanish, Portuguese or Italian descent, but take it from me, in this case, it's Italian. He's a bad one I know all too well, and when I say a bad one, I mean he's a hitman-contract killer from the old days." Warren gently rapped his knuckles against Harris's arm, "Solano could've been *big*, but he committed too many senseless crimes, spending too much time in jail for stupid things. If I bumped into him, you might see he and I talk like we're old buddies, and that's because I arrested him a couple of times for small stuff, but let me think here."

Flipping through the photos, having a look on his face as though amused by the images while he examined them, Warren went on to ask, "Where did you take these?"

"I was doing surveillance at Tokar's weekend home at Lake Laraine…and say, can I still count on some help from the FBI?"

"No, FBI personnel are pulling out of town to track another serial killer running loose somewhere in southern California. Agent Johnson complimented you on your police work, and asked me to tell you he still has agents in the area tracking Garcia and Cordero. He also mentioned they have no evidence to show that Tokar is holding Amanda Kramer, but what you have here may prove helpful in taking the investigation in another direction."

Warren remembered something that made him chuckle. "From what I recall, Solano was released from Missouri state penitentiary in September of last year after serving ten years of a life sentence for murdering a real estate mogul. He was extorting money from the guy, resorting to wasting him after he stopped paying. Convicted of murder only this once, he's suspected in the killings of ten people, which means he's in all probability done even more than that. Detroit syndicate mobsters gave Solano two nicknames for his stentorian, loud voice that demands attention and obedience from his colleagues in crime, and they are 'Louie the Lip', and 'Stormy'. Important advice worthwhile remembering is that if I was confronted by Solano and I saw him reach inside his coat, I'd go for my gun and blow the SOB away, so be careful."

Warren looked at the picture of the other guy with the mole on the side of his face. "Let me ask Bernie Rothman to see if he knows this other guy. He's pretty good at remembering faces and names, sometimes recalling their criminal record as well."

Excusing himself for a couple of minutes to approach Rothman in a nearby cubical, Warren returned, wearing a grin. "Yeah, he knows him, and he remembers Solano too."

Rothman came over to join Warren and Harris, and smirked, "His name is George Sypka, and he's a lot like Solano in that he's a hood who provides muscle for mobsters and racketeers. In underworld circles they commonly know him as Georgie 'the Bull' Sypka. Now Solano hasn't been out of prison all that long and, I think like you said Ron, they let him out after a long stretch because he contracted a cancer. From what I understand, the treatments he'll need are expensive and believing he hasn't much longer to live, they turned him loose."

Knowing Harris is dealing with some bad people, Warren asked, "What can I do to help Len?"

Known for his dry humor, Rothman remarked, "If I may make a suggestion, I think you need to find some new friends, but if you're going to run with that crowd what you need is a bulletproof vest."

Harris knew at this stage he was playing with fire, and he handed to Warren one of the photos of Sypka, "Can you arrange to take this photo of Sypka and make up a lineup selection with others? Then have a uniformed officer pay a visit to Nadia Popovich to see if she can pick out Sypka's photo for identifying him in the assault made against her. And if this proves to be true, place formal charges and get an arrest warrant for Sypka. I understand Nadia is no longer in the hospital, but home now, although it shouldn't be difficult to reach her through her folks. My hope is to at least get one of these two off the street and have him brought in for questioning."

Pulling out a piece of paper that had plate numbers and descriptions for a few cars, Harris handed it over to Warren, "I'd also like to get these plate numbers run. The one I'm most interested in is the one for the late model gray Nissan Altima."

Warren had the license number on the Altima ran in a matter of minutes, "The Nissan Altima is leased under the name of Patricia Wright. I see nothing in her background, she has no criminal record, but it's funny; I remember hearing that name recently, although it may not have been related to police business. Maybe how I've heard the name will come to me later, and if it does, I'll phone you, but all these other cars belong to Tokar, including the burgundy Marquis and the Buick Lacrosse."

"One last thing," began Harris, "if Nadia Popovich makes a positive identification for Sypka, you'll need an address for processing the warrant. I'm certain that both he and Solano are currently residing at Tokar's weekend home at Lake Laraine in Jefferson County, and the lake house address there is 119 North Lake Drive."

From headquarters, Harris went to see Dr. Vincent Dvorak where he had his practice at in a medical office building that was part of the complex for the renowned Barnes Hospital. Dvorak specialized in cosmetic surgery, and judging by the amount of people waiting to see him in the reception room, his services were in high demand, and he waited patiently. When finally getting an opportunity to see Dvorak in person, the distinguished white-haired doctor acted very cordial when they met, and greeted Harris with a smile and a handshake.

Harris caught sight of large photo of Dvorak taking aim with a bow and arrow at an archery range, and commented, "That's a nice photo of you there, Doctor."

Dvorak replied, "Thank you, my hobby is archery and my niece took the cherished photograph. I apologize for the wait, but like I tell everyone else, you should've called first to make an appointment. But enough of my humor, my receptionist told me you're Lieutenant Harris with the police and I wish to know how I can be of service to you."

"I am investigating the disappearance of a young lady named Amanda Kramer. Do you know her or do you ever recall meeting her?"

The doctor put his hand to his chin, "Why yes, Miss Kramer is the private secretary of a neighbor of mine, Anthony Tokar, who owns the casino in St. Charles. I've spoken to her on several occasions, and I'm sorry to hear she's missing."

"You didn't have knowledge that she is missing?"

Dvorak folded his arms and nodded, "Yes, Tokar did mention something about her absence from the casino leaving him in a bit of a pinch, but I naturally assumed she'd returned to work by now. A missing person could turn out to be a mere misunderstanding, whereby the individual who's missing technically is not missing at all, but people are simply not fully aware of what plans they've made. Someone arranging a vacation may make changes in the planning stages of their trip, thinking everyone understands what their upcoming vacation plans are. In this fast paced world, the date suddenly crops up, they leave on their trip, and are soon reported missing. I heard of a similar situation occurring with a nurse employed in this building. I believe that's why the police insist people wait for twenty-four hours before reporting a person as missing."

Harris replied, "That's true. However, Amanda Kramer has been missing for over a week now and her whereabouts are drawing close scrutiny by the authorities."

"You don't think that crazed serial killer D'Angelo did something with her, do you? That's some name for a deranged killer isn't it?"

"We've found no connection between Amanda Kramer and D'Angelo thus far, so that's unlikely, but someone told me that you had words with Miss Kramer while she visited Tokar's weekend home at Lake Laraine."

The doctor's expression turned serious, "No, not at all."

"You are denying that allegation?"

Dvorak remained calm, "I consider Miss Kramer a friendly acquaintance, but I do recall a time when she and I attended a party at Tokar's lake home and she misinterpreted a point I was trying to make. I believe I may have said something that was misconstrued, although I would not say that she and I quarreled or traded words. We were discussing illegal immigrants crossing our border, and while Miss Kramer took a liberal stance, that those people need help, as a physician I'm more concerned about the outbreak of a rare disease. Her concern was mainly with the plight the children are facing, where

I simply pointed out the risk of a new strain of tuberculosis running rampant and overtaking the entire nation.

"I remember Miss Kramer got a bit emotional, and I may have consumed a lot of alcohol without eating something, which may have played into someone thinking there was more to it than that. I'll confess that I'm not the witty conversationalist I once was, especially after having a few drinks, but I never would have said anything directly offensive to the lovely lady. I may have merely made a remark I thought humorous in an attempt to change the topic of conversation and it came out the wrong way, and I might say that this goes both ways. If the person I'm addressing at a cocktail party is feeling their oats, and they aren't doing the best job of holding their liquor, their judgment on what's being conferred may not be clear. People become somewhat incoherent with alcohol and they may come to believe they've heard something said which plain and simply wasn't told to them."

"I catch what you're saying and in one way or another I've had that happen to me, the simple art of communication through the English language doesn't always go smoothly at parties. Anyway, I've taken enough of your time Dr. Dvorak, and I'll leave you to your patients."

The doctor went on to say, "I hope I've explained myself well enough because I certainly would not say or do anything intentionally to make Amanda think I'm an arrogant person. She never gave me the impression that I had actually insulted her, and I have my reputation to consider."

"Well, it may have been as you just said, just a simple misunderstanding, and it wouldn't have required my questioning you about it if it weren't for this girl's disappearance. We're having a difficult time catching a lead on this case, so I'm checking out everyone who had any connection with Amanda Kramer, and your name simply came up. I dated Amanda Kramer years ago, and something that stands out in my mind about her is that she craved Chinese food. It's funny I should recall that particular trait among all others she had, but whenever I took her out for dinner and asked her first where she wanted to go, she'd always insist on Chinese."

Harris looked for Dvorak's response to his comment, and the doctor's reaction was to smile, "There are a good many people who enjoy Chinese food, and I go for it occasionally myself."

"Thank you again, Doctor, and I'm sorry for having bothered you here at your office."

Harris left Dvorak's office scratching his head because to him their meeting was unsatisfactory. After their quirky conversation, he couldn't conclude whether the doctor was a viable lead or not. He wasn't entirely convinced that the doctor's story about a misunderstanding between him and Amanda at the party was true. As far as Harris knew, there weren't any witnesses who could directly corroborate exactly how this conversation went, as he considered it hearsay. Rhonda had more or less given a vague account of Amanda's altercation with Dvorak, but as the doctor had articulately explained, the consumption of alcohol could be the basis for a misunderstanding.

No matter how you look at it, this one disagreement between the doctor and Amanda didn't carry any weight for making out the doctor to be her abductor. What could have made all the difference in the world is if the doctor had flat-out insisted there was no such confrontation between him and Amanda, and at first, Harris thought him to be saying this. However, in the final analysis, this meant that he couldn't cross off the doctor from his suspect checklist for wondering about whether he was truthful with him.

Harris now phoned Rhonda to find out if she could get in touch with Jim Abernathy, the guy Amanda was seeing before she disappeared. He wanted to make arrangements to meet with him. The purpose for wanting to see Abernathy was to show him photos of Sypka and Solano for determining whether they were the ones who roughed him up in the lobby of Amanda's apartment building. Harris had suspicions these two had something to do with Amanda's disappearance, as it appeared on the surface that Tokar had recruited them to pressure Abernathy to stop seeing Amanda.

He told Rhonda an officer is going to see Nadia Popovich to show her a photo lineup selection, and much depended on her identifying Sypka as the individual who beat her up on the shoulder of the highway. If she pointed to Sypka, then the department would issue an arrest warrant, and then the suspect would be taken in for questioning. It wasn't likely he'd give up any worthwhile information, but with his record he'd probably get a long stretch of jail time if convicted for this assault, which may give the prosecutor leverage for making him talk.

When meeting up with Rhonda, Harris showed her two lineup selections of photos he'd put together from his basement photo gallery which he wanted to present to Jim Abernathy. She recognized Sypka and Solano from the time she saw them getting out of the Buick Lacrosse in front of Tokar's lake house. Should Abernathy identify Sypka and Solano as the two men that roughed him up, it would mean considerable progress in the case. If these men were the ones who beat up Abernathy, why did they do it? In light of Amanda's disappearance, they're certain to look suspicious in the eyes of authorities for having been employed by Tokar. They'd seriously injured a man to force him to stop seeing a woman who later vanished and it would be even worse for Sypka with his assault on Nadia Popovich. He'd brutally battered a young girl who closely resembled the sister of Amanda Kramer, and it was no coincidence that all three women worked for Anthony Tokar.

Rhonda still had Abernathy's cell phone number for contacting him, and she called to make arrangements for him to meet with her and Harris on a jobsite where he was working.

Chapter 13
Another Late Night Return to the Lake

Harris and Rhonda saw Jim Abernathy in his work clothes, as he'd just completed putting a finish on a concrete garage floor in a new house. Abernathy, a man of size, washed up at his truck before Rhonda introduced him to Harris, drying off his hands with a paper towel before the two men shook hands.

"Hello, I'm Detective Lt. Harris. I'm here in an official capacity to ask you to look at two lineup selection sheets for the purpose of identifying the men who roughed you up in the lobby of Amanda's apartment building."

Abernathy looked at the first lineup sheet and picked out Sypka from the photo selection, and then he picked out Solano from the second selection of photos.

"There's no doubt in my mind those two are the ones, so what comes next?"

"As long as you're willing to testify in a court of law that they are the two who assaulted you there will be arrest warrants issued and then they'll be taken in for questioning. It doesn't look good for these two because they already have long records and if convicted, they may do hard time. The prosecuting attorney's office is sure to press them to answer why they leaned on you to stop seeing a woman who's recently disappeared. It may not lead anywhere, but there are other factors that should indicate to law enforcement officials that it was Tokar who wanted to breakup your relationship with Amanda."

Abernathy took a moment to comment on the assault. "It was a rainy day when they surprised me in the lobby of Amanda's apartment house. I had just come through the door and didn't think anything of seeing two men wearing trench coats getting ready to exit the building. From out of nowhere I received a crashing blow to the jaw and then took another hard hit from the other fella that left me stunned. The next thing I knew they were both whacking me over the head with blackjacks, hammering me until I was dazed and barely able to stand on my feet. They delivered a few blows to the midsection that took the wind out of me, and I finally fell to the floor, but they still weren't done giving me a beating. They finished knocking the stuffing out of me with a series of solid kicks to my ribs and back—I thought it would never end."

Abernathy looked at Rhonda, "I'd never even seen a blackjack before that day, and then they stood over me holding them in their hands as if ready to give me more of the same medicine."

Harris replied, "Yeah, a bludgeoning by use of those leather beavertail slaps can have a lasting impression. Cops of the gangland era carried them, some military police carry them yet today, and they can resolve a conflict in close combat real quick."

Abernathy's eyes kept going from Rhonda to Harris. "I felt lousy about dropping out of sight at a time when Amanda needed me, but I had serious back trouble for a spell. I couldn't even walk for a few days, but I'm feeling a whole lot better now, and I'd like nothing better than to even the score by catching up to them one at a time."

Harris said, "The big one is named Sypka, the other is Solano, and as you already well know, those two goons play by a different set of rules than the average guy on the street. They showed you they meant business by beating the crap out of you, but their records say they're capable of a lot worse things. A word of warning is that there's a slim chance they may show up again to try to convince you not to testify in court. My advice if you see them is to make every effort to avoid them, for these are criminals who may be packing pistols."

Harris extended his hand to Abernathy, "Let's let the police handle it and give the law a chance to do its job. It's been nice meeting you and Rhonda will keep in touch, reporting any changes in Amanda's situation."

After Harris and Rhonda left Abernathy, Harris phoned Ron Warren, "Ron, I'll be coming by the station to make out a report. Jim Abernathy picked out Sypka and Solano from lineup selection sheets I'd presented to him. You can start arrest warrants on the two of them, and how did it go with the lineup sheet you had an officer show to Nadia Popovich?"

"She confirmed that Sypka was the one who forced her off the highway and assaulted her on the road's shoulder. I have a warrant out for his arrest, but I'm still trying to get a lead on the Chevrolet Suburban he used to nudge her off the highway. The colors dark brown with tan sides hasn't helped because it may be simply listed as dark brown in color, and there are hundreds of brown SUV's on record in the St. Louis area."

Harris then asked, "You didn't happen to recall where you'd heard the name Patricia Wright in connection with those Altima plates, have you?"

"No, I haven't, but it's like something on the tip of my tongue, and I'm sure I'll eventually remember where I've heard the name before."

Harris and Rhonda stopped by the station and it didn't take him long to make out a report related to the lineup selection sheets he used for Abernathy to identify Sypka and Solano. He left the report and lineup sheets with Ron Warren, and then he took Rhonda to dinner at an upscale fast-food diner. While they ate, he told her he was returning to Lake Laraine once more tonight to have another look around. He had hopes some of the same crowd might show up again and his intention was to find out the identity of the individual who had his back turned to him the entire night long. There was also that Nissan Altima he'd seen parked outside Tokar's home with other cars, and he was curious as to who owned it. Thinking that maybe the person he wanted to learn the identity of and the owner of the Altima could be one and the same, he was prepared to spend a few hours out there snooping around.

Harris dropped Rhonda off at her house and then he went home to get some shuteye in preparation for spending long hours at the lake. He had just stretched out on the bed when his cell phone rang and Steve Hastings was on the line.

"Hi Steve, how are you?"

"Just fine and how is the investigation going?"

"Not bad, but progress is slow as usual."

"Look, what I'm calling you about is you stopped by the office of a distinguished surgeon in our community and questioned him when he had a reception room full of patients waiting to see him. You should've called him first before showing up unexpectedly that way."

"Well, I didn't keep him but for a few minutes. What, did he lodge a formal complaint against me for harassment or what?"

"No, nothing like that, but you're talking about a prominent and very resourceful citizen and from what I understand, a personal friend of the mayor's. My advice is that unless you have a strong lead drawing you to this doctor I'd lay off him. Let's try to remember you're on leave for a knee injury and I don't want people upstairs asking questions about why you're conducting an investigation when you're supposed to be out of circulation. Do you get my drift, pal?"

"Yeah, okay Steve, and I haven't any plans to question the doctor again, but if I do see the need to bother him, I'll phone his office to make an appointment."

Then Hastings asked, "So how is the knee nowadays?"

"It's getting better and starting to loosen up."

"Glad to hear it, take care of yourself, and I'll be talking to you soon."

Harris took a one hour nap and then put on a black turtleneck sweater, black pants, and sneakers, but he didn't leave his home to go out to the lake until dusk. He arrived at the lake after nightfall, parking on Dvorak's side of the lake at the same spot he'd taken the night before. Moving along, he peered through his binoculars to view activity at Tokar's house, floodlights were on to show a lot of people cutting loose on a Friday night. He stealthily started across the dam, and stooped to take a cross-legged position near the same bush where he hid the night before, noticing everyone appeared well on their way to getting high on alcohol. Many partygoers gravitated to the decking at the water's edge, and he spotted Tokar in their midst, wearing a brightly colored flowered shirt.

If the individual that had his back to him the night before was in this crowd of partiers, Harris couldn't be sure who he was. As much as he would have liked to examine cars to see if the Nissan Altima was parked nearby, there was too much activity for him to risk venturing any closer.

Watching drunken stragglers wandering about the premises, he caught sight of Sypka, and like the others, the big brute was well on his way to becoming a sloppy drunk. He looked clumsy, falling against a pile of logs stacked neatly beside a retaining wall by the driveway and then limping and staggering around as though he could barely walk. Harris thought Sypka's heavy drinking may not be the only problem this man of size had for affecting his walking, that he may have impairment with his legs, knees, or ankles. He once worked with a fellow police officer who had calcium deposits on his heels which hindered his ability to walk, and Harris was convinced Sypka may have gout or a similar ailment.

Two hours later, the party had run its course and people were beginning to leave for heading home or if they were young and energized, they'd gone on to another party located elsewhere. The party now running on fumes, they'd turned off the floodlights, but there was still one coach light illuminating the land behind Tokar's home. Those few who had hung on were for the most part congregating inside the residence on the upstairs main level, leaving two couples roaming about the yard, but they were soon gone. Harris had begun losing interest in viewing the Tokar home, but he didn't want to leave without accomplishing something for having made a trip out this way.

Sypka had consumed a considerable amount of alcohol and stumbled outside into the backyard with Solano following him, who asked him with a voice that carried well, "Are you gonna be all right, Georgie?"

"I think I'm gonna be sick," Sypka mumbled back, moving to the side of the driveway and crouching low as though getting ready to throw up.

There were no other guests in the yard when Solano replied, "I'll check on you in a couple of minutes, let me know then if there's anything I can get you."

After Solano went back inside the house, Sypka began vomiting, and while heaving up his guts, he heard a man's voice say, "Feeling any better?"

Not recognizing this person's voice, Sypka looked up to see a large object hurled at his head and received a jolting blow that nearly knocked him out. Harris stood over him holding a log from the wood pile, and he clonked him over the head once more to leave Sypka falling forward into the grass where he laid in his own vomit.

Sypka lay unconscious as Harris spoke angrily under his breathe, "You lousy piece-of-shit, I ought to bash your skull in for using that young girl as a punching bag."

The lower level of the house looked deserted as Harris now tossed the log back into the wood pile, and then he gave attention to the automobile parked nearby that was covered with a canvas.

He pulled the canvas back from the vehicle's front passenger side, flipping it over to reveal an older model Chevrolet Suburban, its color was dark brown with tan on the sides. The front passenger side had dents, dings, and scratches from when the Suburban pushed the car Nadia Popovich was driving off the interstate highway.

"Hello," remarked Harris, using his cell phone camera to take several pictures of the vehicle's front end and front passenger side fender where the dents were, making certain he got the license plate number. Draping the canvas back over to leave it how he'd originally found it, he understood how after Sypka had run Nadia off the highway, Tokar simply covered the vehicle as a way to conceal it. Harris thought they would've placed it in storage, but at the same time, it made sense they kept it here, for this is a private, gated lake development not accessible to the public.

Leaving Sypka lying knocked out in the grass, Harris moved from the house to begin crossing over the gravel covered dam, and then he heard someone come out of Tokar's house. Moving along at a fast pace, he heard the outspoken Solano say, "Did you pass out or what?" Thinking Solano was trying to revive Sypka and maybe helping him to his feet, he then barely heard him speak loud enough when remarking, "The side of your head is bloody, are you okay?"

Sypka mumbled, "Somebody blindsided me and hit me over the head with something."

A few seconds later, Harris looked back once more and the floodlights were switched on as occupants of the house were now searching for the culprit who brutalized Sypka.

Harris made it to his car and drove out of the lake community as though nothing happened and without further incident, feeling as though he'd just made a three point shot for the home team. He later phoned Rhonda to tell her he'd located the Chevrolet Suburban used to force her friend Nadia off the road when she was driving Rhonda's automobile. She sounded pleased, expressing optimism that she'd soon hear good news regarding her sister being found safely.

Chapter 14
Rendezvous with a Hitman-Contract Killer

Saturday morning, Harris arrived at police headquarters to catch workaholic Ron Warren at his desk. For a few minutes the two discussed how under questioning D'Angelo had thus far denied knowing Amanda Kramer or Deborah Kutraba or of having anything to do with their disappearances.

Showing Warren photos of the Chevrolet Suburban he'd taken the night before, he pointed out damage to the vehicle's front right fender from the time it was used to force Nadia Popovich off the road.

Harris commented, "I'm eager to find out who the suburban's plates are registered to."

After running the plate number through his desk computer, Warren said, "It's Tokar's Suburban. The plates for that vehicle are long since outdated, and that explains why it didn't show up when I ran a check on Tokar's fleet of vehicles. Good work Len, this is certain to put pressure on Tokar because he's going to have a lot to answer for. First, two goons beat up this Jim Abernathy and afterwards tell him to stop seeing Amanda Kramer who soon disappears, and the suspects are identified as Sypka and Solano. Then there's also the girl Nadia Popovich who was run off the road and brutally assaulted, and the registration for the vehicle that ran her off the road is in Tokar's name. One of the guys involved in both assaults is fingered as Sypka, and you've established a definite link between him and Tokar by locating the suburban, leaving strong evidence mounting against him."

Warren kiddingly continued. "You may be in line for the detective of the year award, and even though we have no such thing, you've certainly accomplished a great deal here. I can't speak for the prosecuting attorney on this, but I'd say Tokar is soon to be targeted for a grand jury hearing, followed by numerous criminal charges."

"Bringing that arrogant bastard down will be a privilege, but I've yet to find Amanda Kramer, and we're still unable to account for the whereabouts of Deborah Kutraba."

Then Warren said, "Len, I just received news that Illinois state police discovered a car in a cornfield outside of East St. Louis, and the deceased person identified in the driver's seat is Deborah Kutraba. She died from a gunshot wound to the head. The car's registration is in her name, and the automobile was found not far from the place where she worked as a nightclub dancer. They first declared it a suicide, but then they notified us of suspicious circumstances and retracted the suicide, claiming it now to be a homicide."

"Did they say what it was that made them change their minds about a suicide?"

"They first found indication the deceased shot herself in the head using her right hand, but she was left-handed, and there may be more they're not yet releasing until they've made a thorough investigation."

Harris remarked, "That was the woman who had the husband and three toddlers."

"Yeah, and her death is certain to devastate that family. I wouldn't want to be the one delivering the news to the husband."

"Ron, I believed from the start that Tokar was behind Amanda's disappearance, abducting her because she knew too much about his affairs. Her knowledge about his illegal business activities worried him for some time and learning she wanted to settle down with Jim Abernathy placed her life in jeopardy. For some time now we've collected evidence leading us to believe that Tokar is at the top of a pyramid structured organization involved in drug smuggling and distribution, and that's why he had Amanda abducted. Just like mobsters from the old days, after you know too much about the organization, there's no way out unless you take a short trip in a coffin.

"Tokar's worries were driving him to desperation, he was in over his head, and he thought one way of reducing his problems was to arrange for her to disappear. He may have been thinking about doing away with her for some time, and when those prostitutes began turning up dead while gaining attention in the news, it sparked an idea. He saw this media spectacle as an ideal opportunity to make her vanish. It took shrewd thinking to use the timing of those killings for abducting Amanda Kramer, and then ordering the Kutraba woman kidnapped to further confound police. These people knew that police would tie the disappearances of those two women in with the others, serving to stifle law enforcement officials.

"They were essentially setting up a serial killer to take the fall for the abduction of Amanda Kramer and Deborah Kutraba. Even after D'Angelo's capture they knew, regardless of the outcome, this deranged killer would remain the chief suspect in their disappearances. Events connected to D'Angelo would serve the purpose of offsetting the investigation, leaving police uncertain about what happened to these two women. It's obvious they'll never find anything connecting D'Angelo to Kutraba and I don't believe they'll ever find evidence linking him to Kramer either. However, the murder of Kutraba and disposing of her body on the Illinois side continues to draw suspicion elsewhere while diverting investigator's attention from the people or person holding Amanda Kramer. Kutraba's lifestyle and social status made her an easy enough candidate to abduct, but killing her for merely this one purpose took cold, cruel, heartless thinking.

"The point I'm trying to make here is that this type of clever criminal planning and manipulation of law enforcement is outside of Tokar's realm of thinking. I'm not saying Tokar wasn't the one who concocted Amanda Kramer's disappearance. On the contrary, I think she vanished because of Tokar's worrisome ways—he had far too much at risk to let her walk away, although I'm not yet convinced she's dead. Tokar may have convinced himself he's evaded an FBI investigation that should've exposed his connection with the drug trade, but I don't see him calculating murder into the scheme of things. He hasn't the diabolical mind or the stomach it takes to abduct people and then, seeing them as expendable, arrange to have them murdered in cold blood as was done with the Kutraba girl."

Warren said, "As detectives, we've all had those kinds of hunches, but even if you are right about everything, where does that leave seasoned investigators on this case? Do you think Tokar's drug people abducted Amanda Kramer and did away with the Kutraba girl to take heat off their organization?"

"That's certainly a possibility, but my guess is Tokar in all probability has done something with Amanda Kramer by putting her away someplace. The timing for her disappearance coincided with the investigation of those prostitutes, as though using their murders to convince people she's dead. Should the police accept the idea that she's dead, they're not going to use as many resources searching for her. I have no problem giving Tokar credit for thinking up that angle, but murdering Deborah Kutraba to throw off law enforcement is something far different. I don't think he did the thinking or planning here, Tokar's mind isn't devious enough for murdering this girl and attempting to make it look as though she'd committed suicide for baffling investigators.

"It took deviant planning and pure evil cunning to murder this girl for practically no reason whatsoever—in my opinion, it's beyond Tokar's logic. This business with Kutraba is something players like Sypka and Solano might have involvement in, but it's not their ordinary line of work and it's not likely they hatched the idea. Those goons aren't the type for thinking up those sorts of things—they are simple soldiers, muscle, and guns-for-hire that do as they're told for financial gain. However, I strongly suspect them of having a role in it because it must've taken two to arrange Kutraba's death, as a second person drove her killer back from the cornfield where she was discovered."

Harris went on to add, "I'm telling you Tokar is getting outside help, and whoever this person is, he's not likely one who delves in the business side of running Tokar's casino. Although you may be right in thinking it could've been his drug distribution racket, those people are capable of almost anything and usually pander to the dirtiest forms of crime. Murder and making people vanish are their signature crimes, and if they believe a woman who knows too much is a threat to their drug business, she's likely to disappear in an instant. On the other hand, if I were Tokar I wouldn't let those people handle it. I wouldn't even want them to know Amanda has knowledge that could bring down their cartel because if they think my managing of things placed the organization at risk they might kill me too."

"Len, you're obviously wrapped up in this case, and you're up against insurmountable odds for learning what's become of Amanda Kramer. If this individual is a drug lord, it could perhaps be someone living outside this country, and it may take nothing less than a miracle to find out what happened to her. I've seen detectives caught up so deeply in a case that it consumed them for the rest of their days, and you may be a candidate for this one doing the same to you. If this Kramer woman's whereabouts goes unfound, it'll eat you from the inside out—I've watched it happen to guys."

Harris was set to leave police headquarters, but before walking away, he asked, "How are those arrest warrants coming along?"

"The county courthouse Lake Laraine is in has a reputation for dragging their feet on such matters as issuing warrants. However, I expect we'll have Sypka and Solano in for questioning within forty-eight hours. I'm also making arrangements to have that Suburban towed within the next couple of hours for providing evidence to that assault. Damage it has to the front right fender from the time the Popovich girl was run off the road makes that vehicle important in obtaining a hit-and-run felony conviction against Sypka."

Harris left the station thinking Warren saw this investigation getting the best of him, and he did feel it important to find closure to this case in order to get on with his life. His wife's death sent him to the borderline of becoming a full-fledged alcoholic, and he knew failing to locate Amanda Kramer would make him a difficult person to live with. If he was to find any kind of happiness with Rhonda, who'd given him one of the bright spots in his life, he knew he must find Amanda soon and find her alive. As much as he'd have preferred to leave Mark Kramer's life in the past, the event was never forgotten, and Amanda's disappearance did much to awaken memories of a tragedy that befell that family. Helpless to do anything to save that young man's life, he'd carried the image of him dying in that alleyway for years, and the memory of his death had made it doubly hard to curb his drinking.

Mark's death haunted Rhonda as well, he knew she was counting on him, and it was of the utmost importance to accomplish something with this case so not to disappoint these people again. To a certain extent, he had a score to settle from his past, feeling as though he owed it to the Kramer family to find out what happened to Amanda. However, taking up looking for Amanda had also helped him to find the stamina to overcome his desire for alcohol, as he'd avoided the urge to drink to see this through for discovering her whereabouts.

Harris had no plans for Saturday, so he again drove out to Lake Laraine to scout around, using his binoculars to survey Tokar's home from across the lake. He saw no activity until he caught sight of Solano, viewing him between Tokar's house and the house next door as he got in his Buick Lacrosse to leave the lake development. Hoping he'd lead him to the place where Tokar was keeping Amanda Kramer, he quickly returned to his car and drove fast through the lake development to reach the entrance, and pulled over to wait for Solano.

Ducking to avoid being seen, he at last spotted the black Lacrosse turning onto the avenue leading to the lake's gated entrance and exit. He went on to tail Solano at a safe distance, lagging behind so he wouldn't be noticed, and followed the Lacrosse as it got on the interstate highway. He had to speed up to keep pace with Solano because he had a lead foot, as though in a hurry to reach his destination. The Buick quickly took to the passing lane on the far left, but Harris stayed in the middle lane cruising at nearly seventy miles an hour.

There came a time later when he was falling too far behind and he had to accelerate, taking to the passing lane so he wouldn't lose Solano. That's when a full-size van traveling much slower cut into the passing lane in front of the Lacrosse to get around a car moving at an even slower speed. Solano had to brake hard, and Harris did the same to keep a safe distance between him and the Buick, but now wondered if he'd made a serious mistake taking to the far left lane. Although he'd begun to drift back, he saw Solano take a long look in his rearview mirror, as though taking notice of the car behind him.

Solano was a professional surely looking out for law enforcement, and having caught sight of the driver following him, Harris thought he may know by sight most of the investigators involved in Amanda's disappearance. It grew worrisome that this hitman-contract killer may have caught sight of him and he dropped back for returning to the middle lane. Harris felt uncomfortable for thinking the man he was trailing had unquestionably given attention to the car behind him after braking a few minutes before. He thought Solano should be alert for that same car and driver he'd seen behind him from now on.

Twenty minutes later, he observed Solano speeding up and he took pursuit of him while keeping his distance. The Buick signaled before cutting across lanes to get off at Hall Street, an exit leading to an industrialized-commercial thoroughfare running north and southbound, where there are many vacant buildings near railroad tracks. Recognized as an economically depressed area, Harris thought this may be where Tokar was acquiring property for planning on building his horserace track. When taking to the exit ramp to get off the interstate Harris fell in line behind a few other cars stopped behind Solano to wait for the light signal to change. With a few cars separating him from Solano, he put on his sunglasses and watched as the old mobster adjusted his rearview mirror to scan cars stopped behind him.

Beginning to get bad vibes about tailing what he regarded as a dangerous man, Harris understood Solano to be an individual that had ways of dealing with people who dared to follow him. However, he had no choice, for he still thought Solano may lead him to where Tokar was keeping Amanda, and his hopes were outweighing the risks, leaving him to carry on.

When the light changed, he went on following the Buick, although hanging back to avoid exposure, and still hoping Solano hadn't seen him when last checking his mirror. Finding himself in a deserted industrial area trying to keep out of view, Harris pulled over to where he was close to the corner of an old brick building and waited there. He hadn't lost sight of Solano, and believed the jutting corner of a nearby building gave him some degree of concealment from the contract killer's view.

He watched as Solano parked in front of an abandoned office building that vandals had broken out sizeable windows in front. Seeing no other cars or a soul in sight in this isolated area, he viewed him entering the office building and from there he fell out of sight.

After giving Solano a few minutes to move into the depths of the office building, Harris drove on to pass by the same office building. Uncomfortable with the Buick Lacrosse being the only automobile in sight, he drove on to turn at the next corner which took him to a sprawling parking lot where he saw an abandoned warehouse and loading docks. Thinking he'd distanced himself enough from the building's entrance so that if Solano exited from the same door he may not see his car, he parked near a side entrance where there was an open door.

Locking up his automobile and starting off on foot, Harris fully understood that following someone you knew made his living killing people is not only foolish, but an ideal way to end your life. Drawing his pistol when entering through the same front entrance as Solano had taken minutes before, he suspected all the while that he was walking straight into a trap. He knew damn good and well that he was stupid for trailing a man with such a deadly reputation, but felt determined to follow through with what he'd started for the sake of the Kramer family.

Upon entering the lobby, he saw how the business life of this office building died out years ago, leaving this vacant shell ready for demolition. The main corridor gave him a choice for turning left or right and he thought he heard something that drew him to the left to meander through broken glass and scattered debris. Feeling nervous and edgy, he still hoped Solano would lead him to Amanda, and if this was true, then whatever was waiting ahead of him was worth facing. Hearing what sounded like metal striking concrete, he thought this sound a sure technique for drawing him deeper into the building. Guided by his instincts, he came to where the main corridor made a right turn to see a long stretch of hallway, but sunlight was not penetrating far enough to see what awaited him.

Not liking this one bit, he paused while trying to give his eyes time to adjust for piercing the darkness, as the length of this corridor appeared infinite. Suddenly hearing a disturbance at the corridor's far end and unable to tell what he was looking at, he froze.

He next saw a shadowy figure, at the same time catching the muzzle flash of a gun firing, and the gunshot ringing out at the same instant a bullet went zinging by his right ear!

Stooping to let one knee hit the floor, Harris knew it was Solano shooting at him and he let go with four shots directed at where he'd seen the flash. Standing alone in the confines of this huge building, he felt stifled and uncertain about his location within the layout of this structure, but he refused to go back the way he'd come. Cautiously giving pursuit, he moved forward slowly to slither along the corridor's wall, and moving deeper into the hallway, he was ready to fire at a moment's notice.

He heard another gunshot that sounded more distant, as if it may have come from outside the building to make him worry about his vehicle. He hurried to find his way out of this dark maze until finally seeing daylight coming through an open exterior door and guardedly stepped outside. He'd exited the building from a side entrance near to where he'd parked his car, and hearing the acceleration of a car's engine and squealing tires, he knew Solano had fled the scene.

Having survived this encounter with a known killer, Harris thought that if Solano didn't know who he was before, by now he must have gotten a good look at him. Returning to his car, Harris learned that last gunshot he'd heard had flattened his front driver's side tire, but even at that, he felt lucky for having eluded this slick attempt on his life. Feeling fortunate Solano didn't fire into his car's engine compartment and hit the engine block, as this could've done serious damage in any number of different ways, he now had a tire to change.

Standing in the sunlight feeling a light breeze, he recalled the sound of that bullet whizzing by his ear and thought how good it felt to still be alive. Had Solano hit his intended target, he'd be lying dead inside that deserted building, and who knows how long it would be before his body was discovered. Removing his sport jacket, he went on to change the flat for putting on the doughnut, and in no time at all was back on the road again. He drove to an automotive repair shop that sold tires, and seeing how the other front tire had wear on the outside, he went ahead with purchasing a new set of tires on the front.

Harris was glad that this episode occurred when he didn't have any pressing engagements, and yet was slightly pissed off about the results of crossing paths with Solano. Not liking the idea of people shooting at him, he was decidedly bent on going out to the casino to try and shake some information out of Tokar. He was dead set on letting Tokar know that he was going to hold him responsible for the next time such an incident occurred.

Arriving at the casino sometime later, he made a couple passes around the parking lot while searching for an open space close to the building in order to avoid a long walk to the entrance. Leaving the house that morning without grabbing his container of pain pills, his knee had begun to bother him after stooping to change out that front flat tire. Seeing backup lights on a car as the driver of the vehicle began to back out of a parking space, he turned on his blinker and waited for the opportunity to take this vacated space. Turning the steering wheel for making adjustments to evenly align his car with the lines, he didn't think he had too far to walk to reach the building's entrance around front.

Harris had just gotten out of the car when he saw a burgundy Mercury Marquis turning into one of the reserved spaces situated on the side of the building. The vehicle looked like one of the cars he'd taken down the license plate number from at Tokar's lake house, and he watched the driver parking a few spaces away from the one he'd taken. He immediately recognized Sypka behind the wheel, but Sypka hadn't noticed him, and knowing officers delivering his arrest warrant obviously hadn't caught up to him as yet, he looked forward to confronting the thug. The big slob stepped out of the vehicle, and Harris thought he'd done well by coming to the casino, feeling the urge to do what he could to antagonize this lowlife jerk.

Chapter 15
Butting Heads with Georgie 'The Bull' Sypka

Sypka didn't see Harris approaching as he went for a door on the side of the casino marked *Private*, which Harris took to be an entrance for prominent customers and selected employees of the gentleman's club. He saw bruising and abrasions on the left side of Sypka's face from last night when he struck him twice with the log, an indication he'd caught him solidly with both blows.

He watched Sypka press a button to have security release the door lock, but before the buzzer rang on the outside to give him access for opening the door, he spotted Harris coming.

Harris called out, "George...George Sypka, I am Detective Lieutenant Leonard Harris and I have a few questions I need to ask you."

Wanting to avoid talking to Harris, he gave up on waiting for the buzzer and started walking parallel with the casino's exterior wall for going to the main entrance at the front of the building.

Harris followed, needling him by saying, "George, sooner or later you're going to have to talk to me, but the fact that you're running off to avoid answering questions makes for suspicious behavior. I'm well aware you have a record, but if you're on parole or probation, you'd do well to stop to answer a few simple questions."

Harris paced Sypka so as not to crowd him. "I saw some bruising and redness on the side of your face, and if you've been getting into fights you need to report that to your probation officer."

Sypka seemed irritable, turning his head to give Harris an angry stare as he approached the corner of the building, turning left to go to the building's entrance. He soon entered the structure with Harris closing in, and they passed shops along the corridor leading to the casino.

Technically out of his jurisdiction, Harris considered that if this confrontation ended in a big ruckus with someone getting seriously injured his superiors would ask him why he didn't wait for the arrest warrant to take effect. However, he knew it may take days for officers to present arrest warrants for apprehending Sypka and Solano, and maybe even far longer than that should those two skip town. This was a definite possibility since this investigation had connections to the murder of Deborah Kutraba, and they may even leave the country to avoid prosecution and prison time. On top of all of this, the fate of Amanda Kramer hung in the balance, and his blood was up as he felt pressed to get answers.

Harris thought it best not to pressure Sypka for stopping until they entered the casino, for he wanted what transpired to be recorded by surveillance cameras. Believing this to his advantage, he raised his voice, "Hey, Georgie—the Bull—Sypka. You must be involved in something pretty serious to want to avoid talking to me, and you're going to talk to me, whether you like it or not. I'm going wherever you go, even if it's straight into Tokar's office."

When coming to the casino entrance, a security guard recognizing Sypka gave him a wave of passage to enter, and Harris followed, presenting his casino card to the guard as he continued his pursuit.

Moving across the casino's main floor, Sypka had a long walk to the gentlemen's club, and he figured that without a membership card to get in the club, security would surely stop Harris. The main aisle they'd taken passed by slot machines on the left and the tables on the right, leaving a far more open viewing space on the right, the entrance to the gentlemen's club in plain sight.

Harris spoke loud enough for Sypka to hear him over the sound of slot machines, "If you think they're going to stop me at the club's door, you're mistaken. When I show my badge, they'll have to let me in, and if security uses force to stop me, I'll have the entire casino shut down. I'd be willing to bet your boss wouldn't want the closure of his casino aired on the news—that wouldn't exactly be what I'd call good publicity."

Sypka suddenly turned around to square off with Harris, angrily clenching his fists and heaving his chest as he moved in a bobbing, short stepping dance.

"Okay, Harris, you've got me, and now I'm gonna tear your head off!"

Having heard Sypka openly make a threat against him, Harris wasn't about to back down and put up his fists in taking a defensive stance. Squaring off with his opponent, they moved about while eyeing each other up, and Harris leaned from his right to his left while holding his left arm up as his guard.

Two security guards arrived to defuse the situation, and Sypka shouted, "Stay back, I'll have him laid out in no time." And not wanting to tangle with the big bruiser, they stepped away.

Sypka took a swing at Harris using a right cross, missing him when he dodged and ducked the punch thrown at him. He was then quick to catch Harris with a left uppercut, clipping his jaw and knocking him back a few steps.

Harris now saw Rhonda standing alone in her uniform, watching with her mouth open, and she wanted to stop the fight, but couldn't. Spectators kept gathering while keeping their distance and all the people gambling at nearby tables cleared away to give space for the two to carry on their fight, and everyone's eyes were on them.

Sypka leaned forward to cut loose with another hard right, but Harris blocked it with his left forearm, and they remained close for Harris to deliver a few quick jabs to Sypka's midsection. He then delivered a hard right to strike Sypka solidly in the jaw, driving him back and leaving him temporarily stunned.

Seeing rage in the face of Georgie 'the Bull', Harris anticipated Sypka to charge him, and when he did, Harris dodged the brawny brute, avoiding his outreached hands while landing a punch to Sypka's ribs. The last thing he wanted to do was end up in Sypka's clutches or on the floor because he knew he'd then take a merciless pounding.

Squaring off again and facing each other to trade more punches, but Sypka's moves had become slow and awkward, while Harris was fast on his feet and showed little signs of tiring. Holding his own to keep Sypka at bay, Harris released a few quick jabs and another hard punch to Sypka's face for giving him a nosebleed, and people watching heaved a collective gasp.

Harris landed a solid right hook against Sypka's jaw, and the jolt jarred him enough to make him think he had to take a different approach to get at his opponent. He knew Harris was working the case to find Amanda Kramer, and he also heard talk that he'd recently taken shotgun pellets to his left knee.

When he got the chance, Sypka kicked Harris in his injured knee and slugged him, leaving Harris backing off, hobbling around as he grimaced in pain, but managing to avoid Sypka. He knew that if Sypka forced him into a corner it would be a one way ticket to palooka city and the big oaf would surely smash his face in.

Sypka, seeing how he'd found Harris's soft spot, chuckled with a sneering expression, "Yeah, I'm gonna fix that knee for you."

Facing off for carrying on this hotly contested fistfight, Harris understood Sypka knew of his injury and had intentionally kicked him in the left knee. Now limping, he wanted to end the fight before his aching knee took more punishment. When anticipating Sypka was going to deliver a kick, Harris lifted his leg in a defensive move, and instead of kicking Harris, Sypka's ankle slammed into the bottom of his shoe. This left the big man reeling in pain, and having grown weak in the ankles, this was Sypka's Achilles' heel. When Harris took the measure of lifting his leg for guarding his knee it resulted in Sypka acquiring a serious injury, leaving him barely able to walk.

Harris took notice of the short distance between Sypka and the blackjack table behind him, and he took three quick steps and dove to plant his foot into Sypka's midsection. The driving momentum and spring in his kick knocked Sypka backwards to send him flying across the blackjack table to crash to the floor.

People were in awe watching how Sypka landed stunned on the floor on the other side of the card table, and Harris came around it, tossing a chair out of his way.

Sypka's dazed state left him vulnerable in how he was slow to recover, and the weakened ankle made it difficult for him to rise to his feet.

Harris gave him a swift kick in his ribs. "Come-on twinkle toes—move that tub of lard and get up or I'm going to kick your guts out. Using a defenseless girl as a punching bag isn't hard for a guy of your size, but it's not so easy when you're up against a man."

Crawling away, Sypka began coming to his feet when Harris grabbed him by the arm, yanking hard for pulling him and ramming his head into the side of a slot machine, denting it.

They scuffled again until Harris cracked him in the jaw, driving him against the front of the same slot machine, and delivering a series of hard blows before Sypka hit the floor.

The crowd had moved far back to get out of the way of their fighting, giving out a loud gasp when Sypka drew a pistol from a holster inside his coat. He fired from his position on the floor, missing Harris and several women screamed as everyone fled the casino in a wild panic.

Harris had ducked to move into the next lane of slot machines, a wall of slot machines paired up in how they were backed up to each other were all that separated the two. Drawing his weapon, he ran hard in this maze of machines for reaching the far end of the aisle to come to the next crisscrossing-intersecting aisle. Closing in on Sypka, while approaching him from the far end of the aisle, the gunman had his back turned to him, peering about as he took to a kneeling position.

He took aim at Sypka, shouting, "Drop it Sypka!"

Sypka leaned back while turning to shoot, but Harris fired twice to hit him in the shoulder and stomach, leaving Sypka to drop his weapon and fall back on his side.

Harris moved forward to kick the pistol out of reach, and holstered his weapon while standing over his adversary. Security began peeking around corners to see if it was safe to come out and Rhonda came running over to see Sypka lying on the floor.

Tokar came out of nowhere with a squad of security, "Are you crazy Harris? Coming in here brawling, tearing the place up, and then having a shootout like this is the OK Corral? You must be out of your mind!"

Harris, still steaming from the fight, directed a question at Tokar in a loud voice, "Do you know this man?"

"Yes, he's in my employment, and this is going to cost you your badge!"

"I thought he was in your employment, your security people gave him a nod for entering the casino when I followed him in to ask him a few questions. Now get this Tokar, your security and surveillance cameras will testify to the fact that this goon threw the first punch, he was also first to pull his weapon, and first to discharge a firearm. Should something happen to those recordings, there are witnesses who can testify to leave me covered, but your man here is going to have to answer for his conduct."

One of Tokar's security people came over to view Sypka's condition to see about giving him aid, and Harris stepped forward. "Leave him alone. He got exactly what he was asking for."

Seeing a big patch of blood on Sypka's clothing and a few droplets collecting on the carpet, Tokar said, "You're not going to allow us to give this man medical attention?"

Knowing or at least expecting an ambulance had to be on its way, Harris replied, "Only if you're a licensed practitioner. Otherwise, he's my prisoner and if you so much as touch him I'll place you under arrest for interfering with a policeman doing his duty."

A squad of policemen stormed the casino and Harris showed them his badge. "This is George Sypka, he has a long criminal record, and why somebody with a record is carrying a pistol is something I'd like to know. You'd be wise to check his pockets to see what else he's carrying, and it wouldn't surprise me a bit to learn he has a blackjack or brass knuckles in his possession."

A police sergeant took Harris's advice and removed a coin roll package of nickels from the pocket on the left side of his sport jacket, and it also held a wad of cash. He then found a leather beavertail blackjack in the right pocket of his sport coat.

Harris looked at the police sergeant, "See what I mean, and I also suggest you confiscate what the surveillance cameras have recorded as soon as possible." Harris turned to look at Tokar, adding, "We wouldn't want evidence disappearing."

At the time an ambulance crew arrived to examine Sypka, Tokar looked at Harris. "Look here, Harris, I hired this man as a security guard, and that's why he was carrying a pistol."

"Don't you usually screen your people, and if you had you would've known he has a record a mile long."

"I hired him through an associate who highly recommended him, and he was given a position to provide me personal protection and not hired on as an employee of the casino."

"I wanted to question Sypka because a man fitting his description reportedly brutalized a young girl on a nearby interstate highway, and it just so happens that this particular female was also in your employment. That's a strange coincidence, isn't it?"

"Do you have any proof this was the man who assaulted that woman?"

"My main objective in life is to provide convincing evidence he did it because I know he did it. And since you made the bold claim you'd hired him for personal protection, I'm hoping this investigation turns up evidence that you paid him to do it."

"People don't usually talk to me that way Harris."

All pumped up from the fight, Harris couldn't stop himself from unloading on Tokar. "If you don't like the way I'm talking to you then you're most certainly not going to like it when the D.A. starts pitching questions at you. The woman who Sypka beat up on the side of the highway has already fingered him as her assailant through a photo lineup. You're soon to learn the authorities know that the vehicle he was driving at the time of the assault has lapsed license plates registered under your name. It's right now parked at your lake house, and I expect they'll be coming with a warrant to tow it away shortly, if they haven't already done so."

Harris got in Tokar's face to intimidate him. "You've got something to think about Tokar—law enforcement officials are sure to want to know why you're hiring blackjack-pistol carrying criminals like him. If this incident today doesn't set Sypka up for a long prison stretch I'll be surprised because with his record there's a good chance that it will. Should the courts lower the boom on old Georgie here, his defense attorney will urge him to make a deal. That means he's going to start looking in his old war chest to see what he can throw on the negotiating table. That thought could give some people sleepless nights, but not you Tokar—you're clean. Sypka is an old buddy of yours who doesn't have anything he can use against you, so you've got nothing to worry about. But if he should know something that worries you, I'd consult with my attorney."

Tokar looked flushed as he turned and walked back to his office, the police sergeant following him to acquire the surveillance recordings. Crime scene detectives arrived to question Harris, and one wearing plastic gloves picked up Sypka's pistol, placing it inside a plastic bag.

The casino was still in disarray from the calamity the fight caused, and when Harris finished answering questions he considered exiting the premises, but saw Rhonda was nowhere in sight.

Chapter 16
A Flirtatious Night at the Races

Looking to leave the casino, Harris didn't want to leave without having a word with Rhonda, but she was nowhere in sight, prompting him to begin strolling down the corridor of shops. Thinking he'd accomplished something by getting George Sypka placed behind bars, he knew with his record old Georgie was over his head in hot water. Assaulting a law officer and discharging a firearm inside a crowded casino, there was little chance for him arranging bail, as Sypka was definitely a flight risk. Harris expected additional arrest warrants should come through for keeping him interred behind bars indefinitely.

He was halfway down the corridor when he heard a woman calling, "Harris, wait up."

Turning around to see Rhonda chasing after him, she came to stand beside him. "I spoke to the casino's manager about getting off early and he said okay, but I'll have to come in a few hours tomorrow."

She straightened his tie and pulled the knot snug to improve his appearance, while Harris gazed at her admiringly.

"I don't know whether I've mentioned it or not, but I'm one of those old-fashioned guys who refuses to date women who work at casinos or nightclubs."

"I figured as much, and I intend quitting the very minute my sister is located."

Thinking he needed a drink badly, he looked in the direction of *the Kentucky Derby Lounge* and saw it to be the closest drinking establishment. "I could use a drink, how about you?"

"I don't think that's a bad idea, especially after what you've just been through, trading punches with Sypka. I recall you mentioning his name the time Jim Abernathy picked him out of a lineup you provided . . . I couldn't believe it when I saw you and him squaring off in the casino."

Walking into *the Kentucky Derby* with Rhonda on his arm, a horserace was just finishing up on the big screen, as a chestnut colored horse beat out a black horse by a nose.

Rhonda asked him, "Is your jaw sore?"

Harris worked his jaw from side to side, "A little, but it's the left knee that's killing me, and I left my pain pills at the house this morning."

Taking chairs at a table, Rhonda removed a medicine bottle from her purse and gave two pills to Harris, "Here, take these."

"What are they?"

"Ibuprofen and they'll make you feel better."

Harris palmed the pills, waiting to get his hands on a drink to wash them down with.

A young male waiter came over to address the couple, "You two didn't by chance just come from the casino did you? I heard somebody got shot in there a few minutes ago. I saw cops coming down the corridor in droves with their weapons drawn, and I thought they were going to insist on evacuating the entire complex."

Harris commented, "We heard there was trouble so we got outta there."

The waiter then noticed that Rhonda was wearing the black top and slacks most of the female employees at the casino wore, "You work at the casino, don't you?"

Rhonda replied, "After the police arrested a man who was said to be the shooter, the casino gave some of the employees the evening off, and I was one of the lucky ones."

Harris rapped the knuckles of his right hand against the tabletop to get the waiter's attention. "Look, if it's not too much trouble, we'd like to order a couple of drinks. Make mine double bourbon on the rocks, preferably *Wild Turkey*, and whatever the lady wants."

Rhonda added, "I'll have a highball."

She nodded in the direction of the big screen as horses were coming to the gate, "You can bet on computer ran horse races here for amusement, if you have a mind to."

Harris glimpsed horses lining up at the gate as the announcer gave their names in preparation for the upcoming race, "I don't play the horses much. As a matter of fact, I don't gamble at all, because as you just saw, money's too hard to come by in my trade, but horses are magnificent animals to watch."

The waiter returned, Harris popped the pills before taking a long drink to wash them down with, and he paid the bill. He last said to the waiter, "Bring us two more."

"Wait Harris, are you sure about that?"

"You want to see my license? I'm over twenty-one."

Rhonda reluctantly nodded, "Bring us two more."

"You looked pretty good in the casino tonight, and I was in your corner rooting for you all the way."

"I thought I did okay, but it wasn't a whole lot of fun getting my teeth rattled. It's been awhile since I've faced off with another guy trading punches in a knock-down, drag-out fight. It must be three or four years since I was in a match with a burly firefighter for a charity event raising money for the Children's Hospital. I thought it was for a good cause and we only went four rounds, but it seemed like ten. I was outta shape then and I suppose still out of shape now, but we weren't out to cream each other that time in the ring, and judges called it a draw."

Rhonda commented, "You held your own against somebody who had at least thirty pounds on you. The fight had drawn quite a crowd until they heard a gunshot, and then everybody scattered, including me."

After taking another drink, Harris asked, "Was there a time when you were uncertain about the outcome of the fight?"

"I was worried the very second I saw who you were up against—that guy was like the Incredible Hulk, but I'm not one to give commentary on a fistfight."

"Why not, give it a try. I mean, you're doing alright, but give it to me straight."

"I've already said you looked pretty good out there, but it obviously was no slam-dunk."

Harris finished his drink at nearly the exact moment the waiter delivered fresh ones and he pointed to his first empty glass as though telling him he wanted another round.

The waiter acknowledged the order, "I'll begin a tab."

Harris started on his second glass, "Go ahead, run with it and tell me how it was out there."

"You're obviously worked up from getting knocked around Harris, and I hope you're not going to get smashed."

Harris looked at Rhonda as though waiting to hear more.

"Okay," she said, looking at the horserace starting on the big screen as horses bolted out of the gate, and the race gave her inspiration to compare the fight to this ongoing contest. "You were slow and a little sloppy moving out of the gate and that had me worried. You were lagging behind in that first lap, and my first impression was that you weren't going to last the race. But then you caught onto the game, kicking up dust as you picked up steam on the straightaways. From then on you made strides, gaining ground on the competition, taking on a strong lead in the last lap to cross the line a winner."

Harris witnessed part of the race, catching on to how she'd injected her words describing the fight to go with the horserace. "Say, you're pretty good. You ever thought about becoming a sports announcer?"

Rhonda watched the waiter deliver the next set of drinks, and looked up at him, "No more for me." She gave Harris a look, "All right, now it's your turn Harris."

Harris put the tip of his index finger to his lips, and then pointed at her, "You want me to read your track score?"

Rhonda smiled, "Well, I did you, and I called it the way I saw it."

Taking a long gulp from his drink, he then gazed at Rhonda. "You've got big brown eyes, but I wouldn't say they're the eyes of a horse, more so like that of an attentive doe."

Rhonda gave him a stare, "I hope you can do better than that."

Harris sat up to take on a serious expression, "Trainers say you can tell a lot about a horse by looking in their eyes, and when I look in yours I see something promising. From what I know of your background you come from good breeding and I'd say you have a reliable track record that's worthwhile betting on." Harris looked at the slacks she wore, one leg crossed over the other. "You've got the kind of sound, shapely legs that are needed for maneuvering in a tight turn or for making long strides on the open track. I don't have any expert knowledge about horseflesh, but if I saw you prancing around before a race I'd be tempted to put money down on you. One thing for sure, I think being in the saddle with you would be a ton of fun."

Rhonda gave him a look, "You're getting real close to crossing the line here Harris."

Harris cocked his head to one side, "I'm just giving it to you straight. That's what you wanted, wasn't it?"

Not altogether displeased with Harris's assessment, Rhonda thought it best to change the subject. "Before you finish that third double, how about telling me what it was that inspired you to become a cop."

"I was playing college football when I injured my knee and finding out I was going to lose my athletic scholarship, I lost interest in getting an education."

"Okay, but was the knee injury the main influencing factor behind you pursuing a law enforcement career?"

"No, something that happened years earlier planted the idea in my head. My parents had divorced, and raising me became a difficult chore for my mother. She'd lean on a neighbor of ours named Arthur Langeneckert to give me guidance, and he'd often sit down and try to reason with me. I wouldn't say he was a father figure to me, but I looked up to him and admired him just the same. He'd often talk to me as an equal, and I remember him best for that. Arthur was a policeman who all the neighbors knew as *Red* because of the red hair he had, but by the time I knew him he didn't have a whole lot of it on top.

"I'd become rebellious, thinking I was hot stuff. I was eight-years-old when I'd begun hanging around with an older crowd, which resulted in my arrest for shoplifting. I wasn't the one who snatched whatever it was we were in trouble for, but since I was in that person's company at the time of the theft, I was still in hot water. The arresting officer kept me in a room at the police station and after my mother arrived, she asked to see *Red*. Upon learning I was in trouble, he became very angry. I'd never seen him so upset, making me ashamed for him to see me in that situation, and after telling my mother there was nothing he could do, she cried.

"Red later came through, doing what he could to get me out of trouble, but he was still angry at me, and I finally got the nerve one day to pay him a visit to thank him. He said, 'Lenny,' that's what he used to call me, 'Someday you're gonna be the smart, responsible individual I know you'll grow up to be. Until that time comes, I want you to remember one thing, there's only one person who's at fault for someone getting into trouble and it's you. You hang with the people you do out of choice, but if you can't see through them to see them for what they are, I can't help you anymore. You can't pick the people you're related to, and you can't pick your classmates or the people who live in your neighborhood, but you can pick who your friends are.'

"This is where the story changes gears because it wasn't too long afterwards that Red was shot and killed in a wild shootout when making a narcotics arrest. My mother and I went to the funeral to pay our last respects, and I was amazed at how many people attended the service. Old Red was a man well thought of by many, and I learned not too long after he was gone that he'd been dealing with a lot of problems.

"You know, St. Louis isn't a city thought of by most to have links with organized crime. The mainline cities with mob connections are Chicago, New York, and Kansas City, but a legendary mob war flared up here in the 1980's. During that time, notorious crime families were in a power grab to take over a Syrian faction of the crime trade and gaining control of the labor unions. Arthur Langeneckert wasn't a Syrian, but he grew up knowing some of the figures involved in this mob war and had gone to school with some of them. From what I understand, the authorities pressured him to socialize with these people for infiltrating their organization to acquire information. They all knew Red was a police officer, but they also regarded him as their trusted friend and occasionally he'd spend time goofing off with them.

"As young as I was at the time, I didn't know a whole lot about the gangland violence rocking the city, but as the violence intensified it gained nationwide attention. A series of car bombings going on around town had drawn attention from the FBI. It was at the height of this turmoil that I'd last gotten into trouble, and little did I know that these mob figures had a growing suspicion that Red was talking to law enforcement. They'd begun harassing him as a way to shut him up.

He'd found a dead chicken hanging from his front door, placed there to put a scare in him. Rumors later circulated that it was a fellow officer who hung the chicken on his door as a prank—some gag, huh.

"In 1979, the Globe Democrat Newspaper ran a story that supervising the unions in St. Louis were bosses in the criminal world that had ties with the Detroit Syndicate directing organized crime activity for the mob. Few had knowledge of it, but St. Louis underworld interests controlled the *Dunes* and *Aladdin* casinos back then, and they were attempting to gain hidden ownership in the *Frontier* casino in Las Vegas.

Harris took a drink, and continued. "As it was, unlike so many others in the crime business, the then big crime boss was dying of natural causes. Shortly before his death, mob forces sought a peaceful transition for long-standing allies to carry on. However, reputed mob enforcers rising through organized-crime ranks coveted control of the St. Louis underworld. They had their own ideas about becoming overlord authority, and violence soon erupted.

"The first in line to take control had just had lunch downtown at St. Raymond's Church, and his black Chrysler Cordoba was blown up on Interstate 55 near the Reavis Barracks exit. Hoping to inherit considerable influence and power, his killers had set up the bomb and detonated it by remote control when following him on the highway.

"Others then conspired to avenge the death of the figurehead who died in that first fatal car-bombing. In 1981, a bomb was planted underneath the car of the big wig that struck the first blow in this war. He lived at his mother's home on Nottingham Avenue, not far from where I live now. Rigging it with a chemical substance made by the DuPont Company called Tovex—a high explosive, they used a remote-control model airplane guidance system to detonate the bomb. The car was blown to hell, resulting in him losing parts of both his legs, and his face was also severely disfigured, but he survived the attempt on his life. Retaliations erupted as each family kept striking back, leading to gunplay on the streets. There was another fatal car bombing involving a Volkswagen Beatle parked in the downtown Mansion House garage. For a time it seemed that there'd be no end to the power struggle.

"In the spring of 1982, authorities began charging principle figures leading the fight to gain control over organized crime. Unnerved by the murders, family members on each side had begun talking and providing the FBI with crucial information. One family murdered one of their own to keep him from striking a deal with the FBI over his involvement in the bloodshed. This became that factions undoing, as within about a year the courts indicted scores of people on state capital murder charges and federal racketeering charges, thus ending an uproariously bloody period in St. Louis' history."

Harris then added, "I didn't mean to carry on, but thinking about Arthur brought back a lot of memories, and that's a true story, all that craziness and killing, and for what. You're younger than me, so you probably have no knowledge of those hair-raising days, and as for that matter, I really didn't either, but it was old Arthur who inspired me to join the force. I primarily took up studying that mob war to learn of Arthur's involvement with the Leisure family for finding how deep he was into that mess."

Harris signaled to the waiter to bring them another round, but his wave went unseen.

Rhonda said, "Don't order another for me. I'm nursing this drink and it'll be my last."

He raised his glass, "Although Al Capone and his Chicago mob still stand above all the rest, organized crime here in St. Louis did their fair share of muscle flexing and saber rattling. It's kind of funny how I haven't thought about Arthur Langeneckert for a long time, and I wonder what he'd say if he'd have known I became a policeman. For a fella who had a lot of weight on his shoulders it was nice of him to take the time to try and talk some sense into me when I was a young kid."

Rhonda commented, "I think he saw potential in you for making something of yourself or he wouldn't have bothered to give you guidance."

The waiter came over, "Nobody's playing the horses, and the manager says he's going to play music. He asked if there's something you'd like to hear."

Rhonda looked up at him and then at Harris, "I feel like dancing to something slow and easy."

The waiter walked away, and Harris said, "I was thinking about having one more drink, what do you say?"

"Uh, I don't think so," and the rich sound of piano playing came through the sound system to travel throughout the lounge, and the song they heard was 'Break It to Me Gently.' She then stood and reached out her hand to him to take for leading her out on the dance floor, and looking into those imploring eyes, he couldn't say no.

Swinging gently in each other's arms to the lazy beat of the song, Rhonda blinked a couple of times from the alcohol fumes.

"Bourbon breath, you're in no condition to drive home, so I'm taking you home with me."

The bartender dimmed the lights, and a crystal ball hanging from the ceiling emitted dreamy light reflections about the place as they made eye contact while drifting with the song's melody.

Harris's eyes slowly swept over her face again and again, periodically looking deep in her eyes. "I wasn't kidding when I said you have the look of promise in your eyes."

For the remainder of the song they gazed into each other's eyes, and when the song ended, Harris continued carrying the tempo while moving as though it hadn't stopped.

Rhonda's brows rose, "The music stopped playing."

Harris kept on looking into her eyes. "What music," and then the next song began, as they carried on with 'Hold Me, Thrill Me, Kiss Me.'

He kissed her gently on the lips and she put her head on his shoulder, her eyelids falling shut as she listened to the song while swaying in his arms.

When the song finished playing, Rhonda said, "I think we ought to head home now."

"The night's young yet, and I've only had a couple of drinks."

"I'd say you've had about six, and they were doubles Mr. Harris."

"Who's counting?"

"I think it would be a good idea if one of us kept track of the alcohol consumption, so I guess I'm the one who's counting—I don't want a crocked cop on my hands."

They went arm-and-arm out to her car, and Rhonda drove off the casino's lot.

"I'll drive you back tomorrow when I go to work and you can pick up your car then." She turned left to take the main road a few miles before turning onto the interstate's entrance ramp with Harris sitting relaxed in the passenger seat.

Chapter 17
An Unexpected Interruption at Dinner

Cruising along the interstate, Harris was feeling the effects of the alcohol. "I enjoyed dancing with you, and I can still hear Brenda Lee singing the lyrics to that *'Break It to Me Gently'* song. How about if I call you *Friday*, my devoted secretary-sidekick, what do you think of that idea?"

Rhonda glimpsed her rearview mirror, "I don't think so Harris. I'm a big fan of film noir, and having watched many of them, the detective's secretary rarely gets him in the end. I remember viewing only one movie titled *The Dark Corner* that has an admirable secretary named Kathleen, who I believe ends up with the private eye. It's not a top-rated detective film by comparison to some of the great ones of the time, and Lucille Ball gets top billing in the credits playing the spunky secretary. Her role helps carry the plot, holding the audience's attention."

Rhonda looked in her mirrors again, checking her blind spot before changing lanes, and hearing Harris beginning to snore, she dug her fingernails into his leg. "You're not falling asleep on me while I'm talking to you, are you?"

Harris perked up, "No, not at all, film noir, the silver screen, I know what you're talking about, but one of my favorite detective films is *The Maltese Falcon*. I seem to remember Bogart shooting a line to his faithful secretary, saying, 'You're a good man, sister.'"

With that, Rhonda squeezed his leg again, digging her nails in deeper than before, a trace of contempt in her voice, "You ever say that to me and I'll kick you in the nuts."

Harris tensed up, "Ouch, when you're hurtful and mean that way to a police detective it's called police brutality."

Rhonda let out a short giggle, "That's not the definition of police brutality."

Harris then leaned over and began kissing her on the neck, while reaching to put his right arm around her waist from the front.

"You're going to have to stop pawing me while I'm driving."

Now sitting straight and acting as though he was pouting, Harris mumbled, "No cooperation."

"What did you say?"

"I didn't say anything."

Her hand then caressed the inside of his left thigh, "I didn't say I don't want to play, but we can't get carried away fondling while I'm driving the car."

"I thought you were one of those multitalented girls."

"I am, but a girl shouldn't have too many distractions when driving."

"Oh, so you're not as multitalented as you may think."

Rhonda's voice changed to a more serious tone, "Luckily, my father hasn't as yet come to my house to stay with me, or I'd have to deal with explaining why I'm bringing you home." She then added, "Harris, way back when you dated my sister, I'd get tingly sensations whenever you'd show up at our house. Since beginning to see you again, I've begun feeling that same way and I think it's because I'm mad for you," and she looked to see his response to what she'd said.

"Are you sure you want to get involved with such an old horse as I am."

Rhonda replied, "You're not all that much older than me, and I'll sock you in the jaw if you dare joke about the feelings I've expressed for you."

"Well, tomorrow morning, when the booze and the pain pills have worn off, I'm going to feel about a hundred-years-old."

When arriving at Rhonda's house, she helped Harris to the entrance and he stumbled through the doorway. She got him to her guest bedroom, and after she took off his sport coat and shoulder holster, he sat on the bed, maintaining a straight sitting position.

At one point he gave her a confused look. "All the time I was married, not once did my wife ever take my clothes off."

Rhonda held a straight face. "Gee, just think of all the fun she missed out on."

Harris shook his head no, "I'm not saying there weren't times she wanted to get me unclothed, but I was cooperative enough that she didn't have to bother."

"Is that so," and after pushing him back on the bed and undoing his belt to pull his pants off, Rhonda presented him with two more Ibuprofen pills and a glass of water.

"What's this, more pills?"

"I'm afraid if you don't take these you won't be able to walk tomorrow when you wake up."

He looked down at the pills she held in her hand. "You may be right," and he took them.

Rhonda went into her bedroom and after showering and putting on a night gown she returned to lie down beside Harris, snuggling up close to him for resting her head against his chest.

Waking Sunday morning, unsure about where he was, but then it came to him, and after getting dressed, he found Rhonda making him breakfast.

He gave her a peck on the neck, "Good Morning. Whatever you're cooking there smells awfully good, and what are we going to do with our day?"

"I don't know what your plans are, but I've got to go to work. I'm ordinarily off on Sundays, but taking off early yesterday meant I had to come in for a few hours today. I have no regrets except that we had another round that ended in a draw."

Harris drew a deep breathe, "I'm sorry about that, but eventually things are going to settle down and we'll have time for ourselves. There was a moment last night when I thought you were going to take advantage of me."

"I don't molest drunken detectives."

She didn't seem to have the spark she usually had, and Harris made mention of it. "You seem placid this morning. I thought you'd be happy—Sypka is in jail and Tokar's little empire is beginning to show cracks in its foundation."

"I am glad you got through that fistfight without any harm coming to you, but I guess I'm beginning to accept the fact that I may never see Amanda alive again."

"Don't say that, and don't even think it, not until they place her bleached bones before you."

Rhonda was on the verge of tears. "You said yourself that time is running against her and I can't go on much longer without knowing what's become of her."

She slapped an omelet with melted cheese, onions, green peppers, and minced ham on a plate to hand to him, pointing to a nicely made table where a tall glass of orange juice awaited him. After he sat down, she joined him at the table.

"I'm picking up Dad today and bringing him out here to stay with me for a spell. I've gone by his house to tidy the place up a bit, but I'd prefer looking after him while he regains his strength and recovers, so he'll be using the guest bedroom."

They were almost finished eating breakfast when Harris heard his cell phone ringing from inside the breast pocket of his sport jacket. The phone identified the caller as Ron Warren, and he'd never before received a phone call from Ron's own personal phone.

"Hello Ron, it seems strange getting a call and seeing your name come up on the ID plate when it's almost always 'Police Headquarters' that shows up when you're calling."

"I'm off duty and I'd prefer not to bother you on a Sunday, but I've got some information that might interest you. Let me first congratulate you on landing Sypka in jail and the D.A.'s office is moving to do everything possible to keep him there. The main reason for this call is to let you know that I remembered where I heard the name Patricia Wright in connection with that Nissan Altima plate number you'd given me. Patricia Wright is Jack Gallagher's fiancée and it came to me last night when my wife and I bumped into the couple when going out to catch a movie show. He must've put the plates in her name to confuse anyone checking the registration number on that car, but it seems obvious somebody paid him to keep track of your movements for a time."

Harris stood and went into the next room to respond to what Ron was telling him without Rhonda listening in. "Yeah, and that somebody's named Tokar. I haven't mentioned it to anybody, but I was shadowing Solano yesterday and he lured me to an abandoned office building where he took a shot at me."

"I warned you about that guy, he plays for keeps and he doesn't have anything to lose now that they've diagnosed him with cancer. My guess is he's picking up easy money working for Tokar to last out the time he has left on this earth, so keep your guard up and don't forget what he's capable of."

Warren added, "You know, I used to think Gallagher was an okay guy, but not if he's running around with the likes of Tokar and the company he keeps. I also thought you'd like to know that Gallagher told me he'd be stopping by the station Monday morning at ten."

"I appreciate that Ron, and I'll try to be there then to have a word with him."

Harris now realized the individual he'd seen with dark hair who'd had his back to him all evening long at Tokar's lake house was Gallagher. It didn't sit well with him that a detective he thought he knew was the person following him in the Altima, but he wasn't certain what he was going to do about it.

When Rhonda drove to the casino for putting in time at work, Harris rode with her to pick up his car. When dropping him off, she said, "I was going to move my father out to my house today, but I don't see how I'll have time. I don't have any plans for the evening, so if you want to meet me at my house after six we'll go out and have dinner together."

Harris responded to Rhonda's invitation. "If nothing unexpected crops up I'll be there."

Harris picked up Rhonda later at the agreed time and she had trouble choosing where she wanted to dine, so he recommended an established Italian restaurant called Alessandro Gianni's on *The Hill* in St. Louis. Located in a traditional Italian-American neighborhood where there are dozens of Italian restaurants, all having an outstanding reputation for good cuisine, he and his wife had occasionally patronized Gianni's.

Gianni's was part of a V-shaped shopping center that had four or five stores, including a variety store and a florist shop with the restaurant situated in the middle. It had been some time since Harris had come here, but remembering how the parking lot out front was usually full with people doing shopping, he drove around back. Going to the rear parking lot was something that had come automatically to him, and it more often than not saved time and the aggravation of finding a vacant parking space.

A misty rain had begun to fall, and after parking the car, he and Rhonda took a central breezeway running alongside the restaurant that gave access from the rear parking lot to the shopping center. There was a rear entrance for the restaurant, although by going this way a person had to go through the kitchen to gain access to the restaurant's dining area, and Harris had never used it. Walking through the open breezeway separating the restaurant from the florist shop to arrive at the restaurant's main front entrance, elevated lights on each side of this corridor provided adequate lighting. They passed a tobacco shop on their right, which was in a nook on the same side as the restaurant, but independent from it and on their left was the florist shop.

Judging by the forecast, Rhonda wore a lightweight windbreaker for expecting it to be a damp evening, and when entering the restaurant, the host helped remove her coat. It looked as though Sunday wasn't one of Gianni's busiest nights, as Harris saw only three other couples dining and another couple sat at the bar having after dinner cocktails. It may have been the threat of showers that kept people from going out to dine.

Harris took a chair that enabled him to view the restaurant's entrance and they ordered two glasses of Cabernet-Merlot wine with their dishes. Sipping on wine and nibbling on bread until their pasta meals came, Rhonda was quiet through dinner.

There was one moment that the expression on her face changed as her eyes looked away, and seeing this, he asked, "What is it? Are you feeling okay?"

Rhonda took a drink from her water glass before saying, "I just noticed a man who looks familiar to me. He's sitting at the bar watching us with cold, piercing eyes."

A wave of concern came over Harris for both Rhonda and himself, "Without looking at him, describe him to me."

"I remember now. He's the guy we saw in Sypka's company when we drove by Tokar's home at the lake. He was the driver of the black car that pulled up in front, the stone-faced one with frosty white hair and black eyebrows, and he's now wearing a trench coat. I remember Jim Abernathy pointing to his photograph in that lineup sheet you presented to him, saying he and Sypka beat him up, and I think you said his name is Solano."

Harris nonchalantly nodded, as if to give the impression they were making small talk while having their dinner. "He probably followed us here. I trailed Solano yesterday afternoon to a deserted building thinking he could lead me to Amanda, and he instead set me up and took a shot at me, barely missing me. Without letting him know you've recognized him, keep an eye on him and let me know if he starts coming this way."

Worried about how this man presented a threat to them, she said, "Judging by the look on his face, I expect he might at any moment pull out a gun and open fire on us."

Harris replied, "He's got that kind of reputation, and that's why it's important for you to tell me if he stands up for any reason."

Rhonda's eyes enlarged. "Before trouble starts, why don't you contact police headquarters and ask that they send a car here to find out if he's carrying a gun. If he is and has a criminal record, isn't that illegal? Can't they put him away?"

"I wish it was that simple, but Solano is a proficient hitman-contract killer, and if they arrest him it will only be a matter of time before he's let out to begin shadowing me again. The authorities released him from the state penitentiary a year ago after doing a ten-year stretch on a murder rap. It's very likely he'll make an attempt on my life before the night is over and you're in danger for being in my company."

Rhonda spoke anxiously. "Harris, I'm scared. Are we supposed to just sit here and finish our dinner, waiting for him to gun us down?"

Harris tried calming her, "Shhh. I can't stress enough the need to know if he stands up from his barstool for any reason whatsoever. I'll have to shoot him before he draws his weapon. I imagine after following us here he parked on the back lot, entering through the rear of the restaurant. While I doubt he'll make a play right here in the restaurant, it's something that could happen. He gets to choose the time and place, and wanting to avoid witnesses to a cold-blooded murder, I'd say he'll wait until after we leave here to catch us alone on the parking lot."

Feeling squeamish, Rhonda leaned forward. "So what are we going to do?"

Trying to put together a plan in his mind, Harris said, "From what little I know about him, he'll shoot it out gangland style and one of us will end up lying in a pool of blood. When trouble erupts, I don't want you caught in the crossfire, so when I stand up to pay the waiter, I want you to go to the variety store and wait for me there. He may think you went to do some shopping at one of the stores out front, and at least I won't have to be concerned about something happening to you."

Getting teary-eyed, she put her hand on his. "Your best chances lie with him believing you have no idea he's here, so I'm staying with you. If I leave here before you do, he's going to know you're on to him, and he might surprise you by firing to kill you the second your back's turned."

Harris finished the rest of his wine while thinking the situation over, assuming it may be to his benefit for Solano to snort a few drinks at the bar for affecting his firing accuracy.

"All right then, but if you're staying with me it's of the utmost importance that you do exactly what I tell you. When we leave to go to the car, he's either going to follow us out the front entrance or he'll go out the backway and be waiting for us on the parking lot. You and I have to exit the restaurant the same way as we came in, doing anything else is sure to make him suspicious. If he follows us out the main entrance, we're going to pass though the breezeway as though going straight to the car like we have no idea he's behind us. It's after we've cleared the breezeway and reached those first few cars in the parking lot that I'm counting on him to lose sight of us for a couple of seconds. At the precise moment we've reached the open parking lot I'm going to make an attempt to take him by surprise, but you keep walking and don't stop."

Rhonda then asked, "We have to be ready for every possibility, and what if we leave and then he heads out the rear exit to catch us unexpectedly in the parking lot?"

"When you and I are going out the door, he'll be watching every move I make, so I'll be relying on you to let me know what you think he's aiming to do. If he's seen moving toward the back exit, after telling me this, I want you to go to the variety store and wait there for me. If that's the case, I'm going to turn around to reenter the restaurant, pursuing him out the back door, and with a bit of luck I may be able to ambush him."

Feeling queasy, Rhonda couldn't sit still. "I'm a nervous wreck Harris. What if he remains seated until we've gone outside before making his move?"

"If he hasn't come out by the time we've reached the breezeway, he won't be exiting the building by the front, and I may have to immediately double back to look inside the restaurant. Here's the thing, if he doesn't come out the front, and we're split up for any reason, you go to the variety store and wait for me there."

Rhonda said, "Should he come out behind us, you're counting on him not to shoot until we've reached the parking lot, but he could start firing before then, leaving us both dead in that open walkway."

"He's a professional and not one to handle this in a sloppy manner. He knows firing a pistol in that breezeway enclosure will amplify the sound to draw people's attention, and he doesn't want that. Another reason for him to wait is because if he shoots and merely wounds me, he'll still have to get by me to get to the parking lot where his car is. He wants to avoid losing time getting pinned down by gunfire in that confined breezeway. The smart move is for him to have clear view of the parking lot, not to come barnstorming out from that breezeway to draw attention and then learn a patrol car is passing through the lot."

Harris saw a worried look on Rhonda's face. "Look, this can play out a hundred different ways, and no matter how many times we go over it, you can bet it won't go as planned. If you don't think you can do this, then simply leave without me and go to that variety store, and that may be the best thing yet for the both of us. Otherwise, if you decide to leave with me, and he's behind us when we walk out the door, you'll walk with me to the end of the breezeway. When we reach the parking lot, we'll separate, but you'll keep on walking. Should you lose sight of me because I doubled back to reenter the restaurant, or for any reason whatsoever, you'll then go to the variety store and wait for me there. It's that simple, and I promise to do all I can to keep you from getting caught in the gunfire. But you still have the choice of walking out and going to the variety store when I stand to pay the waiter."

Dabbing his mouth with his napkin, Harris wondered if Solano is wearing a bulletproof vest, and he thought he probably is, but they'd settled on a plan and he intended sticking to it.

Chapter 18
Facing a Hired Gunman and Shooting it out

Rhonda had last insisted on leaving the restaurant with Harris, and after he paid the waiter, the restaurant's host cloaked her with the windbreaker she wore. Harris looked down while holding the door open for her, and she gave a wave to the host before they walked out of the restaurant together.

Once outside, Rhonda spoke in a low voice, "He was out of his barstool and it looked like he was coming this way."

They hadn't yet made their turn to enter the breezeway when they sensed the restaurant door opening again behind them, and Rhonda's voice sounded squeaky as she said, "Len, I think he's coming."

Harris thought Solano would choose to follow them, and he said nothing as they started down the lengthy corridor walkway on their way to the parking lot. Lighting in the corridor was spaced far apart but adequate in showing the way, and he put his hand out to catch rain droplets as if to show they didn't have a care. The tobacco and florist shops had closed, and distant lights awaiting them at the end of the building where the parking lot was located were bright. They could barely hear the sound of footsteps behind them as they walked, and even though it took them only about a minute to reach the parking area, it seemed like an eternity.

Upon reaching the spacious parking lot, Harris gently steered Rhonda to his left, "Keep walking." He then veered for taking a defensive position between two cars to wait for Solano, and engaged his .45 while squatting. He used his left hand to grip his right wrist for giving added support to steady his aim.

The hitman came out of the breezeway holding his hand inside the lapel of his trench coat and Harris shouted, "Freeze!"

Solano's arm shifted to reach further inside his coat, and Harris fired four times in rapid succession, hitting him in the chest area, and his enemy fell to the ground.

Harris rushed over with his pistol pointed on a downward angle at Solano, ready to fill him full of holes, but he'd critically wounded the old mobster, and his weapon had fallen out of reach. Kicking it further away, Harris saw a series of holes in the man's trench coat and opened it to find he wore a bulletproof vest that had stopped two bullets aimed for his chest cavity. Seeing blood, he then noticed that one bullet had clipped his collar bone and maybe shattered it, and another hit him in his upper right arm near the shoulder.

The rain was now falling steadily and Rhonda came up with her cell phone in her hand. "I phoned the police and an ambulance is on the way."

Beads of raindrops collecting on Solano's face, his cold eyes now had a sad expression, looking back at them for no more than a second before turning away.

Harris stood over him, holstering his weapon. "Those aren't fatal wounds Solano, but they're going to take a long time to heal. Your contract killing days are over and you're sure to spend the rest of your life in prison, which is where people like you belong."

Hearing sirens closing in on the scene, soon police and an ambulance crew showed up to give attention to the situation, and Harris gave information to an officer making out the report. As a crowd gathered, Solano was placed on a gurney and an ambulance transported him to a trauma center where they would treat his wounds before placing him in incarceration.

Harris took Rhonda home and after their arrival there, he sat down in a chair, staring into space while thinking about how the confrontation at the restaurant played out, nearly leaving a man dead. Replaying the incident in his mind, it wasn't easy to shrug off how it could've just as easily gone the other way with him lying dead on the concrete pavement. Shooting purposely to kill a man isn't an easy thing to deal with, no matter what the circumstances are, even when you're firing in self-defense.

Rhonda fixed him a short drink of bourbon on the rocks and when handing it to him, he said, "No thanks, I don't feel like having a drink."

Little was said the rest of the evening until he said goodbye before driving home, and his thoughts kept drifting to the time he saw Solano appear at the end of the breezeway. He spent much of the night replaying in his mind the moment he took aim and fired, the event giving him a restless night.

Harris arrived at police headquarters shortly before 10 a.m. on Monday morning, and seeing Gallagher leaving the station as he walked to his car, he started toward him. Gallagher didn't notice his approach for seeing him maneuvering through parked cars until they met, and he saw anger in Harris's eyes as he slugged him in the chin. He landed two more punches and drove Gallagher back until he fell to the asphalt pavement, lying there stunned by how Harris had attacked him.

"That's only a taste of what you're going to get if I catch you following me again."

A tall uniformed officer, Sergeant Harold Kerns, saw the assault on Gallagher, and knowing both detectives, he came over to intervene. He approached Harris. "I saw everything from over there." He then looked down at Gallagher. "Do you want to register a complaint against Lieutenant Harris with me standing in as a witness?"

Gallagher rose from the pavement, brushing himself off, but didn't say anything.

Then Harris remarked, "I have no problem with that, but you'll have to explain why you've been tailing me at night."

Kerns looked at Gallagher, "You were following Harris?"

Gallagher still gave no reply, and Harris looked to the sergeant. "I had a hitman-contract killer shadowing me for a time, only to soon learn that Gallagher here is keeping tabs on my movements as well."

Seeing things in a different light, the sergeant asked Harris, "Was that you who shot it out with Solano at Alessandro Gianni's restaurant last night? You're also the one who had the gunfight at Tokar's casino, capturing Georgie 'the Bull' Sypka."

Harris replied, "I'm still a little shook up about that ordeal at Gianni's."

Now using a different tone of voice with Gallagher, he reiterated, "I'm going to ask you once more, do you want to make a complaint against Lieutenant Harris with me bearing witness to the incident?"

"No," Gallagher replied.

After that, the sergeant walked away, and Harris got in Gallagher's face. "Tokar paid you to follow me, didn't he?"

Gallagher wouldn't confirm or deny Tokar hired him, but merely stood there.

Harris then said, "You don't have to say it was him. I know he was the one who paid you to follow me." He pointed at Gallagher with his index finger, jabbing it in his chest, "I'll tell you this much, if it happens again I'm beating the crap out of you."

Walking away, Harris entered police headquarters to talk to Ron Warren about the night before when he came up against Solano.

He approached Warren's desk. "Ron, I don't know if you heard about last night."

Warren said excitedly, "Heard about it, the whole station is buzzing about it—you did good, buddy."

"Well, I just wanted to thank you for advising me that you wouldn't cut Solano any slack if you had to go up against him, cautioning me to get the upper hand if I had the opportunity."

"From what I've heard, you played it wisely, and as far as I'm concerned the only way it could've worked out better is if you'd taken him out permanently, but I think he's finished anyway."

"I saw Gallagher outside and smacked him around a little. I don't think he'll be following me around anymore. Do you have anything new to report on the disappearance of Amanda Kramer?"

"No, but I'm sure her family is terribly worried, and I wish I had something."

Harris commented, "I'm running out of leads, and I think she may be running out of time for someone to find her still alive." Then he had another thought. "Do you know if Steve Hastings is in?"

"He wasn't in ten minutes ago when I went to his office to ask him a few questions regarding different cases."

Harris asked, "Can you give me Tokar's home address?"

Warren jotted down the address on a note pad and handed the piece of paper over to Harris. "He resides out in Wildwood on a three acre estate. Even though I've never seen it, that Special Agent Johnson had the place under surveillance when tracking Tokar's movements for learning his business connections. At the time, he couldn't dig up any dirt on Tokar, but he mentioned the guy lived in a nice home. Are you thinking of paying him a visit?"

Harris explained, "I'm considering it, but I'm not quite certain just yet."

After leaving police headquarters, Harris ran a few simple errands before going out to pay a visit to Rhonda for saying hello to her father, who was now staying with her. When arriving at her house, Rhonda answered the door, and they kissed before she said, "Dad still isn't quite his old self—I think the medication he's taking may be making him jittery. He doesn't know about what happened last night at the restaurant, or what went on at the casino. All he wants to talk about is Amanda, but it may be best to avoid that subject to keep him from getting himself worked up."

Rhonda escorted Harris into the family room where her father sat in a comfortable chair, and as Harris stood before him, she said, "Dad, look who's come by to see you, it's Leonard Harris."

Her father looked pale, and his hand shook as he reached to shake hands.

"Hello Harris, are you making any progress toward finding Amanda?"

Rhonda's eyes looked skyward as she understood there was no getting around discussing Amanda, and she went to the refrigerator to bring Harris a cold beverage.

Trying not to get into any details, Harris simply said, "Mr. Kramer, I've been keeping myself busy working your daughter's case, but unfortunately, I have little to report about her whereabouts."

Kramer replied, "I thought you would have learned something by now."

"I understand how you feel, but Amanda's disappearance is complicated in that there's little evidence telling us what became of her. There are video surveillance recordings showing Amanda leaving the casino garage that last night in her car, but no indication of what happened to her from then on. I'm pursuing what leads I have, but they keep taking me back to the casino, leaving me tangled up with Tokar and his people. I've donated time to this case because I'm a friend of the family and I intend to keep on investigating it until she's found. In the meanwhile, if I turn up anything I'll report it either to you or Rhonda, and you never know, a break may come when you least expect it, so don't give up hope."

The elderly gentleman said, "I thought the FBI was investigating her disappearance."

"They were, sir, but they didn't uncover anything with regards to Amanda's whereabouts, and now they're off the case."

Kramer responded with, "I wonder if it would do any good to phone Steve Hastings. He may know if there's anything new regarding the case."

"I went by police headquarters this morning, and people at the station had nothing new to report. Steve Hastings is head of the detective's bureau, overseeing most every investigation, and he rarely has more insight on the progress of an investigative probe than those individuals directly involved in working a case. I was curious about what it was that made you think to phone Hastings when first learning of Amanda's disappearance."

Kramer sat thinking, and finally replied, "I remembered Steve Hastings from the time you dated Amanda. He was a close friend to you and she both, and Amanda had mentioned bumping into him on a few occasions at the casino."

Harris nodded, "I wish I had some words of encouragement for you, but you'll just have to be patient, Mr. Kramer. However, Hastings and I are still close friends and if it will make you feel better to phone him, I don't think he'd object to you giving him a call."

Later that same afternoon, Harris stopped by his house to make preparations to drive out to Wildwood, Missouri to scout out Tokar's residence. Wearing a T-shirt under a black pullover shirt in case temperatures cooled down, blue jeans and comfortable shoes, he saw no need to bring any camera equipment on this trip, but took the binoculars. After driving for almost thirty-five minutes to arrive at an isolated area off a winding two-lane blacktop road, he caught sight of the address for Tokar's residence. He was unable to see much of the house as it sat back a couple hundred feet from the road with an asphalt driveway running back to it, but it appeared large with mature trees surrounding it. The newer two-story structure had a brick constructed front with a tall, arched entrance, but the rest was frame with white siding, and the driveway completed a circle around a cement fountain. Two tall blue spruce trees well-spaced in the yard were aligned on each side of the driveway.

Looking to survey Tokar's home with the intention of spying on him, Harris knew he'd accomplished much by eliminating Sypka and Solano from the equation, but there was no question Tokar had other henchmen. He reasoned someone in Tokar's employment was in charge of holding Amanda in captivity, keeping her fed and looking after her, but eventually they would have to consider a more permanent solution. This went back to the idea that time was running against her and against Harris for finding her, and that was why he decided to come out this way. He thought taking the initiative by coming here to study those in Tokar's circle of loyalists he may learn who Amanda's keeper was. If nothing else, he hoped he may see something for opening up another lead to pursue.

Driving almost another half mile past Tokar's house, Harris soon saw an unmanned, fenced in electrical power station, and he pulled onto a narrow gravel drive used by servicemen. Expecting to leave his vehicle here while he took a brief look around Tokar's residence, he wanted to have the ability to pull straight out onto the road when he was ready to leave. Seeing the lot was L-shaped, he barely had sufficient space to maneuver when backing up alongside the fencing, where dense foliage from low hanging tree limbs would help hide the car.

There was a long time to go before darkness set in, but the winding road on which Tokar lived ran through a valley where surrounding hills helped block the sun, and shadows were closing in fast. Harris stepped out of the car, tucked his .45 semi-automatic inside his belt buckle, and after grabbing binoculars he locked up the car and made tracks for Tokar's house.

The sun barely above the treetops and quickly sinking out of sight, he started cutting through a track of forestry where the canopy of leaves blocked out most of the sun's light. Spying around people's homes wasn't Harris's specialty, and placing the leather strap connected to the binoculars around his neck, he followed a dry creek bed snaking through the woods. He soon saw through the trees a clearing where he recognized the house and the blue spruce trees on each side of the driveway.

Harris carefully made his way through the woods following the dry creek bed that changed course to run around what he saw as well maintained grounds. Skirting the yard while staying in the trees to give him cover, he gained a clear view of how the ground graded to the back of the house where he saw a basement level and garage entrance. The gradually tapering backyard nearly leveled off as it extended for a long way, and he saw no basement lights on where blinds hung at the patio door and windows.

Keeping out of sight while seeing no one as yet, at the back of the house he viewed lights from a broad arched window on the main level. Thinking the home currently occupied, to accomplish anything he needed to find a way to elevate himself to see into the home's main living quarters. Undeterred, surveying the yard left few choices on how to gain a vantage point for viewing the interior of the house, and he spotted two mature magnolia trees spaced a good distance from the house. Believing his days of climbing trees were long since over, he now realized they weren't, but either one of these trees looked easily climbable for giving him the lift he needed.

Seeing how making a climb was the only way to obtain the height he needed, he spoke to himself in a soft murmur, "Harris, your tree climbing days aren't as yet over."

Going to the nearest magnolia tree to begin ascending it, like he thought, the spread in the limbs of the tree were passable for making an easy climb. When he reached a high enough place to where he could see into the house, he clung to the trunk of the tree while taking to a sitting position and then raised his binoculars to his eyes. Not having much difficulty holding his balance, he observed what appeared to be a great room. Tokar sat in a comfortable chair talking on the phone in the company of a somewhat attractive woman. The female looked amused watching the television from a chair where there was a tall floor lamp with a broad decorative shade that had skirting in the form of tassels dangling from its bottom.

Drooping tree leaves made it difficult to see, so to expand his vision Harris reached out and caught hold of a branch, and bent it over until it snapped, which broadened his visual angle. Now having no obstruction, he caught sight of something moving inside the house that he couldn't identify, and taking another look enabled him to see a Great Dane excitedly prancing about the room. Soon noticing Tokar and the dog had disappeared from view, minutes later the Great Dane he'd seen inside the house was now roaming about the grounds sniffing out a strange scent it had picked up. The scent was that of an unknown intruder, and naturally, the animal was drawn to the tree Harris was in.

The dog began barking wildly as it stood on its hind legs with its front paws scratching at the tree bark, and there was little Harris could do but sit tight. He saw flood lights attached to the house come on to illuminate much of the landscape, and spotted the silhouette figure of a male standing while looking back in his direction. Expecting Tokar had a poor chance of viewing him sitting in this tree from such a distance, unless he was to walk into the backyard to find out what was attracting the dog. Hoping not to be discovered, Harris sat still as the dog continued barking excitedly, thinking it made sense that out here it was common for the dog to chase after critters. Surely a squirrel, possum, a raccoon, or maybe even a skunk might venture into the yard to set the dog off this way.

Tokar began clapping his hands to draw the dog back to the house, yelling, "Apollo!"

The animal didn't come the first time its master called, but was quick to go to him on the second call. Not seeing anything worth viewing thus far, Harris considered returning tomorrow evening to see whether Tokar might be entertaining company, which may give him something to study for shedding new light on the case. The important thing was to pick up on a new lead to follow, as he had concerns for how much more time Amanda had left to live, that's if she was still alive.

Chapter 19
A Witness to Murder

Harris connected with Rhonda by phone on Tuesday, refraining from mentioning that he'd gone out to Tokar's home the night before. He also neglected telling her that he was going out there again tonight, but everything connected to Amanda's disappearance drew suspicion to her involvement with Tokar and that casino. She'd vanished without a trace after leaving work one evening, which together with other circumstances put Tokar under the microscope for having done something with her. Amanda wanted to break ties with Tokar's organization to start fresh and settle down with Jim Abernathy, and that obviously didn't sit well with her employer. Walking out on him was a blow to his ego, and her knowledge of his business ventures gave him plenty of reasons for wanting to get rid of her.

Even with all that had transpired to draw suspicion to Tokar, Harris didn't have a stitch of proof that he had abducted Amanda, and it seemed unlikely Sypka or Solano will talk. But law enforcement was putting pressure on Tokar, and he was no doubt feeling heat for having employed Sypka. Solano was a different case altogether. While Harris had photos he'd taken of him at his lake house, there was no proof that Tokar ever employed the old underworld figure. Even though Solano was a hitman and there was evidence he was stalking Harris while carrying a firearm, no proof could be provided that Tokar had paid him for engaging his services. He knew he was on the right track and had accomplished a lot by getting those two off the street, but nailing Tokar wasn't going to be easy. He needed much more if he was going to convict him for kidnapping Amanda. As much as he didn't want to believe Amanda was dead, Sypka and Solano were criminal types who knew how to dispose of a body in such a way that it couldn't be found.

Harris hoped his surveillance of Tokar would produce a new lead for proving where he was holding Amanda, and as slim as those possibilities were, he had little choice but to go out there again. What kept going through Harris's mind was that Tokar had real estate scattered all over the metro area, and if he had her put away someplace, finding out where would be a challenge. He thought the smart move for now was to stick to Tokar for learning more about him and his organization. The law would have to provide solid evidence if they were to convict the casino owner of anything, for he had money backing him to pay for a strong defense by way of a team of lawyers. The FBI's assessment wasn't a bit helpful toward showing that Tokar arranged for Amanda to drop out of sight, and coming up with such evidence was going to be difficult.

Near dusk, Harris returned to the power station where he'd parked the night before, and he dressed in much the same apparel. He carried his .45 tucked inside his belt, putting the leather strap on his binoculars around his neck, and started walking through the woods toward the Tokar estate. Trying to keep his distance from the property line in case Tokar turned his Great Dane loose to wander the grounds like he had last night, he again followed that dry creek bed to his house. Harris didn't have much concern about the dog giving him trouble, bringing with him a can of pepper spray just in case he should encounter the animal when on foot and crossing level ground.

After darkness fell across the land, he came out of the woods to go to that same magnolia tree and climbed it to sit on the same branch he'd occupied the night before. With a clear view of the great room, he brought the binoculars up to his eyes to bring the interior of the house into focus, soon sighting Tokar pacing as he spoke on the phone. His Great Dane was there keeping him company, but there was no sign of the female company he had the night before and it looked like it was going to be a quiet evening.

After a short while, Harris's bottom was getting sore. He sat on that tree limb as long as he could stand it, and it looked as though he was wasting his time. While thinking about heading back to his car, he saw a car's headlight beams streaming across the front lawn, indicating a car had just pulled into the driveway. Although he couldn't see the automobile, his impression was that it had taken to the circle in the yard's frontage to stop directly in front of the house.

No doubt someone had come to pay Tokar a visit, and like a good host he went to the door to greet them and let them in. Less than a minute later, the two were engaged in conversation in the great room, but the guest stood off to one side and out of view.

The tall floor lamp with the large decorative lampshade blocked Harris's view, so he leaned to extend himself, but he still couldn't see who it was.

Annoyed at not being able to see who Tokar's guest was for identification purposes, Harris distinctly sensed that the two were in a heated argument. Alerted by the commotion inside the house, Harris stuck to his perched position in the tree, watching as the two continued trading words. Studying Tokar's movements closely, there were loud undiscernible shouts permeating outside of the house as he began yelling at this individual. The Great Dane started barking, and Tokar gave the dog a command that quieted the animal before the shouting match resumed. Harris still couldn't see who the other person was, and he would've given his eyeteeth to know what was being said, but the conversation was muted.

The visitor whose face was out of view drew a pistol and held it pointed at the casino owner, the weapon's barrel seen extending from his hand. At this eye-popping moment, Harris's jaw dropped open, as he next heard the muffled sound of the weapon discharging twice, and Tokar dropped to the floor.

Harris began descending from the tree. "Holy crap, I don't believe it—I saw a homicide in clear view but never got a look at the murderer!"

He paused when seeing the dog attacking the shooter, the killer lifting the arm that wasn't holding the gun as defense and the dog's jaws clamped on his forearm. The attack continued as the two drifted out of sight, knocking over the lamp, and as Harris hit the ground making a mad dash for the house, he heard two more shots fired.

Drawing his weapon, on his long run across the lawn Harris heard tires squealing as a car sped away, and by the time he reached the front yard he saw nothing but red taillights. The assailant's car sped down the main blacktopped road without him being able to tell the car's make, and that's when he noticed the front door to the house was open. Thinking Tokar may still be alive and be able to speak for giving him the name of his murderer with his last breath, he hurried inside the house.

Walking through a vestibule across an oak tongue and groove floor, he came to the great room, and the lamp that had impeded his view of the killer lay horizontally on the floor. Light from the open top of the lamp lying sideways was directed at Tokar who lay dead in a pool of blood with his eyes open, making for a shockingly awful sight. His eyes were eerily still and staring at the ceiling, and there was no question he was deceased, leaving Harris wondering who the killer could have been. His Great Dane lay dead nearby on the floor, and plainly seeing two bloody bullet holes in its fur, the animal had most assuredly died trying to protect its master.

Harris came forward to feel Tokar's wrist anyway, but there was no pulse, and it looked like an accurately aimed bullet to the heart had done the job. Not only could Tokar not tell him who his murderer was, but he also couldn't divulge where he was keeping Amanda, leaving him high and dry on this case. Catching sight of a spent shell cartridge lying on the floor, without touching it he could tell the casing was for a nine millimeter semi-automatic, and then he spotted other ejected shells.

Standing there, a witness to a murder, and yet he had no idea who fired the fatal shot, and it happened so fast and unexpectedly that it stunned Harris. He only just then realized a car was pulling up in front of the house, and rushed to the vestibule to stand behind a coat tree stand supporting an overcoat that gave him cover.

Waiting and watching the open door, he pulled his shirttail out from his pants, stuffed his weapon inside his belt, and the shirttail served to conceal it. He heard footsteps softly coming to the entranceway and the voice of a female, saying, "Tony, why's the front door open?"

The woman was carrying a brown bag in her hands that indicated she'd been shopping, and it looked to be the same female he saw in Tokar's company the night before. When she entered the great room, he went out the front door, only to hear a bloodcurdling scream that made him pause. He hadn't yet stepped off the front porch, when realizing his duty was to face the music, for if found out that he left a murder scene he'd surely lose his detective's license.

Harris turned at the same moment the woman came running out of the house frightened, screaming, and panicky, but he caught hold of her.

"I'm police, Detective Lieutenant Harris, what is it?"

Speechless, she pointed inside the house, and Harris went back inside to have a brief look around before using his cell phone to call the authorities. Knowing he was in for a long night, he then told her, "I've phoned the police and it shouldn't take them long to get here."

Harris escorted the emotionally shocked woman to a breakfast nook off the kitchen where he had her sit down, and police soon arrived to begin processing the crime scene. One detective escorted Tokar's latest fiancée into the den while Lead Investigator Detective Carl Billings began questioning Harris as they both sat at the kitchen table.

After listening to Harris's story, Billings asked to examine the .45 he carried, and the weapon had been cleaned thoroughly after wounding Solano on Sunday night, leaving no indication he'd fired it since.

The .45 passed the sniff test, and another plainclothes forensics detective named Stafford came to approach Billings. "Shell casings on the floor are for a nine millimeter."

Billings acted reluctant about giving Harris back his .45, but did so, and then the veteran detective resumed questioning Harris. "It was a strange coincidence for you to arrive at a murder scene, showing up at the precise moment it happened."

Harris began, "I had the house under surveillance from the backyard for over an hour when the murder occurred, and even though I witnessed the murder, I couldn't see who shot Tokar. I'd taken an elevated position in a Magnolia tree in the back yard when I saw Tokar and another man arguing, and whoever that other person was fired a pistol that killed him. From my viewing angle I was unable to see the person that pulled the trigger and I last caught a glimpse of the Great Dane attacking the murderer, who apparently shot the dog twice. I ran to the front of the house just as someone drove onto the blacktop road out front, but from that distance I couldn't make out what kind of car it was. I then went into the house to see Tokar lying dead on the floor and felt his wrist for a pulse. A few seconds later, the woman showed up and while she entered the house to view the body, I took a position behind the coat rack in the vestibule. I had stepped outside onto the porch when I heard her scream and then I saw my duty was to stay here, stopping her as she ran out of the house, and then I phoned the police."

Billings commented, "So you actually entered the house and saw the body on the floor first before she did. Why did you leave the woman with the impression you'd just arrived at the house, why not let her see you right from the outset?"

"I wasn't sure if I wanted to get involved after failing to get a look at the killer for providing a description of him—what I'd seen wouldn't prove viable to a murder investigation. I hadn't gone any further than the front porch when realizing it was my responsibility as a law officer to stay and tell what I witnessed while explaining my presence here."

Billings clenched his hands together. "Why don't you do me a big favor and start from the beginning so that all this makes sense to me."

Harris told of his investigation into the Amanda Kramer missing person's case, then mentioning his visit to Tokar's house the night before. He again gave an account of his movements for the evening and explained where he'd parked his car. The two played a question and answer game whereby there were numerous interruptions by phone calls received by the head investigating detective. Harris had to give his story numerous times, but his movements played out with every question to somewhat satisfy Billings that he wasn't evasive and details rang true with what investigators saw at the scene.

Billings then asked, "How many hand guns do you own?"

"I own several, including another .45, a nine millimeter, and a .38 special, but I only have the one firearm in my possession, and there aren't any in my car."

Billings was still curious. "You say your car is parked up the road at a power station. Do you mind if I send a man up there to go through the car?"

"I have no problem with that provided you have a search warrant to do so."

"I can get a search warrant," replied Billings before taking another short phone call.

Believing he'd given sufficient information for Billings to make out his report, Harris replied, "If obtaining a warrant is what you have a mind to do, I have nothing but time on my hands. Like I've already explained, I'm not technically working because of an injury I suffered, and I'm presently looking into a case for the family of Amanda Kramer, who's missing. If you want to verify how I got caught up in this investigation you can phone Chief of Detectives Steve Hastings in metro St. Louis."

Billings nodded. "If your knee is injured so badly, how was it that you climbed that tree out back to look into the house?"

"I managed to climb the tree because I'm desperate to take up with a lead to locate the Kramer woman. If progress isn't made soon, she's certain to end up long forgotten in the cold case files. She may already be dead. . . . If you need validity for my story, in that magnolia tree at eyelevel elevation with the window for the great room you'll find I broke a tree branch for gaining a clear view into the house."

Detective Stafford had finished making a preliminary study of the murder scene, and returned to speak to Billings. "I found blood spatter. Two droplets of blood are spherical and almost perfectly circular, leaving me to think that when the dog went after the shooter and bit him, it drew blood. These droplets are distant from the victim and the dog so it's unlikely it's theirs, which means we've got the killer's DNA. Now we just need to find somebody to match it with to identify our murderer."

Billings asked, "How are you doing with prints from foot tracks?"

"This man's shoes leave prints that are easily recognizable, and the same goes for the lady's dress shoes, but there are tracks from smooth soled shoes which appear to be the killer's."

Harris looked at Billings, who gave Harris what appeared to be his usual snooty expression, and Harris expected him to insist on a saliva swab for getting his DNA.

"Do you have a T-shirt underneath that pullover shirt you're wearing?"

"Yes."

I want the pullover, and if any gunshot residue or blood is found on that shirt there's a strong chance you'll be indicted for murder."

Harris understood the garment was evidence in a murder investigation, and he removed it and stuffed it into a plastic evidence bag held by Stafford, who was wearing rubber gloves.

Now having the bare skin of his arms exposed, Harris commented, "You don't see any bite wounds on my arms."

Billings condescendingly remarked, "Yeah, and that doesn't prove anything. That last call I received was from the D.A. and he wants you to report to his office in the morning at 10 a.m. Do you need the address?"

"No, I've received invitations from Kerrigan and Hall before, but they never seem to amount to anything except to waste everybody's time and the taxpayer's money."

Billings addressed a uniformed officer on the premises. "I want you to drive Detective Harris to his car that's parked up the road at an electrical power station. While there, do a visual inspection of his car's interior and if you see any firearms, hold him there and notify me immediately."

The officer noticed the .45 Harris carried inside his belt, and without asking questions drove him to the roadside's shoulder, completing a U-turn and parking in front of the power station. Harris stood by while the officer used his flashlight to scan the car's interior, and seeing it looked fairly clean with nothing that bore any connections to a homicide, he left.

With that, Harris watched the officer drive away in his cruiser, and started his car, leaving him to wonder where to go from here with this case. However, now he had this pain-in-the-ass meeting to attend to with the district attorney in the morning. It had been a long, drawn-out evening, and the murder of Tokar wasn't going to make the job of finding Amanda Kramer any easier, as leads were drying up fast. Thinking about the blank expression on the murder victim's face and the fixed position of his eyes, he thought Tokar had picked a fine time to get himself murdered.

That same night, he phoned Rhonda and told her that Tokar was no longer in this world, and she wondered if she still had a job, although it really wasn't important to her. It didn't matter because she had feelers out, searching for other means of employment, but she was curious what the results would be with him gone for the future of the casino. He also told her how he'd witnessed the murder, and yet was unable to say who the killer was. Going on to explain that he had an appointment with the County D.A.'s office in the morning, he made mention that he didn't expect the meeting to be a cordial one.

Wednesday morning, as instructed, Harris reported to the district attorney's office, and the secretary-receptionist told him to go right in. His welcoming committee was the current district attorney Raymond Kerrigan, the assistant district attorney Elizabeth Hall, and Detective Billings.

Kerrigan spoke from behind his desk. "Lieutenant Harris, it surely hasn't been so long that you've forgotten Elizabeth Hall and me, and you met Detective Billings last night. He motioned for Harris to take a chair next to Billings, both chairs facing his desk. "We'd like you to give us an account of your movements last night pertaining to the murder of Anthony Tokar."

Elizabeth Hall avoided taking a chair, but instead sat on the corner of Kerrigan's desk while watching Harris with her arms folded.

"Like I had explained last night to Detective Billings, my purpose for being out at Tokar's residence was that I was looking into the disappearance of Amanda Kramer. I had taken a vantage point in a tree in the backyard when I saw Tokar get shot and killed."

He'd nearly finished when Elizabeth Hall interrupted him, "Detective Billings said that you were thinking about leaving the murder scene, why is that?"

"My first impulse was to get out of there, but like I explained to Billings, I saw my responsibility as a law officer to stay on and assist with the investigation. If I had seen Tokar's killer and been able to give a description of him, the thought of leaving would not have entered my mind, but I felt as though I'd fumbled the ball."

"Yes, but could it be that you first initially thought about leaving because you were in a shootout at the casino on Saturday, and then critically wounding another man Sunday night? How do you think this kind of media coverage looks to the average citizen, and how safe do they feel after watching it on the news and reading about it in the newspapers?"

"I'm aware it's an election year, but as far as the people of this area feeling secure, they're certainly not feeling safe when the courts are turning loose gangster types like Sypka and Solano. Those hoodlums shouldn't have been walking the streets with the records they've racked up, and you know it. The prisons are full, and predatory criminals are being let out to keep the most violent transgressors in. In the meanwhile, there are more nutcases running loose on the streets than ever before."

Kerrigan intervened. "Sypka and Solano did time for their crimes and the courts had no means for holding them. The system did the best it could to rehabilitate those two."

"Let's tell it like it really is. You people negotiate with these criminals' defense attorneys and plea bargain to reduce the severity of their crimes. This results in shortened sentences so they can return to prey on the unsuspecting public. Why should anybody feel safe with pistol packing thugs walking the streets? Solano should've spent the rest of his life in jail for first-degree murder and extortion, not to mention the other couple dozen violent crimes he's committed over the years. He was released from prison because he contracted a lethal cancer and the state can't afford to pay for the treatments—that's no reason to release a murderer on the streets. It's not the state's fault he got cancer, let him die in jail from natural causes. But instead you people gave him his freedom and the first thing he does is take up a contract to kill me for pocket money. You aren't making the job of law enforcement any easier by releasing hardened criminals with records a mile long."

"Hall said, "We're not here to discuss the shortcomings of our prison system, we're here to determine whether we should revoke your detectives' license."

Harris tried keeping calm, "If you want to take my license, go ahead, but I don't think it's going to wash with my department, and my guess is that you don't think it will either. Those shootouts weren't my doing, I was merely defending myself, and if you have any ideas about pinning Tokar's murder on me, you can forget it. Billings here can attest that I didn't kill Tokar—he knows every step I made in that house. The bottoms of my feet were damp from tracking across the lawn to leave my footsteps easy to detect, and my footprints don't coincide with the murderer's movements. If he had good reason to think that I murdered him he would've locked me up last night, but there's not a shred of evidence saying I did it."

"I'm well aware of Solano's and Sypka's records," began Kerrigan, "and this office is doing all it can to keep those two incarcerated, refusing them bail while the investigation moves forward. I also know you were once romantically involved with Amanda Kramer, giving you a motive for committing this murder. Tokar was a prominent citizen of this community and your being at that murder scene makes you a suspect. Circumstances leave me no other choice but to insist that Billings takes your DNA swab so we can eliminate you from the list of suspects."

It was an insult for Harris to give a DNA sample, but he understood that this was the district attorney's way of getting the last word, and refusal would show his superiors that he was uncooperative. Billings reached inside the hip pocket of his sport coat to display a plastic bag with two cotton tips inside, and he turned to look at Harris.

Harris snapped back at Kerrigan, "Swabbing me for DNA isn't going to accomplish anything toward solving this case, but I have no objections, providing you have a court order. You people think a lot of Tokar because the casino generates revenue for the county, but the reality is that the people he carosued with are lowlifes and degenerates just like him. Tokar was nothing less than a modern-day mobster, and I'm sure he's made plenty of enemies. If you want to do something beneficial to help Billings with this case you need to get samples from all of Tokar's business associates, which will mean investigating real criminals. You'll rack up a long list of potential murderers cataloging his cohorts, friends and foes alike."

Harris looked to Billings. "I know this wasn't your idea, you have nothing to gain by asking for my DNA, but just the same, you know what you can do with those cotton swabs."

Billings grinned in acknowledgement of Harris's last comments on the subject matter before tucking the sealed plastic bag back in his pocket.

Harris stood. "No doubt the key to solving Tokar's murder and perhaps a few other crimes lie with matching up blood found at the crime scene to a suspect. If you're expecting to compare my DNA to the killer's you need to first convince the police commissioner and chief of detectives that my being at the crime scene warrants acquiring a sample, though I don't think you'll get their cooperation. For one thing, common sense says that if I was Tokar's killer I wouldn't have stuck around last night."

Kerrigan stated insistently, "Comparing your DNA results eliminates you from our list of suspects so we can concentrate our investigation on others."

Harris last looked to Billings, "You're a fellow policeman. Is it possible for you to use your influence to persuade these idiots that I'm not Tokar's murderer?"

Conjuring a thought, Harris asked Billings, "Did the department have time yet to process the pullover shirt I was wearing to test it for blood spatter and gunpowder residue?"

Billings shook his head no.

"If trace evidence examiners get a positive reading on that shirt I'll gladly provide the DNA swab you've requested. Should you otherwise think it necessary to get my DNA, you can get it from the neckline of the shirt I was wearing last night."

Leaving Kerrigan's office, Harris resented them asking him to provide a DNA swab. At the same time, he knew he'd ruffled Kerrigan's and Hall's feathers and there would probably be hell to pay for how he'd just spoken to them. He knew there was a chance they'd pull his detective's license, but he also expected he'd have the support of law enforcement officials and his fellow officers. He also believed Billings agreed with him for giving a refusal, but that detective's allegiance may be more with Kerrigan and Hall for keeping his job and that's why he remained silent. He'd been in the hot seat with the D.A.'s office on other occasions with them trying to use their authority to intimidate him, and it always resulted in a waste of time. However, this time his name was connected to a murder, and he felt slightly nervous about how the meeting went. The shootings with Solano and Sypka, and now involved with Tokar's death, he fully realized the importance of turning up a lead soon before something else blew up in his face.

Chapter 20
Meeting with a Nervous Informant

Harris later received a phone call from Steve Hastings. "Harris, I know it's not your fault for all the trouble you've fallen into lately, but you are treading on thin ice with the department. Right now, you're a hero to officers in the city, but in the county districts your name is shit! It's like you're living in the Wild West here lately buddy, with two shootings over the weekend and now your name is connected to Tokar's murder. I'm standing squarely behind you at this end, but if your name ends up in the newspaper just one more time the people upstairs are going to cut you off at the knees. My advice is to lay low for a spell, speak softly and carry a big stick."

The meeting at the D.A.'s office seemed almost laughable in that he didn't see how things could get much more serious, and he thought what Hastings had told him was good advice. Feeling as though he needed a drink, but what was actually fueling his desire for a drink was mostly that he had no leads. The problem was that he didn't have time to lay low, that someone's life was hanging in the balance. He had to continue the investigation for the Kramer's sake, for Amanda especially, since she was the one missing. Tokar's murder complicated matters in that as a result of his death the bottom had fallen out of this case, and he didn't know where to go from here. It helped to keep his mind occupied for keeping off the booze, but everything fizzled out with this homicide, and he now saw a difficult road ahead for carrying on with this case.

The casino, private gentleman's club, and the casino's hotel went on operating, as there were safety nets in place to see that these institutions kept on generating business. Keeping the casino going was a complex corporation intertwined with shady investors who had connections to organized crime. An investigation showed that people of wealth had put up money to front Tokar, and found to have a controlling interest they worked the ropes so that Tokar didn't look like much more than a puppet. Unions had invested in the corporation too, and while the casino remained operational, people of high status shifted into position to take control of the conglomeration. It was these people near the top of the pyramid who benefited from Tokar's death, leading law enforcement officials to think them likely candidates for reaching out to take down Tokar. Investigating the money people who had a big take on the casino's profits was going to make finding Tokar's killer nearly impossible, and for a time it drained police resources. Harris was nearly alone in trying to learn what had become of Amanda Kramer and he was giving it all his mental concentration.

With all that Tokar possessed in this world, the glamour of a huge casino machine sucking money out of people's pockets, and his infinite real estate holdings, in reality it was a house of cards. The vast hodgepodge of business dealings had all become difficult to manage, for while it made money, it also took a great deal of money to maintain its operation. Thinking he could do better on his own, Tokar skimmed off the top, while at the same time purchasing real estate for making his dream of a profitable horserace track a reality. However, when calculating the value of the real estate he'd accumulated it added up to little in that banks were holding the mortgage on most of it. After the accountants were through, their adding and subtracting put Tokar at a net worth of less than a half million, when most people thought he was worth millions. If he'd gone on to acquire great wealth through the distribution of illegal substances, he'd still go in the ground like the average slob who worked his tail off for a lifetime.

Harris had acquired a listing of property owned by the Tokar Corporation, and spent a couple of days poking around these buildings. He'd begun to wonder if Tokar and his business partners had thought it best to simply do away with Amanda Kramer rather than hold her someplace captive as he had believed. There was no way they'd let her move on while she had knowledge that could in some way hurt Tokar's organization. If that was the case then they may have gotten rid of her in any number of different ways. Organized crime had methods for making people disappear, even if it was simply to wrap them in chains anchored in blocks of concrete and let them sink to the bottom of a lake. This is another reason of many why Harris couldn't get Lake Laraine off his mind, and why he felt drawn to go back to that lake. Still mystified by how Dvorak disappeared when Harris was hiding in the basement of his lake house, as much as he felt relieved for having avoided the doctor, he couldn't put that episode out of his mind. He'd never stopped wondering what became of him to vanish in such a strange and mysterious way.

Not knowing all the facts made Harris wonder if he may be off base in how things unraveled with Tokar and Amanda. He theorized that their relationship may have soured and how she may have grown demanding of him, perhaps wanting a lump of money for forgetting all she'd learned. A hefty sum of money could make for a big help in someone wanting a fresh start in this life. Harris hadn't seen Amanda in ages and for that reason he couldn't be sure she hadn't become greedy, telling Tokar she wanted a bonus at the time she told him she wanted out. Even her own sister Rhonda had said that in more recent times Amanda had become somewhat selfish by how she lived for herself. In a way, she may have been standing up for getting what she thought she'd earned and deserved by having given support to the casino owner. If Amanda threatened Tokar for forcing him to pay money owed to her, while leading him to believe she'd otherwise turn over harmful information to the authorities, he may have killed her in a fit of anger. If that had happened, then she may be at the bottom of that lake or buried deep in the woods near his lake house, but this was merely speculation he didn't want to dwell on.

Money can make people do strange things, but with Tokar eliminated from the picture, whatever had caused Amanda to disappear didn't seem to matter so much now, only that she needed to be found. At this point in time, he hoped he could at least find her remains to bring closure for her father and sister. If Tokar had anything to do with her demise, he'd paid the ultimate price, for Harris was convinced without a doubt that he was responsible for her vanishing.

The last few times Harris came to visit Rhonda and her father, the old man pestered him about his daughter's whereabouts, and he never had enough answers to satisfy him. He thought Rhonda's father was expecting a big bill for his investigative services, while thinking the detective wasn't doing enough to earn it, so Harris avoided stopping by for a time. This gave him more reason to turn to drink, but he remained focused on the case, holding out for something unexpected to surface that would give him a worthwhile lead to follow.

When everything seemed to grind to a standstill, word came that while the FBI had Salvador Garcia and Rafael Cordero under surveillance, the Camacho Cartel ambushed two bureau agents trailing them. Tokar's old cronies knew agents were following them for some time and getting sick of it, they had affiliates of their organization close in to do away with them. They were riding along in their white four-wheel drive Cadillac Escalade near railroad tracks off Hall Street when they stopped, the agents following them stopped too. That's when Camacho members came out of nowhere to start blasting the agents while they sat in their car. The men were killed as their vehicle was riddled with bullets from high-powered assault rifles, and the people who did it believed they had nothing to fear.

Hearing about the agent's deaths over his car radio, Harris stopped by the station to confer with Ron Warren about this latest turn of events.

Warren said, "This is just the beginning. The authorities have been preparing to close in on cartel operations for months, and the bloody murder of these agents started things in motion. Federal agents working in conjunction with military units are activating a huge net being thrown over Puerto Rico and other Caribbean Islands, while sting operations are unfolding on the waterfronts of Miami, New York, and New Orleans."

Harris asked, "While I'm here, Ron, do you have anything for me?"

Ron shook his head no, but then he said, "There was a guy calling for you earlier, saying he had something important to tell you, but he wouldn't leave a number. He called something like three times, and I spoke to him the last time he phoned. Getting the impression he was a desperate character and rattled about something, I hope I did the right thing by giving him your cell phone number."

Harris left the station wondering who may have called. From there he went out to visit Rhonda and her father and Mr. Kramer had the television on watching the news. The media was in a big uproar about the killing of those FBI agents here in St. Louis, and arrests being made in Puerto Rico, as well as action being taken at the waterfronts of various U.S. cities. Watching this ruckus on the news for an hour, he kept his cell phone handy in case he received a call, and it was well into the evening when a call finally came.

Seeing a number on his phone's ID plate he didn't recognize, Harris went in the next room to answer it, "Hello."

"Is this Detective Harris?"

"Yes, it is."

"You may not remember me, but my name is Allen Schaeffer, and I was employed as business manager of the casino under Anthony Tokar."

Harris's eyes lit up, "Yes, Mr. Schaeffer, of course I remember you."

Schaeffer nervously carried on, "Some important papers have come into my possession which might interest you. As soon as I'd learned of Mr. Tokar's untimely death I went to his safe and removed documents covering a wide range of business affairs he was involved in. I have those documents in a briefcase and I'm prepared to turn them over to you, provided I'm guaranteed immunity from prosecution. I know my former boss was guilty of tax evasion, but I also know some of the shady characters he was in cahoots with were criminals, and this information is sure to interest the authorities."

Harris thought this could be the big break he'd been waiting for. "I promise to do all I can to help you Mr. Schaeffer, but you need to be aware of what's at stake here. Do you think there may be something in those papers to shed light on Amanda Kramer's whereabouts? This may be of great importance in that her survival may hinge on what you're carrying in that case. Recalling the last time you and I spoke, I tried stressing that someone withholding information about Amanda's disappearance could be held in part responsible in the event of her death. Neglect on your part to turn over that documentation at such a critical time could result in your criminal prosecution in connection with a murder. Whatever accounting or tax problems you're concerned about, the penalty can't be near what a capital murder charge will carry."

Hearing no response, Harris became worried Schaeffer might hang up on him, that he may be pressing his point too hard, although he had little choice but to try reasoning with him. He toned down his voice, "This woman has been held against her will for a long time, and a matter of minutes can make the difference as to whether or not she survives this ordeal. While my first consideration is for this woman's safety and welfare, part of my concern is for you as well. Should she die, are you going to tell a jury that you refrained from turning over this briefcase to ensure you had protection from tax evasion charges?"

He went on to speaking assertively. "We're wasting precious time here talking, and what I suggest is that we get together immediately in private to go through those papers. Should we find nothing to clue us on Amanda Kramer's whereabouts, from there I'll set you up with a good lawyer to represent you, and I'll be at your side every minute to provide assistance. I'll do whatever your attorney asks bearing witness to the fact that you were cooperative to law enforcement, and I'm certain my testimony will help to relieve your legal problems. This attorney will contact the authorities to arrange for your immunity, but from this moment on this woman's life is in your hands and it's important we get together this very minute to examine those papers."

Schaeffer's voice sounded more frazzled than it had before. "Okay, I trust you for doing it your way. Ever since taking that briefcase from the casino I've been worried sick I'm being followed. I've read the papers to know some of the men connected with Tokar's organization are contract killers, and I'm sure there are others who'd kill me for what's in this case."

"That's all the more reason for you and me to get together right now."

Harris heard Schaeffer speaking to someone. "Who's there with you?"

The sound at the other end became muffled before Schaeffer replied, "I'm with a friend I've confided in, and he prefers that I don't give out his name. He may come forward at a later date to give testimony pertaining to what he knows about Tokar's business ventures, but right now he wants to remain anonymous."

Feeling urgency to meet with Schaeffer, Harris didn't want his paranoia about people following him to cause him to cut off the conversation before settling on a meeting place. Making him uncomfortable was that he didn't know who was with Schaeffer or what this person's role was in this, but he knew he had to exercise patience for gaining his confidence so he'd comply.

"Okay, tell me where you are and I'll come there, or if you'd feel safer meeting at a mall or an open parking lot where there are people that's fine with me."

"I believe I'd feel safer meeting at an isolated area, and from there I can follow you to a destination of your choosing. I presume you're a detective living within the city limits, and if you like we can go to your home to examine the papers. I don't live far away from Clifton Park, located south of I-44 and west of Hampton Avenue. Do you know where that is?"

"Yes, I do."

"At the furthest south end of the park is a lake where there's a playground, and I'll be parked on the street there waiting for you in thirty minutes."

Harris marched out of the house, simply saying to Rhonda, "I've gotta go."

From Rhonda's house he knew he'd have trouble driving to this park in thirty minutes if he kept to the speed limit, so he drove at high speed on the interstate and made good time. With nightfall closing in, he drove around the park with minutes to spare for arriving at their meeting place. He discovered a lone white compact car parked on the street at a bend in the road where he saw a kiddy playground, and thought the car had to be Schaeffer's.

Seeing streetlights reflecting off the nearby lake when getting out of his car, he went on to approach the vehicle's driver's door. The window was down, and he recognized the individual slumped in the driver's seat as Schaeffer, a bullet hole in his left temple, the car's interior a bloody mess. A pistol left lying on the floorboard suggested suicide, but Harris knew better, and he also believed an investigation of the scene would provide proof to police that it was murder. Schaeffer was apparently correct in his paranoid state of mind to think people were following him. However, there was also that person who was in his company when Harris last spoke to him on the phone, the friend he'd confided in who didn't want his name known.

Walking around to the vehicle's passenger side, he saw no briefcase in the car, and returned to the driver's door, glimpsing Schaeffer's corpse once more. Removing a handkerchief from the hip pocket of his sport coat, he used it as a glove to cover his right hand as he carefully took the key out of the ignition. He then proceeded to open the trunk lid to see if the briefcase was there, but it wasn't, and he returned the key to the ignition.

Schaeffer was gone, and whatever was in the briefcase was also gone and perhaps disposed of, leaving him to contend with another killing. Harris was bothered about how he should deal with Schaeffer's death, a man he hardly even knew, for he didn't want his name connected with another murder. He also didn't want someone to discover Schaeffer in the daylight hours when strolling about the park, as it could even be a child who looked in the car to see him in this condition.

He finally decided to go to a public phone to report to police where to find this dead person in the park. He told it as though he was a passerby who didn't want to get involved in a homicide and left it at that. Not wanting to do it this way, but he had no desire to get hung up in the investigation of Schaeffer's death when Amanda Kramer could still be alive and desperate for someone to rescue her.

Trying to fit together the puzzle pieces in his head, he went home to ponder Schaeffer's death and how it came about. In doing so, it occurred to him that the person who committed the murder could be someone connected to the casino. Sitting at the kitchen table, the bottle of bourbon right there in front of him, but it was as though it didn't even exist, for Harris's mind was on details about the case for finding Amanda. Finally lying down and falling asleep, he dreamed of the moment when he was cornered in Dvorak's basement, the anxiety he felt about the doctor closing in as he waited in the utility room. He awoke feeling mystified about how Dvorak disappeared, but again somewhat relieved the doctor didn't open that utility closet door to find him snooping around in his basement. People don't simply vanish into thin air, and this is something that baffled Harris. He felt a strong need to learn how Dvorak, for all practical purposes, seemed to vaporize from his basement. Sitting up on the side of his bed, he kept wondering how this came to be, making him think there may be a secret doorway or hidden compartment in that basement.

Chapter 21
Learning about the Secret Place

The sun had come up and Harris showered for starting his day. Considering the death of Schaeffer would surely shake up the authorities, he picked up a newspaper from a newsstand before entering his favorite greasy spoon to have breakfast. Yes, Schaeffer's murder made the morning news, reading the headline in big, bold print: **Another Death Connected to Tokar's Casino**.

Drinking coffee and consuming a BLT with melted cheese, he felt caught up in this case, and yet again thinking about Dvorak's vanishing act, he turned his thoughts to Lake Laraine. The doctor's strange disappearance that day wasn't the only thing drawing him to drive out that way though. He was still thinking Tokar may have engaged Solano and Sypka to dispose of Amanda's body at the lake development. Her body may have been interred in a shallow grave on one of the undeveloped wooded lots. They may have weighed her body down before letting it sink into that lake, and it wouldn't be the first time mob figures did it while the victim was alive and pleading for mercy.

Heading out that way, on his travel to the lake he thought about how it looked as though Amanda's disappearance would, in all likelihood, never be solved. It was disparaging to think he'd used all of his investigative skills to learn what happened to her, and yet there seemed little chance of finding her. He also thought about how not finding her would surely impact the lives of Rhonda and her father, for they'd never really gotten over Mark's death. Surely finding Amanda's corpse at a later date wouldn't be much help toward these people finding closure for moving on with their lives. Not wanting to fail them, he knew the only way to turn things around for making a life with Rhonda was to find Amanda alive. Otherwise, this girl he loved was certain to have emotional problems plaguing her for the rest of her days. The haunting remembrances of a brother senselessly shot to death, and now her older sister in all probability murdered, it didn't seem likely she'd ever get over these losses to find true happiness with him. He wondered what kind of life there can be for two people who love each other, for there'd be no way to console her when dwelling on these heart wrenching events.

The security gate card Harris had in his possession still worked for giving him access to Lake Laraine, and he took South Lake Drive to park near the circle where he'd left his car before. He gave Dvorak's weekend home a look when passing by it, and unless the doctor's car was in the garage, he wasn't there. Making certain he took his locksmith set with him, he walked back to Dvorak's home to once again let himself in for taking a look downstairs in the basement. After entering the residence, he soon afterward switched on the basement stair lights and descended to the large paneled room in the lower level. Standing before the broad faced fireplace, he examined it and the mantle, and then turned his attention to shelving on each side of it, seeing a collection of books and various decorative objects nicely arranged. Nothing seemed out of place or unusual, not until he caught sight of a silver urn, which he thought may contain one of Dvorak's close relations.

Harris thought there may be a secret door here at the fireplace, but he saw nothing to suggest this, as the shelving looked well-crafted and solidly built. He again thought how this side of the house was closest to the garage, the overhang of the garage roof attached to the house to leave a breezeway between the two structures. There was every indication that this is where the foundation of the house ended, as he'd seen how the chimney ran up and out of the roof like any other normal brick chimney.

Spending more than a prudent amount of time here in the basement, he thought he ought to leave before having another close encounter with Dvorak like the last time when he was inside the house. He left the premises in the same condition as he'd found it in, turning the knob to lock the front door.

Walking out into the sunlight, Harris saw the same elderly white-haired gentlemen he'd seen before in the yard across the road from Dvorak's residence. The man was busily watering flowers with a hose, and not paying the slightest bit of attention to him. He then noticed the man's wife in the corner of the yard wearing a wide brimmed sunhat as she pruned rosebushes. Still fishing for information about Dvorak, he had nothing to lose by conferring with these people, and he crossed the road to enter their yard.

He casually approached the man, "Hello, my name is Harris, and I was admiring your bungalow from across the road there. This is a great lake development and my guess is you folks have lived here for quite some time."

The man nodded, pulling the water hose along as he went on with spraying a bed of flowers.

His wife came over to see what Harris wanted, looking at him suspiciously through her sunglasses. "What can we do for you?"

"Well, like I was saying to your husband, my name is Harris, and my reason for being here at the lake is that I'm investigating the disappearance of a woman. She was an acquaintance of your neighbor Dr. Dvorak, and I was wondering if I may ask you a few questions pertaining to the doctor's routine when coming here to the lake."

The woman was snippy with Harris, "We hardly know that man. We've maybe only spoken to him once in the time he's owned that house."

"While that may be so, but perhaps you wouldn't mind answering a few routine questions, as I assure you I won't take up much of your time."

"We scarcely know him, so I don't think we can tell you anything of importance. I wouldn't talk to him Bill." And with that, the woman went back to tending to her rosebushes.

Harris quickly concluded that these people's reluctance to speak to him made it clear that the doctor wasn't on a friendly basis with them, nor were they in good standing with him. He brought out his detective's badge and presented it to the man, "Just so that we understand one another, I'm no friend of Dr. Dvorak. He's a suspect in this woman's disappearance, and I'm trying to dig up evidence to win a conviction against him. My primary purpose for coming out this way is for learning how often he comes to this lake house, and sometimes the smallest detail goes a long way for breaking a case."

The man twisted the hose attachment on the end of the line until it sprayed a misty shower, adjusting it further until no more than a drip came out. He grinned when turning to Harris. "You used the term *trying to dig up evidence*, you don't think he killed her and buried her here at the lake?"

Thinking he was hitting it off with the old gentleman, he nonchalantly replied, "I've been in this business long enough that nothing would surprise me. Part of what drew our attention to Dr. Dvorak is that he's a friend of Anthony Tokar, the owner of the gambling casino, and this girl who disappeared worked as Tokar's private secretary."

The man nodded, and spoke with a Midwestern drawl. "We heard about him getting killed and I've seen the girl's photo in the newspaper—Kramer. That casino hasn't gotten any good publicity with all the things I've read in the paper, and he and his associates used to have wild parties out here all the time. The business manager was thought to have committed suicide in a park in the city, but I heard it announced on the radio that police changed their report to concede it was a homicide."

"Yeah, and his death may somehow be connected to this girl's disappearance. That's why law enforcement has its nose to the ground checking out all of Tokar's friends and cohorts. You were right about the girl's name being Kramer—Amanda Kramer. Making my job difficult is that there are all sorts of rumors flying around, and crucial leads are drying up fast. Separating speculation from the real facts isn't easy, and that's why it's nice to talk to down-to-earth folks like you and the missus. I shouldn't mention this, but I interviewed the good doctor at his medical office and just between you and me, I didn't think he was straight forward with his answers. For that reason I can't scratch him off my list of suspects, so that leaves me out here poking around for learning what I can about him."

"I'm sure the life of a detective isn't an easy one, and investigating a case can get quite complicated and monotonous. And say, I was going have a cold beer, have you time for one?"

"I'm on duty, but I don't think one refreshing cold beer can detract from my duties on a warm day like today."

"By the way, my name is Bill Ellison, and my wife's name is Suzanne."

The two shook hands. "Detective Lieutenant Leonard Harris, but my friends call me Len."

After the man introduced his wife to Harris, Len responded in a friendly manner, "I'm sorry for intruding on your day, Mrs. Ellison."

They went around to a screen enclosed back porch where Harris drank a beer with Mr. Ellison, and after discussing various general topics he asked again about what they could tell him about the doctor."

"The wife and I really don't know Dr. Dvorak all that well, but he comes to the house almost every day and at the strangest hours, often long after dark and into the night."

Harris saw photos hung on a wall of Mr. Ellison standing with men beside eighteen-wheeler transport trucks parked in a row.

"Were you a truck driver?"

"Only for a short time, but I owned a transport trucking business."

"I see," and then he recognized the name Ellison on the side of one of the trucks. "Sure, I recall your company." He then gave attention to a photo on a table that showed the couple stooping with a white German shepherd sitting between them with its ears perked up. "That's a beautiful dog. I had a German shepherd when I was young named Greta, but she wasn't white. They make the most loyal pets, and they're very protective—if a stranger came in our yard, she'd take their leg off."

The woman said, "Fluffy was our dog's name, and she was a good-natured, friendly animal, but she was killed. She'd never leave the boundaries of our yard, and rarely did she bark at strangers, unless they were looking to come on our property. We used to have a house in the county with a big yard and only came out here on weekends, but we now live here at the lake."

"I heard you say the dog never left the yard, did it get carried away with chasing a squirrel or rabbit and get run down by a car?"

Mr. Ellison replied, "We can't say for certain because we have no proof, but we think the doctor shot her with a bow and arrow. I rushed her to a vet to have the arrow removed, but she died on the operating table, and we still have the arrow. The doctor was the one person she never took a liking to, and when he'd come to the mail box to collect mail she'd run out to the edge of our yard barking at him. I'd immediately call her in so she wouldn't be a nuisance, and he'd always give her the same angry stare, but we couldn't prove he caused her death."

Thinking about how the dog's life ended, Harris remembered the photo he'd seen in Dvorak's office of the doctor posed at an archery range shooting a bow and arrow. He soon thanked Ellison and his wife for their hospitality, and Mr. Ellison walked with him to where his property line ended at the road.

Harris commented, "I wish I could afford to live here at the lake, some of the homes are gorgeous and it seems so peaceful here."

Ellison replied, "The large lakefront houses are ridiculously high priced, partly because many are brick, but the bungalows are affordably priced for working class people. The house we live in is plenty big enough for just the two of us. A bigger house just means all that much more upkeep."

"I recall reading a newspaper article telling about the lake's history, and it made mention of the unique architecture of some of the homes. The columns writer told of the developer having a fetish for glamorous Laraine Day, and that he named the lake in her honor."

"That story about the actress is mere speculation, although while there are variations for the name Laraine, the spelling matches hers, and the lake's development came at the top of her popularity. However, many of the homes here are of unique architecture. I was told the man who built Dvorak's home was one of the designers of NORAD in Colorado Springs. Some call it the Cheyenne Mountain Directorate or Cheyenne Mountain Operations Center, code named Crystal Palace during the Cold War. The facility is housed in a mountain, and is the nation's Air Warning Center and Missile Correlation Center. The way I understand it, he and his wife were originally from the St. Louis area, and coming back here to retire, they had the home custom built. The house is brick, but the foundation, including the floor for the main level is reinforced concrete—it's a bomb shelter, built to withstand a nuclear attack from the Soviet Union."

"Say, that's interesting stuff, and you're a regular fountain of information.'

"Those are just things I picked up from living here at the lake."

"Just the same, I'd say the *Kennedy Missile Crises* had the general public living in fear of an all-out nuclear attack. I remember seeing historical film clips about the school children drilling for *'duck and cover'*. One thing I noticed when circling Dvorak's home on foot was that there aren't any windows for the basement, which now I understand why. And those people must have spent some serious money having the house built that way."

Ellison nodded yes, "I imagine so."

"Well, I'll be saying farewell Mr. Ellison and thank you for your time and those little tidbits of information about the lake."

The two shook hands and Harris went on his way, returning to his car. He took a few minutes to use his binoculars, scanning Tokar's home on the opposite side of the lake, but he saw no cars there, no one in sight.

His cell phone rang, and seeing it was Rhonda calling, he answered it by saying, "Hi, how are you?"

"We're doing just fine. Dad and I were wondering if you'd like to come out to the house to have dinner. I'm making spaghetti."

"Why sure, I'd be delighted to take you up on that cordial offer. I was visiting Lake Laraine, hoping to learn something helpful for picking up a new lead, but no such luck. I poked around Dvorak's house for a spell while interviewing neighbors, and I intended checking out Tokar's place once more, but I suppose I can come back tomorrow. Viewing it from Dvorak's side of the lake, that house looks deserted."

"How's the knee?"

"It's bothering me quite a bit now that you ask, probably because I've been on my feet for hours."

"Dinner will be ready in less than a half hour, so don't keep us waiting."

Harris got in his car and started its engine for leaving the lake, and passing by Dvorak's house, he gave it a look, "A bomb shelter, who would've thought that."

Driving along headed for the lake's gated entrance, he kept thinking about that house and the way it had been built years ago during the Cold War era.

When he'd nearly reached the security gate, he saw Dvorak's black Lexus moving at a fast clip for approaching the gate, as the doctor was making his entrance into the lake development. Harris put on sunglasses, stroking his chin as a way to keep the doctor from recognizing him while he used his access card to pass through the gate.

Watching Dvorak stop to insert his card for entering from the other lane, Harris believed he hadn't been spotted, and he watched the doctor drive on in the opposite direction. Suddenly, it hit him, as learning that house had been built as a bomb shelter helped him to conclude there must be a hidden passageway or secret compartment near the fireplace. He'd examined the fireplace thoroughly for finding such a compartment and saw no indication of one, but thinking of the time Dvorak disappeared, he was convinced there had to be a compartment of sorts.

Turning around to return to the entrance, he again used his card to reenter the lake development to follow Dvorak on South Lake Drive. Lagging far behind, he accelerated to pick up speed, but was unable to see the black Lexus until catching sight of it parked at Dvorak's home, although the doctor was nowhere in sight. He had apparently hurried to enter the house and Harris was left wondering how to handle this situation. Driving on to park in the same place he'd left his car earlier, he started walking back to Dvorak's home. He had his locksmith set and checked his .45 automatic to make sure he was ready for trouble.

Chapter 22
Entering the Doctor's Lair

Before entering the house, he used his cell phone to call Ron Warren, "Ron, this is Harris. I believe Amanda Kramer is being held captive inside Dvorak's weekend home at Lake Laraine, and I'm going ahead with entering the premises. I just learned minutes before that his house was built as a bomb shelter during the Cold War days. Just between you and me, I've been inside his house on one other occasion, and while I was inside poking around, the doctor arrived. Trying to avoid a confrontation, I hid in a basement utility room, and it just so happened that the basement was where Dvorak was headed for. Just when I thought he'd catch me in the house, he vanished into thin air. People don't just simply vanish, which leaves me thinking there's got to be a hidden compartment somewhere off a fireplace room in his basement."

Ron replied, "If you're right, you'll be declared a hero, if you're wrong, your goose is cooked—you'll lose your detectives' license for going in there without a warrant. If the doctor is injured as a result of your entering that house without you locating the Kramer girl, you may end up in jail or even prison. You know that guy's going to sue you for every penny you've got."

"If the doctor hadn't disappeared that one day, I wouldn't be sure, but he did and he's in there now. You know as well as I do that it's only a matter of time before he murders Amanda, and this could be the hour he's decided to do away with her."

"Did you consider that you may be right, but this doctor may be waiting for you and you'll be the one getting ambushed, and he has the legal right to shoot a home invader?"

"I'm going in, Ron. Now listen carefully, if I phone you back for assistance, tell officers and medical personnel to take South Lake Drive. The house is brick and on the left near the end of the drive, and the mailbox in front of the house has the name *Dvorak* in bold print with the number 114. Have you got that?"

"I've got it, and if I don't hear from you in the next fifteen minutes I'm calling for the cavalry. I may phone you back before making that call, so let me know as soon as you can how things are."

"If I'm wrong, I'll still give you a call back, but then it's Dvorak who'll make the call for the cavalry, and my career in law enforcement is down the drain."

"That's a good argument for getting a warrant before going in there."

"Ron, that'll take hours and maybe even days, and in all probability that girl hasn't got that much time left. Look at all the days she's been missing, and all along he's been coming to this lake house at odd hours."

Signing off with, "Wish me luck," he stuffed his phone in his coat pocket.

Finding the door locked, he used his locksmith tools to get in and, leaving the door unlocked, he went straight to the basement door to descend to the lower level. Lights were on, and he moved cautiously with his .45 in hand, making short steps as he approached the paneled fireplace room. Having seen no sign of Dvorak, he began closely examining decorative objects displayed on shelving on both sides of the fireplace, and that's when he saw a Moroccan jeweled lantern. Usually found on the inside of these decorative pieces are candles, but in this one was a small ceramic angel, appearing timid as a praying, winged female, childlike in stature.

Studying the caged angel, he saw what looked like a lever behind the antique lantern, and moved the piece aside. When pulling the lever, a vertical row of shelves shifted, jutting outward to expose a narrow cavity, and he cautiously ducked to enter the passageway.

Moving forward quite slowly, he held his weapon pointed at what lay ahead of him, and saw how this pathway led to a lower level beneath the garage. Remaining alert, while bewildered by what he'd found, he kept his eyes open wide. He came upon a room painted a dingy white with a sink that had a dripping faucet centered against a wall. Turning to his right, he saw a compact refrigerator, a chest of drawers and curtains fully draped back on the left and right. To his left he saw Amanda Kramer sitting dazed on a twin bed, one of her wrists and an ankle chained to an eye screw anchored in the concrete wall. With nothing covering her except a sheet draped over her shoulder, her arms and legs were exposed, and purplish spots in the bend of her arms gave evidence of drugs injected into her to keep her subdued.

Amanda's eyes had dark circles, and she looked at him in dumbfounded awe and disbelief, while Harris spoke in not much more than a whisper, "Where's Dvorak?"

She didn't speak a word or move a muscle, but her eyes looked to the far end of the room.

Suddenly, a gunshot rang out, and Harris's right hip jerked with the entrance of a bullet!

He saw curtains in the far corner gently swaying from a bullet passing through them, and catching a glimpse of black toed shoes below, he fired three rapid shots.

Dvorak fell to the floor, taking the curtains down with him, and there was no doubt Harris killed him.

Harris now doubled over in excruciating pain and crumpled to the floor. His eyes turned to Amanda, but she looked to be off in another world, seemingly unaware of goings on, as though having no idea what was transpiring before her was real.

She finally looked at him as if recognizing him, and said simply, "Harris."

He pulled out his cell phone and dialed Warren, "Ron, I'm shot. I discovered Amanda Kramer alive, but Dvorak is dead—I killed him."

"Help is on the way."

He then looked to his phone, hitting the memory key for dialing Rhonda and pressed the speaker button before leaving it lying on the floor. The excruciating pain fast growing intolerable, trying as best as he can to keep from convulsing, he heard Rhonda's voice, and said, "Can't talk."

His hands wrapped around his stomach in trying to offset the pain, and he took to a slow rocking motion as a way to deal with it. Hearing Rhonda calling to him, he finally reached with one hand and slid the phone across the floor to Amanda's feet.

Rhonda still calling to him, he said, "Pick it up." He again repeated those same words to Amanda, "Pick it up."

Amanda grasped what he wanted her to do and reached down to pick up the phone, and hearing her sister's voice, she said, "Rhonda."

Grimacing in pain, Harris raised his left hand to see blood covering his palm and fingers, and with time running out, the room began closing in, growing dim as sound became muffled. He tasted blood in his mouth, another indication the end was near, and everything went to spinning before turning black and he lost consciousness.

For a moment he saw police and an ambulance crew hovering over him. He was being moved out of the house on a gurney, and the rocking motion making him sick, he blacked out again.

Harris didn't return to the land of the living until hours later, and sore as hell, he felt and looked like crap, but he was also grateful to doctors for saving his life. For a few days he lay in bed, and during this time he became anxious to get out of the hospital, but the surgeon who removed the bullet absolutely refused to release him. One day giving nurses a fit, the doctor came and told him straight out that if he didn't stay put he'd put him out by shooting him up with morphine. To which Harris replied, "I know some people who can get the drug for you at less than wholesale cost."

In the end, the medical staff prevailed and Harris took it easy for a spell.

The next day, Rhonda came to the hospital to pay Harris a visit, bringing him a change of clothes, as he'd asked her to do. She made the mistake of telling Harris that Amanda was getting out of the hospital and as requested by authorities, she'd be going down to headquarters to be interviewed later in the day. Detectives had questioned her while she was under a doctor's care, but now feeling more like herself, she agreed to be interviewed. Dvorak had given Amanda powerful doses of tranquilizers to control her and break down her ability to fight him, and while not considered perfectly healthy, doctors saw no lasting effects from the drugs.

Harris once again demanded to be released, and this time he wasn't backing down. Telling Rhonda to give him space, she did, going to the nurses' station to ask for doctors to intervene.

The doctor came to his room. "Harris, how is it I spend more time trying to keep you in bed than I do attending to most of my other patients. You're not going to be happy until you tear out that sewing job I did putting you back together on the operating table. You don't look stupid, but you certainly aren't using good sense by not listening to me."

Harris moved slowly when tucking in his shirt and zipping his pants up, "I've got to get out of here, doc."

"If you're crazy enough to walk out of here when the doctor is telling you that you're playing with fire, then you'd better heed my warning to move about slowly. You're going to experience hellish pain when that wound opens up and you're bleeding all over the place, and then what? You'll be right back here on the operating table starting from square one."

Harris sat down on the bed. "It's not in my nature to sit around, and I've been lying here for days. What more do you want me to say?"

The doctor took Rhonda aside and gave her prescriptions for medicine, discussing how and when to change the dressing, and gave instructions for Harris to follow when showering.

Harris was now fully dressed, but out of breath, and when a middle-aged nurse came in with a wheelchair he gave her a hard stare. She returned a determined look, and said in a grumpy voice, "You go out of here in this wheelchair, or I'll break your legs. What's it going to be?"

"I'll take the wheelchair."

The interview was for three p.m., and Rhonda arrived with Harris in time to hear Amanda give an account of what she'd gone through to a female investigator. Joining a dozen or so officers and detectives behind a one-way mirror, the interviewer had patience in giving Amanda pause before she made a statement in response to a question.

There was quiet as everyone listened, and Harris bumped into Ron Warren, who whispered, "Hey, I was going to come and see you at the hospital, but I've been swamped. Holding together the detective's bureau hasn't been easy these last few days. Maybe you can answer something for me. Has your buddy Hastings ever taken treatment for depression? Even some of the girls in the office say he's falling off the deep end in how the guy comes to the office and is unresponsive when they ask him questions. This all began a couple of days ago, and we don't know if his wife is leaving him or if he lost a family member, or what, and he won't confide in anyone." Warren pointed at the floor. "Hastings should be here listening to this."

Before Harris responded, Rhonda signaled for quiet as the interviewing detective asked Amanda a question. "Did you encounter anyone besides Dvorak when you were held captive in that room?"

"There was this girl named Debbie who he kept with me for a time, but then he took her away and I thought he released her."

The detective responded, "This young woman was Deborah Kutraba, the mother of three children, and in all likelihood she was murdered the night she was taken from that house. However, I want you to think carefully when answering as to whether there were any other males who came to that room where you were kept?"

"There were two other men who came to my dungeon room besides Dvorak. Once Tokar came and he told me it wouldn't have come to this if I'd been more cooperative. I thought he'd return and I intended to beg him to give me my freedom. I'd have sworn to do anything he asked to get away from Dvorak, but he never came back, probably because the FBI was investigating him. One other male came, and although I have no idea who he was, he was a man of size, perhaps making two of me. Dvorak kept giving me injections to keep me doped up and he blindfold me before this man came. He had cigar breath, and something else I distinctly recall is the scent of a powerful aftershave or cologne he wore, reminding me of tequila."

Harris and Warren looked at each other, Warren speaking in a low tone of voice, "Are you thinking the same thing I am?"

"As much as I'd prefer not to, I suppose I am. Let's talk to Hastings."

When leaving the room, Harris saw Gallagher standing next to the door, but didn't acknowledge him as he entered the corridor. Gallagher came out directly behind him with Warren following, and Gallagher was trying to get Harris's attention, finally grabbing him by the arm.

Harris turned around to give Gallagher an angry stare, his eyes then turning downward to the hand placed on his arm, and Gallagher released his hold.

"Len, I just wanted to apologize."

Not wanting to listen, Harris turned his back on Gallagher and began walking away, but Warren passed him to stand in his way.

"Hey, come on, Len, this'll only take a second, Gallagher's trying to do the right thing here."

Harris retorted, "I haven't time for him."

Sidestepping Warren to go to Hasting's office, Harris heard Gallagher raise his voice. "I know you think my trailing you was a lousy thing. I'd never ordinarily divulge the name of an individual who employs me, but it was Hastings that asked me to keep you under surveillance. He had the odd idea you might have been responsible for the disappearance of Amanda Kramer."

Harris froze, and a strong feeling of betrayal was like a cold, hard slap across his face. He nodded to Gallagher, "Okay, what happened is forgotten. Thanks."

Turning to nearly bump into Kerns, a uniformed police sergeant, Harris looked to see that the officer had his handcuffs readily available on his duty belt.

"Kerns, come with me and Warren, we're going to pay a visit to Hasting's office and I want you to be the arresting officer."

Kerns grinned. "You make it sound like Hastings is going to be the subject we're arresting."

Harris replied, "It is Hastings who's going to be arrested."

Kerns grin wiped away, he now looked confused with his forehead wrinkled, his eyebrows running together as though thinking some serious shit was about to occur.

Harris, Warren, and Kerns passed through Hasting's secretary's office before bursting into the chief of detective's office, and Hastings sat before them at his desk looking sad and sorry eyed.

Wearing a look of anger on his face, Harris spoke demandingly to his old friend, "I'm placing you under arrest for the kidnapping and rape of Amanda Kramer. I can't believe you'd do such a thing Steve, and you were the one who put me on this case."

Hastings sat speechless, but finally spoke up. "I should've known better than to think you were washed up, Len—you were a mess drowning in the bottle after your wife's death. I put you on Amanda Kramer's case primarily to get her father off my back because the old man kept annoying me, calling and asking for help finding her. It occurred to me that you'd be perfect for acting in the capacity of a private investigator. I didn't think you'd get anywhere investigating your old flame Amanda's disappearance, who I thought was once the love of your life. I also knew the death of her brother was something that hit you pretty hard, leaving me to believe you'd soon fall off the wagon and start drinking again. As a result of you falling flat on your face, nothing would get done and the investigation would go nowhere, at least not as far as anything you'd be able to turn up."

Looking pathetically broken, Hastings continued, "I underestimated you old buddy—you hung tough on solving this case. There were times I thought you were going to put your own neck in the noose by stirring up trouble. All the shootings you were involved in, and the time you told the D.A. where to stick it. Yeah, I started hanging around the casino and the gentlemen's club where I got to know Tokar and Dvorak. I should've known better than to fall in with that crowd. And even though I knew it, I couldn't walk away from payoffs I'd taken from Tokar for burying evidence about his nefarious affairs with organized crime. Then Tokar's empire started showing cracks, and as much as I knew it was going to crumble, I still couldn't walk away. Dvorak did cosmetic work on Fran in his office for pennies on the dollar, and I felt I owed him. At the same time, I knew if either of those two got into trouble they'd sell me out for a reduced sentence. When learning the FBI was focused on Tokar, I knew the end was coming, but by then I was in deep, never dreaming it would all come down to this."

Harris said, "You're finished Steve, destroyed by your own mishandling of this office, and I'm changing that arrest report to say kidnapping, rape and murder. You killed Tokar in a desperate attempt to save your own ass. You killed him when thinking he was going to spill everything for making a deal to reduce his prison sentence. They found blood in Tokar's house from when his dog attacked the killer. Those droplets of blood are going to put you away for the rest of your life, and you may even get the death penalty. But I'll tell you how wrong you are about Tokar and Dvorak; you probably think they roped you in and you blame them for putting you in this predicament, but that's not so. You're every bit as disgustingly sick as they are, and how is your family going to take this news? Your wife and children, and your mother and father are still alive, Steve, and they're going to be crushed to learn they've raised a perverted monster for a son."

Hastings looked up at Harris, and without hesitation opened the top drawer of his desk to grab a .38 revolver. Warren and Kerns moved to stop him before he put it to his temple, but the gun went off.

Warren stepped back, holding his arms outward and to the side while assessing the spray of blood spatter on him, and remarked, "Crap, this sport coat is ruined."

The chief of detectives now dead, Harris thought Hastings had taken the easy way out, and it may have worked out best for his family that he ended it this way. In the days ahead, he stayed at home as he continued recovering, doing a lot of thinking about loose puzzle pieces and how they fit for closing out this case. That following Sunday, he received a phone call from Rhonda asking him if he'd like to meet with the family for dinner at Alessandro Gianni's, and he accepted. She told him she'd made reservations for 7 p.m., and he said he'd be there.

Chapter 23
Fitting Together Remaining Puzzle Pieces for Tying Up Loose Ends

Harris hadn't been to Gianni's since the shooting, and parking around back, he stopped for a moment at the spot where he shot it out with Solano to ponder the incident. He entered the restaurant nicely dressed in a navy blue sport coat and tie to see Mr. Kramer, Rhonda, Amanda, and Jim Abernathy sitting at the table, and they were all glad to see him. They placed their dinner orders with the waiter while making small talk, and salads were brought to their table.

In entered Ron Warren and his wife, and when Harris saw him he shook his hand and congratulated him on his advancement to chief of detectives. They were asked to join Harris and the others, and the couple accepted.

Warren went on to make a confession. "I asked my wife where she wanted to go for dinner and she told me she wanted to go the restaurant where Harris wounded that contract killer, so here we are."

The restaurant's formally dressed manager overheard what Warren said, and recognized Harris by having seen his photograph in the newspaper. He came over to their table and made mention that business has picked up since the shooting of Solano, and everyone chuckled in how the statement reverted back to Warren's comment. He returned to their table minutes later with a complimentary bottle of red wine and left it on their table, smiling as he said, "With gratitude from Gianni's."

When Warren had a chance to speak to Harris privately, he said, "Harris, I'm still trying to figure out who killed who in order to find closure to this investigation. You were on top of things as they were happening, so maybe you can enlighten me."

"I can tie together some of the loose ends for wrapping this case up for you, but I may not be correct on every detail. To get the story down pat you have to go back to when Amanda told Tokar she was leaving him for a fresh start in life. This was a blow to Tokar's self-image, but more importantly, he worried about her turning informant for law enforcement. Tokar wasn't the kind to get involved in kidnapping and murder, but when he told his worries to his friend Dvorak, the doctor offered to make Amanda disappear. This idea interested Tokar because he saw his problems mounting, as the drug cartel he was in business with would've surely killed Amanda to silence her forever. However, if her murder drew attention from the FBI, it could result in suspending their drug enterprise trade, and if this happened they may have also considered getting rid of Tokar for protecting their interests.

"Tokar hadn't thought things out very well for agreeing to Dvorak's scheme, and later realized how ugly it was to throw in with the devil. The cold, calculating doctor had an uncontrollable obsession and insatiable desire for Amanda, and he wanted to keep her stashed away in his basement for fulfilling a twisted fantasy of his.

"Dvorak had shrewdly planned that a serial killer would be blamed for Amanda's abduction, who was D'Angelo. He further tried to divert the police's attention with a second abduction, and lured a young girl to his lake house who he'd met when carousing night spots on the Illinois side. He may have been scouting for months with the idea of kidnapping a girl, planning it long before he'd begun holding Amanda, and he had success with Deborah Kutraba because she desperately needed money. She may have known Dvorak to be a wealthy, prestigious doctor, and he possibly drew her to his house with the promise of a large payment for a massage. She fell into his trap, and he kept her with Amanda for a time, probably keeping her car hidden in his garage.

"What Dvorak hadn't banked on is that the deaths of D'Angelo's victims involved crossing state lines, and this meant the FBI's involvement. With the added resources of the bureau, D'Angelo was soon caught and incarcerated, and while they knew he'd murdered prostitutes, they couldn't be sure about Kramer and Kutraba. Dvorak, again, trying to outsmart law enforcement officials, decided to do away with Kutraba, as her shooting death on the east side was a ploy for drawing investigators attention to Illinois.

"Dvorak needed a helper for getting rid of Kutraba, as he'd have to have transportation from the cornfield where her body and car was discovered to his home. He'd met Solano through Tokar, and as you well know, he was a murder-for-hire killer willing to do most anything for good old American currency. Dying from cancer with little time left on this Earth, Solano needed money for living the good life. I believe Dvorak followed Solano into Illinois, and he'd driven Kutraba's car with her in it. Solano, having no conscience about killing, shot her in the head, and the doctor drove him back to the Missouri side.

"All of these events were driving Tokar crazy, his world was closing in on him, and it may be that he really loved Amanda and agonized over the position he'd put her in. He wanted to get away from criminal activity and open a legitimate horseracing track, and had long since invested in his dream by purchasing real estate to build it on. The FBI breathing down his neck for drug trafficking, he saw his only way out was to spill everything he knew to the authorities, throwing everybody under the bus for leniency in his sentencing. The cartel operation, Dvorak's insane sexual perversions, and Hastings burying evidence against Tokar for the exchange of money made the icing on the cake, all making for a nice package to present to the FBI.

"Hastings must have read in assorted discussions he'd had with Tokar that this was coming soon, so he paid Tokar a visit and shot him to death at his house. I'm sure you recall Hastings explaining much of that before blowing his brains out, and that stuff about the doctor doing cosmetic work on his wife for pennies on the dollar was true. I think he gave her a facelift and surgical liposuction, and judging by a photo I saw of her, she looks pretty good. For this, Dvorak won Hastings loyalty and allegiance, as Steve felt indebted to him, and the two became the chummiest of buddies, often partying together. Steve didn't wake up to how much shit he was in until it was too late."

Warren put his index fingers to his temples as though trying to put everything together in his mind. "Okay, I think I've got it all except one thing. Who killed Schaeffer?"

Harris took a sip of wine. "In the time Dvorak rubbed shoulders with clients of the gentlemen's club, I believe he may have formed a friendship with Schaeffer, and won his confidence. I think Schaeffer was impressed with Dvorak's credentials, a distinguished cosmetic surgeon for the celebrities. Dvorak envisioned himself as having rock star status, and having risen to fame, his giant ego needed people sucking up to him. And while Schaeffer was a mild-mannered workaholic, he also pandered to the doctor for having respect and admiration for him. A charismatic, intelligent person, and no doubt the doctor had smarts, when Schaeffer took those documents from Tokar's safe he sought the doctor's advice.

"Schaefer had no idea that telling Dvorak he intended delivering that briefcase to police made for his demise, as the doctor thought those papers may contain information about him as well. Someone was in Schaeffer's company when he and I discussed over the phone a meeting place, leaving me to later consider it was the doctor, and he followed Schaeffer to the park without him knowing it. He snuck up on Schaeffer as he sat in his car and put a bullet in his head, and while we may never know what was in those papers, my guess is the briefcase got destroyed."

Warren nodded. "It fits because Dvorak's warped mind had likely developed a paranoia that something might turn up to implicate him in Amanda's disappearance."

Jim Abernathy tapped on the water pitcher with a butter knife to get everyone's attention, and looked at Amanda. "I'd like to take this moment to make an announcement." He presented to her a ring with a big stone. "Amanda, I never want to lose you again, and I'm asking for your hand in marriage. I promise to always be there to love and protect you."

Amanda looked as though she was going to cry, nodding her head yes before kissing him, and he put the ring on her hand.

Harris looked at Amanda and Rhonda's father who looked very happy at hearing this news.

He then commented, "How about that Mr. Kramer, not only did you get Amanda back, but now you've got a new son-in-law to boot."

Abernathy chuckled, repeating Harris's words, "A new son-in-law to boot."

"Well, it's the truth, isn't it?"

Warren had another bottle of wine brought to the table and he went on to fill everyone's glasses. "Hear, hear, I think it appropriate that we all raise our glasses to share in a toast to this newly engaged couple who have so much to live for."

They all stood to raise their glasses to Amanda and Abernathy, and Mr. Kramer was allowed to give the toast, saying, "May you have a long and happy life together."

When they'd finished the toast, Rhonda tugged on the sleeve of Harris's sport jacket to get him to sit down next to her. "You look familiar to me. Don't I know you?"

Harris gave her a strange look, temporarily closing one eye. "I'm not sure, but you look like someone I once knew."

"I'm only asking because you and I haven't spoken to each other all evening long."

"Yeah, well, you can see how the night's gone. We're now celebrating your sister's engagement, but one of these days, and not in the too distant future, we're going to have time for ourselves."

Rhonda turned a serious expression. "Harris, it seems I've heard that line on more than just one occasion. I don't know if there's real closure to all this or not, as for one thing, where does it leave us?"

He sat there contemplating how to respond to the question. "That's a good question, and you know I never tallied up the charges for all the detective work I did on this case. You don't think your father would mind giving your hand in marriage as payment for taking care of the bill?"

"I don't know what he'd say, but I could go for that."

"Should we make an announcement?"

"I don't think so, I wouldn't want to butt in on Jim and Amanda's night, and anyway, you not only don't have a ring to give me, but you're still wearing your old wedding band."

He slipped the ring off his finger, offering it to her as a symbol of his love and to initiate their engagement, but she declined.

"I want a rock at least as big as the one Jim gave to Amanda."

"Oh, so that's how it is."

Rhonda nodded, and then Harris commented, "How about if we go to the jewelers tomorrow and you can pick one out that fits your fancy."

"That will work." She then added, "Amanda and Jim are taking Dad home, but I've long since lost track of what round we're into, and the last few, as you well know, ended in a draw. It's early enough that we can continue the match at my place for determining a winner. What do you say to that proposal?"

"It sounds as if you're taking advantage of my good nature—I've seen that glint in your eye before, and those bedroom boxing matches can get brutal. My heart and mind are into it, but I don't know about my body—I don't know if I'm in shape to get in the ring with you."

Rhonda grabbed his tie and pulled him close for them to kiss, and afterwards spoke in a reserved manner. "Don't be such a wuss, Harris. Some light sparring isn't going to hurt you, and regardless, we have to get you back in training for the big bout that's coming up."

Harris nodded with a grin, "Big bout that's coming up."

"Yeah, at my place you can chase me around the ring a few times or, if necessary, I can chase you around some. But I'm going to win this time, and I'm counting on you to ring my bell."

She pulled his tie again to draw him closely for another kiss, and Harris said, "You win."

Warren stood behind them, motioning for everyone to take notice of the pair kissing. "Get a load of these two. There must be something going around, and it's catching."

THE END

you need to ad mor